THE
UNNAMED WAY

IAN W. SAINSBURY

Cover design by Hristo Kovatliev

For Mum (always reading)
and Dad (Bertrand Roy)

Join my (very occasional) mailing list, and I'll send you the unpublished prologue for The World Walker: http://eepurl.com/bQ_zJ9

Previously...(contains spoilers for books one, two, and three)

Musician Seb Varden has been dragged into a world he never knew existed. Alien nanotechnology indistinguishable from magic has been used—consciously or not— by individuals and organizations throughout the history of our planet. The nanotechnology, accessed by visiting sites called Thin Places, is known as Manna. In The World Walker, Seb learns how to cope with the new powers he has been given by an alien benefactor and avoid those who wish to use him or see him dead, notably a very powerful Manna user known as Mason.

In The Unmaking Engine, now living anonymously with girlfriend Meera Patel in Mexico City, he is initially powerless to stop himself being summoned and questioned by the Rozzers, an alien race on their way to Earth to destroy their failed experiment—humanity—and try again. The Rozzers are scientists who carefully control the evolution of new species in the universe by seeding planets with Manna before introducing cellular matter with the potential to develop into intelligent life. Seb prevents them by reprogramming The Unmaking Engine. Instead of wiping out humanity, Seb's intervention means the Engine rewires humanity's DNA so that future generations will no longer be able to use Manna. The Rozzers are appeased, but his actions come at a huge personal cost for Seb: he has to allow his entire body and brain to evolve and become, fully, a World Walker (or T'hn'uuth.) In the process, he again fends off Mason, discovering that he is, in fact, his brother. After Seb removes the brain tumor that caused his personality to warp so thoroughly, Mason takes the name John and joins his brother and Mee on the small island of Innisfarne, off the east coast of Britain. What should be a time of relief and celebration turns sour as Seb becomes increasingly distant with Mee, finally disappearing from Innisfarne entirely, possibly against his will. Mee has just discovered she is pregnant.

Many years after The Unmaking Engine, in The Seventeenth Year, we meet Joni, Seb and Meera's daughter. Conceived before Seb sacrificed the last of his physical humanity to become a World Walker and save Earth from the Unmaking Engine, Joni discovers she has unusual abilities of her own. She is resistant to Manna, which is good and bad. Good because it can't really be used against her, bad because she can't Use it herself - to heal or be healed. Her other ability involves the multiverse - which Seb discovered he was using every time he Walked. Joni can *reset* the multiverse, returning to a point she has consciously created, where the universe branches into two possible futures.

Joni uses her ability to escape from Adam, a psychopathic remnant from the Acolytes Of Satan - the organization which tried to kill Seb in The World Walker. Adam's belief in a demigod which created the Earth and may yet return to rule it fuels his desire to rid the planet of the most powerful Manna users to prove his worth. If not Seb Varden himself, who is missing presumed dead, then why not the next best thing - his daughter? Joni is aided in her escape by her mother and Sym - a personality construct originally created by Seb who has been pursuing his own agenda in the years since Seb vanished.

Mistakenly believing Adam to be dead, Joni and Mee return to Innisfarne where a disguised Adam kills her uncle John and prepares to kill Joni. Seb returns and saves Joni. Sym kills Adam.

Seb prepares to tell Mee and Joni—the daughter he has never met—where he has been the past seventeen years. It's an incredible story, involving a mysterious alien artifact he as brought back to Earth with him: the Gyeuk Egg. It's not over yet...

MAIN CHARACTERS CONTINUING FROM BOOKS 1-3

Seb Varden

Orphan, musician, World Walker and our unlikely hero.

Meera (Mee) Patel

Seb's girlfriend, a singer and Manna user. Pot-smoking, foul-mouthed and brilliant.

Joni

Seb and Mee's daughter. Conceived before Seb's final

evolution to T'hn'uuth status, she has unexpected abilities, namely a resistance to Manna and the power to return to a previously chosen *reset* point in her own timeline and re-live the subsequent events, changing them if necessary.

Sym

Artificially constructed by Seb to passively observe Walt Ford in The World Walker, Sym can live online or symbiotically within a host (hence his name). He can also take over a host body if necessary. Although his personality is based on Seb's, he has a more ambivalent relationship with morality than his creator.

Billy Joe

A T'hn'uuth (World Walker) who evolved from the Rozzer species thousands of years ago. In The World Walker, he awoke from a dormant state on Earth in order to accelerate Seb's own evolution into a World Walker, giving him extraordinary powers.

The Gyeuk

A swarm-mind, artificially intelligent. Just as nanotechnology provides the physical makeup and power of the T'hn'uuth, so it provides the countless tiny intelligences that go to make up the group mind of the Gyeuk. The Gyeuk's ambitions and motives remain opaque. It was a Gyeuk ship that carried the Rozzers on their destructive mission in The Unmaking Engine. As Seb found in his encounter with H'wan (the ship), the relationship between the Gyeuk and the T'hn'uuth is characterized by a slight unease on both sides.

Chapter 1

The moons were full that night. Usually, this would be considered an auspicious omen. Usually.

Two figures, silhouetted against the evening sun, walked into the meeting circle and faced the three Elders. No other tribe members were present. Sopharndi had requested a private audience for herself and her son. The orange tinge of sunset gave the illusion of warmth, although back in the settlement fires had been burning for a few hours already.

Sopharndi stood silently before the Elders. She could not quite bring herself to lower her eyes, despite her love and trust for those who led her tribe. She fidgeted while they bowed their heads. The thin scar on her chin itched, but she resisted the urge to scratch it.

Beside Sopharndi, Cley started his tuneless humming. When, at five years old, her son had first started this curious habit, Sopharndi had felt a wild and desperate hope pierce her broken heart. Perhaps Cley wasn't a Blank after all. Maybe he was just a late starter. After all, he was able to feed himself a little, and sometimes he seemed to show interest in a bright flower or the flight of a particularly raucous lekstrall. But the humming, despite hours of patient coaxing, had never led to a single intelligible word, and Sopharndi had felt her hopes slip away, replaced by the quiet despair that accompanied her every waking hour and haunted her dreams. She wondered why the Singer had chosen to inflict such cruel and torturous punishment on her and her blameless child. Sopharndi had always tried to live according to Her silent song. Perhaps trying wasn't good enough for the Singer.

Laak, Leader of the People, raised her head and held both palms toward Sopharndi and Cley.

"Sopharndi has asked. The Elders will answer."

Laak dropped her hands and took a step forward. "You are a mother. Your love for your son is a reflection of the love the Singer has for all of us. We honor this, Sopharndi."

The two Elders flanking Laak were parents and grandparents. Hesta had two boys. Gron had outlived both of his children and was bringing up his granddaughter. Laak's daughter Cochta was strong of arm and was considered by most to be the obvious next First, replacing Sopharndi when the time came. Some suspected Cochta's desires were greater still, and she intended to follow her mother as Leader. When Sopharndi looked at Laak, she saw a woman entering her final years, her strength beginning to ebb away. Cochta was certainly strong enough to lead but lacked her mother's patience and wisdom. The girl had a little too much to say for herself.

Better too much than nothing at all.

She looked at Cley, then automatically took out a cloth and wiped away the saliva spilling from the corner of his mouth. He stopped humming for a second while Sopharndi dabbed at his face, then picked up where he had left off. Sopharndi looked back at the Elders and—just for a moment—saw a flicker of pity in Laak's eyes.

The decision had gone against her, then.

"It is our way," said Laak. "We cannot make an exception."

Sopharndi, Hesta and Gron intoned the age-old response. "As the Singer wills."

Cley would have to make the Journey. He would go into the Parched Land. For any other of the People, it was just a ritual marking their transition from adolescence to adulthood. For Cley, it was a death sentence.

Without another word, Sopharndi took her son's hand and led him back to the settlement.

Chapter 2

Innisfarne

When Seb opened the door of the crofter's cottage to find Jesus Christ standing there, he was—for a moment, at least—nonplussed. He regarded the figure in silence. Jesus looked back at him steadily. The slowly falling snow was part of Seb's reason for his lack of reaction. There was something uncannily familiar about the scene.

"Seb," said Jesus, with a friendly nod.

"Jesus," said Seb, returning the nod. Being brought up by nuns made politeness habitual.

And it's Jesus, *for Chrissakes.*

Seb spent a moment trying to unpick the sheer *wrongness* of that last thought before mentally shrugging and giving up. He was dressed for the weather, his usual jeans and T-shirt supplemented with a thick woolen sweater, a greatcoat that looked like it belonged in nineteenth century

4

Russia, gloves, hat, and scarf. He had no need for clothes for warmth, but he was making a determined stab at being *normal*. On his back was a knapsack, inside which—carefully wrapped in an old blanket—was an object that had been created by an Artificial Intelligence made up of a swarm of beings that were both many and one, countless light-years away from where he stood now, outside a cottage on the tiny Northumbrian island of Innisfarne. Looking at Jesus. Maybe this whole attempt at *normal* wasn't going perfectly, but Seb could be a stubborn and resolute man, and he wasn't done trying just yet.

The man in front of him, dressed only in a loincloth, his head crowned with thorns, bloody wounds on his hands and feet, looked every inch the Catholic Christ of Seb's childhood. But icons or statues didn't place Jesus in a snow scene. It wasn't that Catholics were shy about portraying their savior in myriad ways. Seb had seen images of Christ as a shepherd, a teacher, a stern judge, a healer, a friend to the poor and needy. He'd seen statues where the man of sorrows pulled open his own chest to reveal a stylized, golden, sacred heart. He remembered one of the sisters pinning a page of a magazine to the noticeboard at St Benet's, purporting to show the face of Christ in a pretzel.

But *snow?*

"So, yeah, Seb," said Jesus. "Hey. What's happening?" Despite the sub-zero temperature, the apparition didn't shiver. *Apparition* was the wrong word. Seb had no doubt that, were he to place a hand on that wound on the man's side, he would feel warm flesh and blood. Not that he intended to try it.

Instead of feeling as if he were in the presence of a miracle, Seb felt irritated. Snowflakes were settling in the figure's long, deep-brown, lustrous hair, with its unlikely shampoo-commercial shine. The beard covering the chin of the otherwise flawless white skin was neatly trimmed. Jesus's barber was obviously a perfectionist. The eyes were an unlikely shade of cornflower blue.

Why did it seem so—

Then, suddenly, he had it. Sister Theresa's office. On the windowsill. Next to her bowl of plastic rosaries, which she had handed out with unrelenting generosity and optimism to everyone she met.

A snow-globe.

When he had been very small, way before he was attending any classes, Sister Theresa had sometimes let him sit in her big leather swivel chair. She was in charge of the orphanage accounts and had spent hours every day hunched over bills and receipts. A bad back didn't allow her to sit still for extended periods, so she had made sure she stood for at least ten minutes in every hour. And that had been when the two or three-year-old Seb, looking at picture books or playing with donated toys in the corner, had been allowed to sit in the big chair, his outstretched feet not even reaching the edge of the leather. As the only resident orphan abandoned on their doorstep just after his birth, he had enjoyed certain privileges.

While she'd stretched her recalcitrant spine, or moved paperwork from an eternally refilling in-tray to a similarly overloaded out-tray, Sister Theresa would hand Seb a plastic rosary—because not to do so would just feel plain *wrong* to the dutiful woman—and, after a few seconds during which he looked at her wide-eyed and ever so slightly reproachfully, she'd cave in and give him the globe. She did it just to see the child's face break into that broad, delighted smile that not a single Sister in the place could resist. They weren't going to spoil the boy, *God forbid*, but if an opportunity arose to take any action that would produce that wondrously uplifting expression on Seb's chubby, innocent face, well, who could blame them? If any Sister in the place had ever harbored any doubts about their calling, a few seconds' exposure to that boy's smile would set them right.

So, maybe once a week, when it was Sister Theresa's turn to babysit, Seb would get the chance to shake the snow-globe, and watch the tiny flakes swirl around the figure of Jesus, as he stood in a frozen gesture of blessing. But that figure had been robed. Seb couldn't remember any other details apart from the blue eyes of the plastic statue. All other colors had long disappeared, the materials used in the globe's construction having been chosen for cheapness, rather than durability. Over the years, the figure of Jesus had become as white as the scene around him, only those two minuscule flecks of blue remaining in an almost featureless face. The contours had worn smooth, no details discernible. Christ's plastic form had literally become part of the world inside the globe, little by little, shake by shake, his own body falling around him with the flakes of snow.

Seb found he was losing patience. His Manna was providing information he had already half-guessed.

"Jesus Christ was a Middle-Eastern Jew," he said, "not a Woodstock hippy."

Piercingly blue eyes narrowed into a slightly petulant glare.

"I thought you'd *like* it."

The voice was pleasingly soft and nondescript, unmistakably American, but geographically vague. The kind of accent an actor playing Christ might settle on.

"Well, you thought wrong. I don't."

Jesus mumbled something and rolled his eyes. Then, with such swiftness that it seemed to happen instantaneously, the figure lost about a foot in height, its skin darkening to a sun-baked brown. The eyes were dark now, the eyebrows bushy and wild. The beard now looked unkempt, matted with blood. The face was completely different, older, weathered…tired. For a moment, Seb felt a deep sense of shock as the Christ he had sometimes pictured as a teenager, rejecting the toothpaste commercial poster boy he kept seeing, stood before him, silent and solemn. Then the man winked, and the spell was broken.

"Well, are ye going to invite me in, then?" said Jesus, the voice now accented, although Seb couldn't place the dialect. There was something maddeningly familiar about it. Then, suddenly, he had it. Jesus had now, for no good reason, adopted a strong Scottish accent.

"I'm going out," he said. "Whatever you want, it can wait."

He opened the door wider and stepped aside. The figure—with a childish giggle—walked in, then paused, surveying the room. The roaring fire's dancing orange and red light revealed fairly sparse furnishings. There was a wooden chair, a table that didn't match and an old chest in the corner. A dented stove and a plain, iron bed completed the picture.

"Make yourself at home," said Seb. The man, who was now shorter than him, looked up and smiled.

"You haven't asked why I'm here."

"I know why you're here, Fypp."

His visitor seemed unperturbed by the use of the name.

"It's time. We need to look at the Egg."

Seb shifted the knapsack on his shoulder and shook his head.

"Later," he said. "I have to be somewhere. We can look at it when I come back."

The figure of Christ rose a few feet into the air, looking briefly annoyed. Then he leaned back as if supported by an invisible cushion and folded his hands over his stomach.

"Sure. I can wait. I've done my fair share of waiting over the millennia. Billenia? Trillenia? Am I making up words now? Ye go tell them whatever it is you have to tell them. Then we'll talk."

In the doorway, framed by the falling snow behind him, Seb turned.

"Please don't look like this when I get back," he said. "It's in pretty bad taste."

Jesus tutted.

"There's no need to be touchy about it. It's just a bit of fun, och."

Och? Seb didn't reply. Jesus sighed and pouted.

"Oh, have it your way. Perhaps I had ye figured wrong, laddie. Maybe you're boring after all."

Seb stepped out into the snow.

"Fypp, you may be a lot of things, but empathetic isn't one of them."

A halo had appeared above the figure's head. Jesus grabbed it and tossed it toward the fire, where it landed neatly on the poker in its brass stand. He applauded his own skill.

"When you're as interesting as me, what's the point in caring about what anyone else is feeling?"

"Hmm. Well, here's a heads-up for you. Being boring sounds really appealing to me right now." As he pulled the heavy door closed behind him, he caught one last comment from the floating figure.

"I only thought if ye saw me looking like this, ye might get a kick out of it. Even think it was good news. Good News - geddit? No? Just me?" The accent shifted again. "Jeez, tough crowd."

Seb closed the door and trudged away from his visitor toward the Keep, toward the woman he loved and the daughter he'd only just begun to know.

It was time for him to tell them the truth. Whatever that was.

Chapter 3

Joni stepped out of a small, stone building as Seb approached the Keep. She hugged him briefly, and he felt the same curious tightening of his chest and his throat that afflicted him every time she was near.

She smelled like home.

He had seen news stories and PBS documentaries about fathers who discovered they had a kid after years of not knowing, and despite his certainty that he was being emotionally manipulated, he had always cried.

Mee had caught him at it once, drying his eyes in front of the TV as a man was confronted with a ten-year-old son he had never met.

"Wuss," had been Mee's only comment. Seb suspected she never watched those shows herself because she would end up bawling, but he'd allowed her to keep her illusory sense of superior emotional balance.

His situation was a little different from those in the documentaries, of course. He had stepped away from the planet for a few weeks. Or seventeen years. Or a lifetime. It was all relative, apparently. It didn't feel relative to Seb, though.

He held Joni for a long moment and tried just to enjoy that moment, rather than lament the lost years. It would be all too easy to blame himself for allowing Joni to grow up without a father, but he knew he had been given no real choice. He was here *now*, he had choices *now*. What else was there?

"I want to show you something," said Joni, and pulled him gently toward the outbuilding. Seb could smell coffee. Good coffee.

Inside, a heavy iron vice was fixed to the edge of a large workbench. On the wooden surface, there were a couple of notebook pages with measurements and diagrams scribbled on them. Coffee mug rings were everywhere, but they looked like they had been placed carefully, making some kind of intricate pattern.

Joni saw Seb looking. "You need to squint, Dad."

Seb stepped back and duly squinted, smiling automatically when he heard the word "Dad." He wondered if he would ever get used to hearing it, or loving it. He guessed not.

At first, the hundreds of dark rings still looked just like they had been arranged in arbitrary sequences, just as someone might doodle while thinking. Then, as Seb allowed his vision to blur slightly, they suddenly coalesced, forming an unmistakable shape. The worktop now clearly displayed a pair of eyes, one of which was winking at him.

"Oh," said Seb softly.

Joni smiled at him and brushed some sawdust from the surface onto the floor.

"We didn't see it for a long time, Mum and I. Kate still won't come in here, not since Uncle John—." Her voice tailed off, and she swallowed hard. Seb took half a step toward her, then stopped, unsure. How is a new father supposed to behave when his baby girl is nearly seventeen years old? Where was that section in the books on parenting?

Joni, now looking up at the rows of clean, oiled tools hanging in place on the wall, had either failed to notice Seb's awkwardness or was pretending she had. Either way, he was grateful.

Pieces of driftwood and detritus rescued from the sea were piled up in one corner. Joni picked up what looked like the iron ring from a barrel and turned it in her hands as she spoke.

"This was his workshop. He loved to work with his hands. He always had a project on the go. Did you know that Uncle John made a lot of the furniture in the Keep?"

Seb shook his head.

"He taught himself. Said he wanted to do something good, something productive, however small. He repaired everything, and if he couldn't repair something, he'd drag it down here and make it into something new."

Seb had only known his brother for a few weeks before, well, before—

Before you let yourself forget who you were. Before you let yourself get pulled away from here like a dog running to his master's whistle.

Seb shook his head. No point beating himself up over what was done, and he knew the choice to leave Earth had never really been his.

So you say. But look what you've come back to.

His brother was dead. John had lived most of his life trapped in a mind ravaged by a cancerous tumor. He'd been no more than a terrified, passive observer to the horrors committed by the sick, diseased personality that controlled his brain and body. Then, only weeks after Seb had freed him from the torment he had suffered for decades, Seb had disappeared. And now, the only link to a family Seb had never known was gone. John had died protecting Joni. John had been a father to her when her real father didn't even know she existed.

Seb saw that Joni was crying. He felt a strange tightening of the skin on his cheeks and placed his fingers just under his own eyes, finding water drying there. Then a drop of moisture trickled down until it touched the pad of his forefinger and he realized he was crying, too. He blinked deliberately and watched Joni's face smudge into abstraction for a moment until his vision cleared.

Tears?

Seb didn't want to think too hard about what was going on.

Emotions, Sebby, that's what going on. But you don't have emotions anymore, right? Not now. You've changed.

Seb took another small step toward Joni. How could she look so much like Mee, yet be so completely and utterly herself? A rush of feelings arose which he couldn't identify, let alone begin to name. Well, that wasn't quite true. There was one feeling he could name: awe. He looked at this human being that could only exist because Sebastian Varden had met Meera Patel. He looked, and he felt that sense of awe snatch him up and shake him, showing him how every moment could be simultaneously mundane and unimaginably vast, full of riches.

No good fooling yourself you're just some guy, Sebby. We're way past that. You took on the powers of a god. You coulda said no.

When he had sabotaged and reengineered the Unmaking Engine, he had chosen to relinquish every last particle of his original body, allowing himself to fully become a T'hn'uuth, a World Walker. It had been a one-way ticket. There had been no real choice as far as he could see. On the one hand, the future of humanity. On the other, your typical damaged, flawed, scared individual, clinging on to the last scraps of what made him human.

Before then. You made the decision way before then. Remember?

Seb remembered. Of course he remembered. It wasn't a moment anyone was likely to forget. The moment everything ended, and everything began. The offer of life from the glowing alien figure who had saved him from suicide.

Yeah, but he gave you a choice.

The choice between life and death.

Still a choice, buddy.

That day in the Los Angeles hills, he had said his goodbyes. The goodbyes he could bring himself to say, that was. Death had chosen him months before. He had just finally accepted the fact and decided he would decide the when and where of it.

When Billy Joe had appeared, when he had taken Seb's hands and brought him back from the brink, he had paused before giving Seb the power that would not only restore him but set in motion changes that could never be undone. He had paused. He had waited. Waited for Seb's answer. Yes or no. Seb had known saying yes would have consequences, he had known it would mean walking a path no human had ever walked. In that frozen moment, he had known there could be no turning back.

You coulda said no.

Seb felt a smaller hand on his, gently pulling his fingers away from his face. He looked down at Joni.

"It's okay to cry, you know," she said. "It's good to cry."

She buried her face in his chest and wrapped her arms around him. Seb put one arm around his daughter's shoulders. Slowly, he brought his other hand up to her head and gently stroked her hair. As well as hearing her sobs, he could feel them in his chest as he held her. After a few seconds, he realized he was sobbing too.

They stood that way for nearly ten minutes, a father and his daughter. Then Joni slowly disentangled herself and wiped her face with a tissue before blowing her nose loudly. She reached into her pocket and pulled out a clean tissue, offering it to Seb. Even as she held it out to him, his tears disappeared, his puffy eyes instantly losing their red tinge and returning to normal.

"Oh. I forgot," said Joni, putting the tissue away. "That's going to take some getting used to, you know."

Seb smiled. "Says the girl who can revisit her own timeline and try again."

Joni grinned. "Yeah, I have to admit that's pretty cool." She took down two tin mugs from hooks above the coffee pot.

"Milk? Sugar?"

"Neither, thanks."

Joni poured two black coffees and handed one to Seb.

"Mum's still a tea drinker. Uncle John said you were a coffee snob, too. He liked it when Mum talked about you. The times she wanted to talk about you, that is. He found out more about the ways you were similar, even though you'd never known each other. He liked that."

Seb sipped his coffee. It was as good as it smelled.

"Your mum didn't always like to talk about me?"

Joni chewed her lower lip before replying. Seb watched, fascinated. He found everything about her fascinating. He hoped that feeling would never get old.

"Mum had to find a way to deal with it. With being gone. She always thought you'd be back, but she thought it would be days - weeks, maybe. No longer than a month. She said it had happened before. By the time I was old enough to understand, she didn't like to talk about you too much. Sometimes, she let herself think you were never coming back. For a few years, she believed it. They were bad times. When she was like that, it was easier not to mention you, not to risk Mum going—"

Joni paused for a few seconds.

"You okay?"

"Fine. It's just, well—"

She stopped again and Seb was aware of how little he knew about his daughter's life up to now, how much catching up there was to do. And how much he could never catch up on, however hard he tried.

"Mum had some bad times, but I should let her tell you about that. If she wants to."

Seb nodded, but didn't speak.

"When I was twelve, she told me about the Rozzers, about what you did. I'd grown up pretending you were the king of the fairies. When I found out who you really were, what you'd really done, it was even better than I'd imagined."

Seb shook his head, not wanting to speak.

"Although..." Joni smiled at him, one eyebrow slightly raised. The expression was so like Mee that Seb felt the customary grip of time loosen suddenly, the ground shifting under his feet.

"Although what?" he said.

"Well, I'd probably keep quiet about the fact that you're personally responsible for Year Zero. Not everybody's entirely happy about the end of Manna use."

On her visits to the cottage, Joni had told him about the effect of Year Zero. Seb had watched documentaries and news stories, scanned over a decade-and-a-half of media, both traditional and social, piecing together the story of the years he had missed. There were tales of hope and horror, selfishness and self-sacrifice. As usual, humanity had displayed its ability to fuck things up, but there were inspiring stories buried in amongst the fucked-upedness.

He realized his train of thought had taken on more than a hint of Mee's colorful vocabulary. So when he heard her voice, it took a few seconds to register that it wasn't part of his internal dialog.

"Oi, Varden, you said ten o'clock. It's five past. You've already kept me waiting seventeen years, I'm expecting a little more consideration from now on."

Seb looked over at the doorway. Mee had one hand on her hip, the other holding a spliff, blue smoke curling from its end. He looked at the face of the only woman he'd ever loved. He knew she looked older. The lines around the eyes and mouth, the backs of her hands, a softening around her belly and hips. But, if anything, she looked more beautiful than ever. He said nothing, but she saw the look on his face and blushed before looking away. She turned and started to walk back to the main building.

"Come on, you two, before my tea goes cold. And Seb?" She waved the spliff in the air but didn't wait for an answer. "I hope you've brought the sodding Gucci Egg, or whatever you call that arsing thing. Can't believe you let Joni see it before you showed me. You better rethink your priorities if you want to get back into my pants."

"Mum!" protested Joni, going bright red. She looked at Seb, and they both burst out laughing, before following Mee to the Keep.

Chapter 4

Years, months or weeks previously...

Seb opened his eyes. There was no light at all. *Pitch black* didn't even begin to do justice to how dark the darkness was. It was as if a completely dark room had been placed inside a dungeon buried hundreds of feet beneath the ground. At night. In midwinter.

In fact, although Seb had felt something akin to the physical sensation of opening his eyes, no such thing had actually happened. As he looked around him into the utter blackness, he became slowly aware that he had no eyes to open, no head to turn, no face, no body. All he had was awareness. And a memory. A specific memory.

The memory was this: he was standing on a beach, his head tilted a little, looking beyond the rolling sea toward the pinpricks of stars in the clear night sky. As he gazed upward, it was as if someone was slowly turning down the volume of the scene. The roar of the sea—the most prominent sound—became a hum, a murmur, then nothing. The wind in the trees behind him dropped away and was replaced by the kind of silence Seb had only experienced before on pre-dawn hikes in the mountains.

Along with the silence came a feeling of being enclosed. He started to look around but found he couldn't do it. His physical body seemed beyond his control. There was a moment of confusion as Seb experimented, trying to turn his head, wriggle his fingers or shrug his shoulders. It was as if his body had petrified, like an ancient tree. He felt planted on the rocky beach, solid, permanent. His awareness, his center, was contracting to a diamond-hard core buried deep within his mind. His physical body seemed distant and unimportant.

While this was going on, the scene became light, the day dawning far more quickly than usual. Within a few minutes, it faded again toward darkness. Then the process repeated, faster this time. Soon, day and night cycled so quickly it was as if someone was flicking a light switch on and off.

Once, Seb thought he saw Mee's face looking up at him, but it flashed by so quickly he wondered if he had just imagined it.

Without warning, one of the micro-days turned to night, and everything froze. Seb felt his awareness, this tiny, tightly-packed core of everything he was, suddenly become utterly still, his thoughts disappearing into nothingness just as the daylight had.

A moment passed. It might have been less than a second or more than a week. As there were no external physical stimuli, no sense of his own body, no breath, no thoughts, Seb had no way of measuring time. Although the absence of thought was something he associated with the deepest part of his practice of contemplation, this was utterly different. It was a moment of preparation, of energy building. The fraction of a second before the shot-putter heaves the ball away, the high diver leaps into the unknown, or the fighter unleashes his best punch. Everything came to a standstill. The world stopped turning. Seb finally lost his last shred of awareness; his sense of self.

Then, with an explosion of energy encapsulated in a nanosecond, everything came to life, everything happened. He was a flat stone skimmed across the surface of galaxies, a javelin hurled at the perfect angle, a ball-bearing nestling in the leather strap of a catapult stretched nearly to breaking point, finally released and sent spinning toward a distant target.

At the same time as this frenetic burst of activity, there was a concurrent sense of intricate folding together, a patient and gentle coaxing so that the universe might allow the otherwise impossible to occur.

Next, the gap between here and there, between then and now, between thought and action.

Then, nothing. Nothing but a sense of awareness and the deep darkness, far from home.

SEB ACCEPTED his lack of a recognizable body without fear. He swiveled non-existent eyeballs in sockets that weren't there and looked down at hands he knew he wouldn't be able to see.

It was too disorientating. Seb decided he *did* want to see his hands. Even as the thought came to him, he saw a change in the darkness, a shading of deep gray lightening as it took on some definition, becoming first an outline, then semi-solid versions of his hands. He opened and closed his fists a few times.

I must have eyes, then, if I can see my hands. Although...maybe not. The actual business of interpreting reality goes on in the brain. Seb knew that what he thought of as *seeing* was, more accurately, his brain telling his consciousness a story based on the visual stimuli currently on offer. He knew the human brain was capable of filling in the blanks in a picture. If it could do that, it was also capable, surely, of giving him the illusion of hands, eyes, arms, a body. He was assuming his brain was present. But knowing his brain was no longer human, instead a sophisticated simulacrum made up of nanotechnology faithfully duplicating his every neuron, synapse, and connection, made him pause and question even that. The nature of consciousness was still a matter of intense debate among scientists, not all of whom believed it necessarily resided in the brain. As he mentally reassembled his body, his limbs becoming visible the moment he pictured them, Seb wondered what those scientists would make of this. His consciousness was undeniable, but a physical brain might not be involved.

Once his "body" was back, he calmly assessed the situation. A small part of him still registered how ludicrous this calmness was. He inferred that he had—somehow—just traversed an unimaginable distance. He had arrived at a place to which he had not consciously chosen to travel. He could be in danger. And yet the human instincts of fight or flight in this completely unknown place were entirely absent.

It was still dark.

Seb knew he had left the Earth. He had Walked. But, unlike previous occasions, there had been no clear sense of a destination when his journey began.

And this doesn't feel like the times when I was grabbed by the Rozzers.

Seb grinned as he tried to imagine the fun Mee would have had with that last thought. He felt the physical sensation of skin tightening at the corners of his mouth. Now that he had accepted the idea of a body, every nuance seemed normal and natural.

He had felt a distant call those last few weeks at Innisfarne. An invitation—no, a summons—that could not be ignored. His awareness of this summons had grown more and more palpable. Eventually, the call had consumed him. He no longer knew who, or what, he was, and the call felt familiar, as if a family member was trying to get hold of him. As an orphan, the urge to respond to that feeling had been particularly strong.

He looked at his body again, the only thing visible in the gloom. He knew it wasn't real. Whatever *real* was. He thought for a moment, then imagined a mountain, the base of which was covered in trees. A large lake completed the initial picture. As Seb thought it, it happened. The mountain appeared gradually, like an old-fashioned photograph in a darkroom, its bulk solidifying and gaining definition with every passing second. The trees grew like stop motion animation, densely packed at the foot of the mountain, and thinning higher up. Seb turned from the mountain and looked to his left. A lake appeared, mist clinging to the water. Between the lake and the first line of trees stood a small wooden cabin, smoke curling from a chimney on its dark roof.

Seb looked at the scenery. It was idyllic. He remembered the version of Richmond Park he had shared with Seb2 and Seb3 when he had first been given Manna. That had been a scene recreated from a strong memory. This was different. The place Seb was looking at didn't exist anywhere outside of his own imagination. Until now.

He took a step forward. His feet were bare. The ground was soft, mossy, and yielding. The air was cold and fresh, but his body felt warm enough, despite the fact he was only wearing jeans and a T-shirt.

Seb jogged down the slope to the edge of the lake. Kneeling, he scooped up a handful of the perfectly clear water and splashed it onto his face. It felt just as ice-cold, shocking and refreshing as he had expected. He scooped up a few more handfuls and soaked his face and hair. Then he stood and shook himself like a dog. He felt incredibly alive.

He looked at the cabin and changed his mind about how he wanted it to appear. Under the current circumstances, a need for privacy—or protection from the weather—was unnecessary. The roof and outer walls disappeared, leaving a single room exposed to the elements. A simple wooden table with five chairs around it. A rocker in one corner. An upright piano. A wooden bed with a simple cotton cover thrown over it. There was fresh coffee brewing; Seb could smell it. He jogged up the three steps leading to the deck and walked into the room. He poured the coffee from an old-fashioned ceramic pot on top of the range. He drank from a thick china mug. The coffee was perfect. He sat down at the table and sipped, looking slowly around at the scene he had created.

It looks like a modern theater set for an edgy, contemporary take on The Waltons.

"Night, John-Boy," he said. "Don't forget we're taking Pa to Alcoholics Anonymous tomorrow and we need to talk about those gender reassignment leaflets we found in the dresser."

After a while, he looked back at the table. Five chairs,

including the one he was sitting on. Why had he conjured up *five* chairs? Why not just one? If more than one, why not four, or six? Five seemed a strange number to arbitrarily put round the heavy oak table.

It was at that moment that he first became aware he wasn't alone.

Chapter 5

At first, Seb wondered if he was imagining things. Then he remembered that the entire scene was—effectively—a product of his imagination, and laughed, slightly uneasily.

He scanned the area anyway. Around the tops of the trees, there was a slight sway as a light breeze passed through the upper branches, but there were no birds or animals. Evidently, Seb's imagination had neglected some of the details. Even as he considered this, there was a sudden eruption of sound and movement from one of the trees as a peregrine falcon took flight, swiftly climbing until she was a brown speck against the deep blue of the sky. Seb watched her fly, then his attention was caught by a second movement at ground level.

He stood up abruptly. He was right. There *was* someone out there.

Seb was sure he'd seen a figure dart behind a tree. He got up from the table, jumped lightly down from the decking and strolled toward the edge of the clearing. He was used to the lack of fear, but now he wondered if being scared might have its uses occasionally. After all, he was a long, long way from home, in a place created by his own imagination, and something was here that didn't belong. It was as if an author had suddenly found a character in her book that she hadn't consciously created. And yet his primary reaction was curiosity.

As he reached the first trees he stopped, listening. For a few seconds, he heard nothing. Then, distant birdsong began to fill the silence, as his subconscious continued to add details to the scene. Seb stood very still, waiting. He knew he hadn't been mistaken. He *had* seen something. *Someone.*

He waited for whoever it was to show themselves.

Eventually, he heard something. A few yards away. It was a giggle. More specifically, a child's giggle. Seb's eyes widened. He looked for the source of the sound but saw nothing. He took a few steps forward and entered the forest. As he did so, there was a flash of yellow and red as a small figure launched itself from behind a nearby tree and sprinted uphill and out of sight.

"Hey!" called Seb, and followed, jogging up the slope. He lost sight of the colorful figure a couple of times and stopped, only to catch another glimpse before setting off once more. After a few minutes, he thought he'd been outrun and stopped to catch his breath. Then he remembered that breathing was just a habit he hadn't completely lost, stopped panting, and stood in silence.

A tiny sound to his left—a twig snapping, perhaps—made him swing round. The figure was climbing a tree, as fast as any squirrel, darting round to the other side of the trunk as Seb watched.

"Gotcha," said Seb, and walked over. He placed his palms on the trunk of the tall hemlock. Hundreds of millions of microscopic barbs sprang out of his hands and hooked into the bark. The same process repeated on his bare feet as he climbed quickly upwards. Toward the top of the tree, about twenty-five feet above him, he could make out the small figure crouching behind a screen of branches.

"Who are you?" He peered upward. There was no answer.

Slowly now, he climbed the last few feet that separated him from the mysterious interloper. He reached forward and gently moved aside the branches obscuring his view. There was no one there.

Seb frowned, and eased himself onto the branch below, sitting with his back against the gnarled trunk. This vantage point gave him a great view of the clearing, the cabin and the lake beyond, sparkling in the sunlight.

A streak of color flashed below him as the child—it was definitely a child—flashed out of the trees below and sprinted toward the cabin. The sound of breathless giggling reached Seb. It was such an infectious noise that, despite the bizarre circumstances, he also started to laugh. How was he ever going to catch this imp?

A memory flickered through his mind. A CCTV image of a woman using Manna to transform her shape some-how. Not quite flying, but gliding. The woman in question had just tried to kill him, but that hadn't stopped Seb admiring the trick she used to make her escape. He'd never tried it himself. Now seemed as good a time as any.

Seb hurled himself away from the tree. The branch he had leaped from was over forty feet from the ground, but the power behind his jump took him an additional twenty feet into the air before gravity (gravity *he* had created?) kicked in, and he began to fall. Immediately, he spread his arms and legs wide as he'd seen skydivers do when wearing a "flying squirrel" suit. Unlike those skydivers, Seb could increase his gliding prowess by lengthening his body and bones while decreasing his weight. When his arms and legs were eight feet long, a skein of thin tight skin now connecting wrists to ankles, he angled his body downward and skimmed through the air like a paper airplane, aiming directly for the cabin.

At the moment he had jumped from the tree, he had momentarily lost sight of his quarry. As he shot through the air on his makeshift wings, he looked for the child but could see no one.

Ten feet short of where the front door of the cabin might have been in a real building, Seb snapped his upper body upward, simultaneously opening his arms and legs as wide as possible. This induced a stall, which brought Seb to a dead stop twenty-three feet in the air. The subsequent drop would certainly have broken both ankles, if not both legs, if he hadn't been able to alter his own physical makeup, as well as that of the ground, cushioning the impact as he landed. Not that he *really* had ankles and legs, he reminded himself.

I'm gonna have to start accepting all of this at face value, otherwise I'll drive myself crazy.

He stepped into the cabin's single room and looked around, listening intently. He thought he heard a quickly stifled giggle. He smiled and sat in the rocker in the corner. He was yet to father any children of his own, but his friends had provided ample opportunities for him to experience the world of what Mee referred to as "ankle biters." Although his visitor was surely not an actual child, it was behaving like one, so Seb decided to play along.

"Hmm," he said aloud as he rocked, "this is all very interesting. I *thought* I saw someone in the trees, but now I'm not so sure. I got fairly close, but all I saw was a strange looking monkey."

Another stifled giggle. Seb pinpointed the sound. It was

coming from under the bed. He pretended he hadn't noticed and carried on rocking and talking.

"Yes, definitely a monkey," he said. "Probably looking for bananas. No bananas in those trees, though. I keep all my bananas in my boots, like everybody else does."

This time the giggle was louder, and no attempt was made to smother it.

Seb walked over to the piano. A pair of boots had now appeared on top of it. He picked them up, held them upside down one at a time, and shook them, before replacing them.

"Oh, no. I'm all out of bananas. I'll have to play the banana song."

Sitting at the piano, he played the version of Chopin's Death March that used to reliably reduce Mee to tears of laughter. By simply taking the key out of the minor into major and speeding it up, the somber melody was transformed into a happy, carefree tune.

When he'd finished playing, Seb stood, picked up a boot and looked inside.

"Aha!" He reached into the boot, pulled out a banana, peeled it and began to eat noisily and appreciatively. "Mm, yum," he said. "Delicious!"

Reaching up for the second boot, Seb peered into it and sighed loudly.

"Another banana," he said. "Too bad I'm not hungry anymore. If I knew where that funny monkey had gotten to, I'd feed it. Oh, well, guess I'll just leave it here, then." He placed the boot carefully on the floor between the piano and the bed. He started playing again but looked back over his shoulder.

After a few seconds, a small face appeared. It was that of a small girl - eight or nine, perhaps. Her head was shaved, and her features were Thai, perhaps Vietnamese.

Although, Seb conceded as she crawled out from under the bed, his guess may have been influenced by her clothing. She was wearing the saffron and red robes of a Buddhist monk or nun.

She crawled as far as the boot and sat up, legs crossed underneath her body. She giggled again when she saw the banana sticking out of the boot, then reached in and took it. Without stopping to peel it, she took four quick bites in succession, grinned happily while she chewed, then threw the last piece after the rest, even the stalk.

She looked up at Seb, her brown eyes wide and unblinking.

"Hello," said Seb. "My name's Seb. What's yours?"

She swallowed the rest of the banana and looked at him quizzically, before shaking her head.

Abruptly she sprang to her feet like a startled cat, took two brisk steps toward Seb, put her hand on his face, and felt the contours of his features just as if she were blind. Then she took a step back and smiled broadly. Seb smiled back at her.

Her voice, when she finally spoke, was exactly how Seb expected it to sound. In this place, he wasn't sure what he was responsible for creating and what was outside of his control. He certainly hadn't consciously created *her*, but the voice conformed so precisely to his expectations that he couldn't help wonder if he was behind it.

"You're *young*," she said. "This is going to be so much *fun*."

She turned and ran to the edge of the cabin's wooden floor, before looking back over her shoulder at Seb.

"I'm Fypp," she said and jumped lightly to the ground, which yielded like water. She sank out of sight and vanished.

Chapter 6

The People had no guards watching their southern border.
There was no need. Less than half a mile from the meeting
circle, the increasingly patchy vegetation yielded
completely to sand, rocks, and the occasional patch of
scrub. No enemy had ever attacked from the Parched
Lands, and no one from the People had ever returned if
they ventured further than the Last Mountain. The little
water that was available vanished along with the southern-
most blacktrees, no more than a few hundred yards past
the mountain.

At midnight, Sopharndi and Cley walked together in
silence. Cley had even abandoned his humming, perhaps
—somehow—sensing his mother's tension. No one else
would have noticed anything amiss in Sopharndi's manner
as she walked. Her head was high, her eyes looking
unflinchingly ahead. Her hard, muscular figure cast a
sharp-edged shadow by the light of the Sisters, the tight
cluster of stars which lent summer nights such as this a
silver-blue radiance. The three moons were almost aligned.
This would usually be considered an auspicious sign, but

Sopharndi allowed herself no unrealistic feeling of optimism.

The Parched Lands stretched as far as the eye could see, the emptiness eerily beautiful in the night light. That beauty would become a deadly landscape by day. Dehydration would kill you within a day and a half unless you found water, and that water was usually jealously guarded by deadly creatures. Not so deadly that they couldn't be easily dispatched by an average fourteen-year-old. But Cley was far from average.

Sopharndi slowed as she reached the edge of the desert. She turned to her son and wiped the corner of his mouth. He didn't look at her. He never really had.

A small group had gathered at the edge of the Parched Lands. Six, maybe seven figures watched from the shadows of the last few trees. Sopharndi wasn't expecting to see anyone but showed no outward sign of surprise. Then a familiar voice called softly from nearby.

"It's a shame, Sopharndi. Such a warrior cursed with an idiot child. The Singer chooses a strange way to honor our First, does she not?"

Sopharndi didn't even look up. Cochta may have hoped for a reaction under such circumstances, but she would be disappointed. Sopharndi was too good a fighter to waste useful anger by allowing herself to feel it now when it might usefully be channeled into a killing blow later. Cochta's confidence was a weakness and—when she finally dropped the taunts in favor of issuing a challenge— Sopharndi would exploit this knowledge.

She looked at Cley's face for a few seconds. He looked so like his father, the hard skin ridged pleasingly around his deep orange eyes. Beautiful eyes, but empty. No hint of his father's passion. A Blank, no more. As recently as Sopharndi's grandmother's day, Blanks had been driven out into the Parched Lands as soon as their condition became apparent. Some had barely learned to walk. To Sopharndi's secret shame, she had sometimes wondered if that might have been the kinder outcome. If not for Cley, for her. The dark moments when such thoughts had surfaced had been few, and she had responded by loving her son more fiercely than ever as this might save both of them. Now came the reckoning. Now she had to watch him go, a boy who couldn't even feed, let alone defend, himself.

The watchers from the trees were silent as she whispered in Cley's ear.

"Go to the Last Mountain. Stay for two nights, then return. Find shade in the day. Take water from the roots of the blacktrees or the small pools you will find on the mountain. Snakes and smaller lizards can be driven away, but keep your distance. You cannot outrun a skimtail. If it attacks, you must kill it. The flesh of its throat is soft, and its blood will sustain you."

Cley showed no sign he had heard her, his head moving a little from side to side as it always did. Sopharndi knew he couldn't understand her, yet still she spoke.

"On my Journey, I killed an adult skimtail and its blood told me what I would become. I left home a child. I came back a warrior. Now I am First."

Sopharndi searched his face for any glimmer of understanding. She didn't know where this desperate, pointless hope came from, but it was there. Even now, she had *hope*. It seemed to her, at this moment, that nothing was crueler than hope. She raised her voice as she spoke the traditional words of parting.

"You are my son, Cley. It is time for your Journey. Leave us only to return. We will wait for you. Listen to the Singer, for She will lead you."

Cley looked ahead, seeing nothing. Sopharndi gently

poured the last of the liquid from his waterskin into his mouth. He swallowed automatically and didn't react when Sopharndi kept the skin, instead of looping it back around his shoulder. No supplies were permitted for the Journey, other than a knife, and flints to make fire. Enough to ensure any normal adolescent would survive the experience.

When he didn't start walking immediately, Sopharndi took his shoulders, faced him directly toward the Last Mountain and gave him a tiny push. He moved then, walking steadily away from her, one foot after the other.

The observers made their way back to the settlement, but Sopharndi didn't move. She stood utterly still, her red-flecked pupils focused on Cley. She watched her son for over an hour until the wind that moved across the land disturbed the sand enough to make the plodding figure vanish completely. Only then did she turn and quietly make her way home, a mate-less warrior who had just sent her only child to his death.

Chapter 7

Hours passed, but Fypp didn't come back. Seb wondered if she ever would. He had created everything else in this place, wasn't it possible that he had created the playful child who'd visited him, too? He toyed with the idea for a while before rejecting it. Fypp was just too unexpected, too unpredictable, too *solid* to be a product of his subconscious. Although he wasn't sure if *solid* was the right word to describe someone who could disappear, passing through the ground like it was mist.

I thought I *was the only one who could do that.*

Seb looked at the patch of earth where Fypp had vanished. He stood in the same spot for a moment, then sank into it as she had done. He found himself in blackness again, disembodied. He opened his eyes back in the cabin. He shrugged. Whoever she was, whatever she wanted, he felt sure she'd be back.

There was a prayer stool propped against the piano. He took it onto the stoop and knelt, quickly deepening his attention and allowing stillness to envelop him. The stillness, the silence underneath the surface, was always there, and Seb found he needed to be enveloped by it just as much now as he had when his body was regular flesh and blood. His practice hadn't changed much—if at all—in the decades since he'd started. It simultaneously grounded, humbled, and moved him just as it always had done. Naturally, it also still alternately infuriated and bored him too. He sometimes questioned why he still kept this ancient practice at the center of his life. Sitting still, back straight, in silence. And yet he kept coming back to it. It was the only surviving remnant of his upbringing in a Catholic orphanage. No dogma, no ritual, no community. Just this sitting in silence.

Minutes passed. Maybe hours. Seb's sense of time was warped in this place. He wondered if any time was passing at all. He had read somewhere that time lost its linear nature at the quantum level, that it became something far more mysterious and unpredictable.

I might open my eyes, find myself back in bed on Innisfarne and no one would know I had gone anywhere.

He thought of Mee and part of him was dismayed to find that he was able to do so dispassionately. He knew she was safe. That was good. But his thoughts were no longer colored by her constant presence. That warm awareness of the love that had slowly blossomed between them was there, but it was compartmentalized, not all-pervasive. He suspected this would, under normal circumstances, be a worrying development, but he also knew he had changed, was still changing. He was still Seb. But he was also T'hn'u-uth, a World Walker, and he didn't yet know how Mee might yet fit into that picture.

Seb realized he had followed a train of thought, getting caught up in it, rather than just acknowledging its existence and allowing it to go its own way. He had fueled the thought by clinging on to it, and it had grown, gained impetus and, finally, taken over. With the discipline born of years of patient, repetitive and often tedious practice, he returned his attention to his breath and let the mental edifice he had created drift apart, lose coherence and finally dissolve like so much mist. Silence grew once more, filling the space left by the evaporating thoughts.

What happened next was something entirely unexpected, utterly novel and yet seemingly completely familiar. Seb *felt* a greeting. No one said a word, there was no polite cough to announce a presence. His eyes were shut, so he didn't see anyone coming toward him. He just felt a reaching out, something aimed at his Manna, the nanotech that not only made up his physical body, but trailed around him like an invisible cloud. The approach, the greeting, was careful and polite. Almost formal somehow. It was the equivalent of a butler announcing a guest at a well-heeled gathering a hundred years ago. Someone was here, saying hello, introducing themselves. And Seb knew instantly that it was another World Walker.

He opened his eyes, wondering if he was about to see the tall, gray, glowing figure of Billy Joe - the only World Walker he had ever met. But even before he looked, he knew his visitor wasn't the alien who had saved his life. The greeting he had just received was as individual as a fingerprint, and it didn't belong to Billy Joe.

Seb turned and looked at the lake. The water was gently lapping at the shore. About fifteen feet out, there was a dark shadow, gaining definition as it moved slowly closer. Seb stood and watched it approach. At first he wondered if it was some kind of fish, but when the head broke the surface, it was humanoid in shape and features. A hairless black scalp glistened and shone in the sun. The eyes—a bright blue, were small for the size of the head, which was about a third larger than a man's. The nose was

barely there at all, just a slight bump with twin ho..
which, as he watched, blew out two huge sprays of water.
The mouth was more human, the jawline strong. As it
strode out of the shallows, its body was revealed; massive,
slab-like muscles covering much of its torso.

The ground shook a little at every step once the figure
was clear of the water. It stood about eight or nine feet
high. It was as if a bodybuilder had eaten a wrestler. Now
that Seb could see more clearly, he could tell that there
were muscles in places human physicality couldn't support.
The figure was naked. It was certainly male. Either that or
he had discovered a novel way to carry a squirrel. Seb
winced and felt entirely inadequate. The thought made
him smile - he was obviously still capable of feeling some
human emotions.

The colossal figure was also smiling - perhaps
mirroring the expression on Seb's face. It came to a halt
just outside the limits of the cabin and spoke. Its voice was
exactly what Seb had expected from the size of the reso-
nant chamber in that massive chest. Deep, sonorous and
loud. Seb felt the words in the pit of his stomach as much
as he heard them with his ears.

"Hello. I am Bok."

"Seb."

Seb wasn't sure what was expected of him at this point,
but Bok's movements were confident and assured. He
stepped lightly onto the decking of the cabin. Seb half-
expected the huge figure, who looked like he'd been hewn
out of some kind of dark metal, to crash through the wood
to the ground beneath. In fact, the floor didn't even move
as he stepped across the room and lowered his huge bulk
into a chair, which illogically refused to fall apart in an
explosion of splinters.

After spending a few seconds wondering if he was

ake an attempt at small-talk, Seb decided to
fore he could do so, Bok's enormous head
slightly to one side. He was evidently watching
ning over Seb's shoulder. Seb turned and immediately saw what had caught the attention of his guest.

An old woman was walking slowly across the grass
toward the cabin. She was tall and very thin, the outline of
her skull clearly visible through the almost translucent skin
of her face. Her features were covered in wrinkles, giving
her the appearance, Seb thought, of a gnarled and ancient
tree trunk. Her nose was her most prominent feature. She
had long, straight gray hair hanging down to her waist.
She was dressed simply, and—it seemed to Seb—symboli-
cally, in an ankle-length dark green dress with long sleeves.
In one hand, she carried a wooden staff, in the other, a hat,
which she placed on her head as she stepped into the
cabin. The hat was also dark green. And pointy.

As she stepped into the cabin, she cackled loudly, as if
to dispel any doubt of what kind of creature she was. Seb
looked for a black cat and a broomstick, but neither were
in sight.

"Kaani," she said. Seb just stared back at her. The
silence grew oppressive. "I already know Bok," said the
witch, indicating the dark giant beside her.

"Oh," said Seb, finding his voice. "Sorry, ma'am. I'm
Seb."

Another silence followed, broken finally by the
rumbling voice of Bok.

"He is young, Kaani, and—whatever your opinion of
his provenance—you will not help matters by being
obtuse."

Kaani glanced in Bok's direction and sighed.

"I do not know how I look to you," she said,
"because you are creating my appearance through

cultural filters and your own prejudices. What you see here,"—the witch waved an arm, indicating their surroundings, "is visible only to you. I see something very different, as does Bok. For us to communicate at all, it is best to create a familiar environment. The same applies, to a certain extent, to the physical appearance you have chosen for each of us.

"I didn't choose any—"

The old woman held up a hand. Her nails were long, dark, and dirty.

"What you see of Bok is a crude representation of his actual form. The same goes for me. Your consciousness shapes our being into something comprehensible, using tropes and images common to the species from which you evolved. You would consider us *archetypes*."

Seb wondered if his confused expression could be interpreted as such by Bok and Kaani. Evidently, it could, as Bok elaborated on the witch's words.

"My species of origin lives in liquid on a planet with a higher level of gravity than average," he said. "Your image of me is based on the information shared by our Manna - which is communicating between us constantly. My image of you is produced in the same way. I doubt you would recognize yourself if you could see through my eyes. Kaani,"—he nodded in her direction—"was born on a world which initially condemned Manna use as evil, and considered those who used it as practitioners of dark arts. Your view of her is formed partly by how you interpret this information."

"So I'm creating all this?" said Seb, knowing as he said the words that it was true. "Then where are we, really? And what do you actually look like?"

"To see us as we are," said Kaani, "you would need to spend time among us as a species. And, of course, you must realize we have more in common with each other than we do with the species which spawned us."

"Hardly," said Seb to the witch. He glanced at the massive figure beside her. "No offense meant."

"None taken," rumbled Bok. "But Kaani is correct. *You* still identify with the species you were born into. To a small extent, you always will. Your physical appearance is unlikely to change radically, though it is possible should you wish it. But you are of no species now. You are T'hn'uuth. As are we. I have been T'hn'uuth for - seven hundred and twenty-six years. Kaani for many thousands." Seb realized the slight hesitation from Bok might be due to him converting his measurement of time into one Seb would understand. The complexity of such a calculation and the speed in which he achieved it was astonishing.

"Of the two others," Bok continued, "the oldest has been alive for billions of years. How long have you been T'hn'uuth?"

Seb felt a strange twinge of social embarrassment.

"Nearly two years," he said. The witch cackled. Seb made an effort not to think of her as a witch, but it wasn't going to be easy. She had a wart on the end of her nose, after all.

"You have much to learn," she said. "The universe is open to you, but you must see it, listen to it, and experience it, before you can begin to understand it. This will take time." She turned to Bok. "And yet his vote carries as much weight as mine, or yours."

Bok nodded, gravely. "You are toying with us, Kaani," he said. "You know our ways, you know how this must unfold."

Kaani folded her arms and looked up to the sky.

"I was witnessing the birth of a star," she said. "The

42

council's concerns seem rather trivial in comparison. I do not thank it for the interruption."

Bok just looked at her impassively, although Seb had yet to see evidence of any other kind of expression on the slab-like face.

"It is the first time in nearly two thousand years that we have been called into session," he said. "The council does not ask much of us."

Kaani made a dismissive noise. "And it was Baiyaan who was the cause of that session too, as I recall."

Bok seemed disinclined to reply. Kaani seemed about to speak again, when she was interrupted by a sound from the trees.

All three of them looked as a small figure leaped from the top branches of one of the tallest trees, spread her limbs and began to glide toward them. As she came closer, Seb recognized Fypp, her small face bearing a delighted grin as she swooped straight at them. Just as it seemed inevitable she would crash, she flipped herself upright, using the stretched skin between wrist and ankle to act as air brakes, slowing her sufficiently to alight on the table, take a few steps, and stop.

"Whoo!" she said, turning toward each of them in turn, and bowing. She jerked her thumb toward Seb. "This one taught me that. Great, isn't it? He's going to be fun. Been ages since we had a young one."

Kaani looked at Seb. "You've met Fypp, then?"

"She came by earlier," said Seb.

Kaani tutted at Fypp, who had now gone over to the piano and started jabbing notes at random.

"She can't even stick to protocols she initiated," she said to Bok.

"It is her prerogative, Kaani," he said. "As the eldest."

Seb looked at Bok. "Wait. Did you say 'eldest'?"

"Yes," said Bok. "Fypp has been T'hn'uuth for billions of years. She has watched planets evolve new life, she has seen solar systems collapse into white dwarfs, she has borne witness to the first attempts of countless species to reach the stars."

"And yet, she's still a pain in the ass," said Kaani. Fypp giggled from the piano, then sat at the table with the others.

"Kaani's just jealous because she's forgotten how to have fun." She grinned at the scowling witch. "She'll remember, eventually. It's not as if there's any rush."

"Billions of years..." repeated Seb, weakly, as Fypp picked her nose and flicked boogers at Bok, who endured it with the dignity of a true stoic.

No one spoke for a few minutes. The only sounds were distant birdsong and the tiny, almost metallic *ping* as the tightly and carefully rolled contents of Fypp's nose bounced off Bok's head.

"Where is Baiyaan?" said Kaani, directing her question at Fypp, who responded by sighing theatrically.

"Oh, all right," she said, and made a gesture with her left hand. "It's always the quiet ones that cause all the trouble, isn't it?"

They all looked at the figure now standing directly behind the fifth chair. It was about seven feet tall, thin, humanoid in appearance, although hairless and without any discernible mouth. Its large black eyes could have been looking anywhere, but Seb felt the force of its gaze and experienced a physical shock of recognition - his heart pounding and his eyes widening as he stood and took a hesitant step toward the alien who had saved his life, given him unbelievable power, then disappeared.

It was Billy Joe. And he was in chains.

Chapter 8

Innisfarne

Mee and Joni looked at Seb. The kitchen in the Keep was silent other than the old station clock ticking away the seconds over the cracked Belfast sink.

Joni rubbed her eyes.

"I was just wondering if there's ever been a stranger family. Mum can use Manna like a boss, I can travel back along my own timeline and you can hop over to the other side of the universe using magic alien powers."

Seb watched Mee stretch, extending her arms over her head.

She still looks like a cat when she does that.

She sighed, expelling lungfuls of air in a long, controlled *pshhhhhh.*

"Was he okay? Billy Joe?"

Seb nodded.

Mee screwed her eyes shut, then opened one, her gaze fixed on Seb. She laughed suddenly, shaking her head.

"What is it?"

"Oh, I was just thinking about Skanky."

"Who?"

"She was a kid at my school. At the beginning of term, Miss Harrington used to get two or three kids to come up and say what they'd done during the summer holidays. I remember one year, Skanky—Jane Dankworth was her real name—got up and said she'd ridden an elephant through the jungle and we all laughed at her. None of us were rich, but Skanky was poorer than most - tall, pale, streak of piss that she was. She had to walk a couple of miles to school to save on bus fare, and her shoes were always too small and worn through because they were passed on from her older sisters. She got everything third-hand, poor Skanky. Anyway, when she started talking about these elephants, and how her mum and dad shared one, but her sisters and brother and her, they got an elephant each, we all started howling with laughter. The thought of Skanky affording to go further than Margate for a holiday was funny enough, but elephants? She couldn't make herself heard over the racket. Miss Harrington tried to quieten us down, but you know what it's like when a roomful of kids starts laughing. There was no way we could have stopped, even if we'd wanted to.

"Anyhow, Skanky just went quiet and stared at us like she hated us all, which was fair enough. Then she sat down. About a week later, she didn't come in. Miss Harrington said her family had moved out of London. Later on, I found out her dad had won the pools - they were millionaires. She'd gone to some private school, and they'd moved to a mansion in Berkshire. She'd been telling the truth. They'd been to India during the holidays. The thing is, when I thought back to the day she had told us about the elephants, I'd looked at her feet. Her shoes were brand new. I must have *known* she was telling the truth, deep down, but I laughed along with everyone else at poor old Skanky."

Seb raised an eyebrow. "And you're telling me this why? Because you don't believe me?"

Mee laughed again. "You know I believe you, Seb. It's just the contrast suddenly hit me. I couldn't believe a poor kid from East London had ridden an elephant, but right now I have absolutely no doubt that you've been playing the piano for a banana-loving Buddhist kid who is billions of years old while waiting for three other immortal super beings to arrive. One of whom is a prisoner."

Seb nodded again. He looked at Mee. She held his gaze for a moment, then looked away. She was visibly struggling with a constant torrent of emotions for which no one could ever fully prepare. He was alive. He was back. She must know he still wanted her. And, hopefully, she still wanted him. But he wondered if the weight of the last seventeen years of not knowing if he was alive or dead was threatening to overwhelm her. She needed help. She needed something. She needed—

"I need a cup of tea," she said, looking back at Seb. "Better make it a strong one."

Seb glanced at the table, and a mug appeared, the dark brown liquid within a steaming blend of freshly steeped Assam and Ceylon leaves. He gestured at his and Joni's tin mugs and they were instantly refilled. Joni grinned and picked hers up, sniffing it.

"Wow. That smells as good as the real thing."

"It is the real thing."

She replaced the mug on the table. "Better not. I'd

already had two mugs when you arrived this morning. Mum says a third coffee always sends me nuts."

Seb snorted. "Go ahead. I've just made a tiny amendment. The caffeine will disappear after you swallow it. So you'll get the full taste without the buzz."

"Good," said Mee, as Joni sipped appreciatively. "Cos, seriously, three mugs and she's absolutely off her tits."

Chapter 9

Seb walked forward until he stood just a few feet in front of Billy Joe. Part of him was glad of the alien's habitual silence because he was certain he'd never be able to begin to find adequate words to express his feelings if he had to engage in conversation. He was alive because of Billy Joe - or *Baiyaan*, a name which immediately seemed more fitting for him. Or her. Or it. Seb remembered something about the Rozzers cycling through genders during their series of rebirths from a shared genetic pool. Then he accepted the fact that he had always thought of Baiyaan as male and decided he may as well continue to do so.

He remembered the moment Baiyaan had grabbed his hands when he was bleeding out on the Verdugo mountains. The moment when he had been pulled back from the brink of death. He had been shown an incomprehensible glimpse of something vast, something that connected all life, all worlds, all universes. He had said yes to all of that. He had taken the first step in becoming what Baiyaan was: a World Walker, a T'hn'uuth. The Roswell Manna had completed the process. Apparently. But Baiyaan felt almost as alien to Seb now as he had back then.

The only thing Seb felt utterly sure about was the alien's basic goodness. That first encounter had involved a sharing of minds, a complete opening up by both of them. As the alien had shared his consciousness with him, Seb had become aware of a complex history, a far-reaching perspective reached over millennia. What he hadn't found in Baiyaan's consciousness was any hint of evil - no selfishness, not even an urge to convert others to his own way of thinking. Seb knew that his own personal code of ethics was far less firmly established. He had moved—was moving—away from a worldview that centered around his own ego, but it was a process, not some kind of achievable goal. Seb had been brought up a Catholic but had read enough outside that particular faith to believe Jesus wasn't the only historical figure who had somehow emptied himself in order to become something greater. He had never thought about it more deeply than that until meeting Baiyaan.

The chains that secured Baiyaan's wrists and ankles were iron. There was no padlock. Seb knew the restraints weren't real in any physical sense, but the fact that his subconscious had placed them there meant that the alien was being held captive in some way.

"You chained him up?" said Seb, looking down at Fypp, then across the table at the others.

"Of course," said Kaani.

Bok nodded slowly.

"We have little choice," he said. "Baiyaan did the unthinkable when he acted unilaterally. We have heard his reasons, we have accepted you as T'hn'uuth, but now the council must decide."

Seb felt his Manna interacting with Baiyaan's. The

sensation was so powerful, he couldn't marshall his thoughts for a few moments. Baiyaan's presence affected him profoundly. He had the same deep sense of peace, stillness, of *rightness*, that he very occasionally felt when in contemplation. And yet alongside this, he still felt confused, off-balance and plain angry about what was happening to the alien.

"He's on trial?" he said.

Bok nodded. "Yes," he said. "We—his peers—cannot let his conduct continue unchecked. The council must decide what, if anything, is to be done."

Fypp took a couple of quick steps forward and, with a child's natural athleticism, did a handstand. She walked back and forth on her hands for a few seconds, her saffron robes hanging down and concealing her face.

"Baiyaan has been interfering," she said, her voice muffled. Briefly, she put all her weight onto one hand so she could move her robes away from her head, tucking them into her belt.

"He's interfering in order to stop the Crozzghyooni'ii Nssstaa interfering."

Seb wasn't sure if Fypp had said a name or cleared her throat.

Kaani flicked a cold glance toward Billy Joe.

"He doesn't seem to fully appreciate the irony," Fypp said, overbalancing. She stopped herself falling by planting both feet squarely onto the piano keys, producing a chord of which Bartok would have been proud.

"Huh?" said Seb, which was the only response he felt capable of coming up with.

Kaani rolled her eyes, but Bok put a massive hand on her arm and looked over at Seb.

"Please excuse us," he said. "We may be ancient, but age alone does not necessarily produce greater patience, or, indeed," glancing pointedly at Kaani, "basic manners. You only recently evolved, so—"

Kaani sniffed dismissively. Fypp giggled again as she righted herself, then skipped back to Seb, reached up and held his hand. Seb looked down at her, then back to Billy Joe, whose silent presence seemed to dominate the space.

"You know the Crozzghyooni'ii Nssstaa as the *Rozzers,*" said Fypp. "Baiyaan's species of origin. The ones who zip about all over the place, creating life, leaving Manna lying about to help kickstart a new species' evolution."

Seb regained a little composure.

"Sure," he said. "The Rozzers. Yeah, I remember them. Hard to forget. Wanted to wipe out humans because we didn't conform to their standards."

"*They,*" said Kaani, drily.

"What?"

"*They,*" the witch repeated. "Humans. *They* didn't conform to the Rozzer's standards. Not *we.* You're no more human than I am, T'hn'uuth."

"That's what you pick out as important in what I just said," said Seb, feeling a dull flush of anger. "Not the fact that the Rozzers were about to commit mass murder. Would have committed mass murder, if I hadn't stopped them."

Kaani stood up and leaned forward, her knuckles cracking alarmingly as she placed her gnarled hands onto the table.

"And now we come to the crux of it," she said, looking straight at Seb. "The reason the council has been convened. You ignored the covenant."

"What covenant?" he said. "I don't know what you're talking about."

Bok's voice rumbled. "Which is why Baiyaan, rather than you, is in chains."

Seb let go of Fypp's hand.

"Enough," he said, with enough authority that everyone turned toward him. Fypp even managed to suppress the giggle that was threatening to burst out. "What is Billy J—, Baiyaan, accused of? And what, precisely, is the council?"

There was a brief silence. Then Bok spoke.

"May I?"

Kaani sneered at him. "Well, your people always were the diplomats, weren't they?"

Bok seemed to pay no heed to her remark. He waited while Fypp and Baiyaan both sat down. He waited again until Seb pulled out the one remaining chair and joined them.

"The Rozzers are the universe's oldest known species. Every form of intelligent life that has developed interstellar travel owes its existence to their ongoing stewardship. Before they began their program, species would evolve in ways that, more often than not, led to disorder, violence and, on occasion, war that threatened to escalate to a galactic level. Baiyaan is accused of—on your planet—preventing the Rozzers fulfilling the task they have performed for billions of years. He did this by creating you."

Kaani interrupted.

"A T'hn'uuth should not be *created*. A T'hn'uuth should spontaneously *evolve*. We are wildcards, rare but *natural* genetic leaps. Baiyaan has done that which he asks us to prevent in his own species of origin. He has interfered. At least, he has if we continue to accept—" she waved a hand toward Seb, "—*that*, as one of us."

Fypp stuck her tongue out at Kaani. "We already voted on *that*, you old witch," she said, "and you lost. So drop it, okay?"

Seb noticed a different quality in Fypp's voice, and the air seemed briefly charged between the two females as Manna facilitated different levels of communication. He sensed a struggle of some kind, but it was quickly over. Kaani looked away.

Bok spoke up again, his sonorous tones still measured and slow.

"As for the council, you are looking at it."

Seb looked from Bok to Kaani, Fypp, and Baiyaan.

"The four of you?" he said.

"No," said Bok. "The council is comprised of all known T'hn'uuth."

It still took Seb a moment to catch on.

"Me?"

"You," confirmed Bok, as Kaani practically snarled with displeasure. "And now you must be shown the facts. Then we will vote. A simple majority will settle the matter. It is not a question of guilt or innocence, as such. Baiyaan has taken action that altered the future of intelligent life on your world."

Seb frowned. "You say it's not a question of guilt or innocence, but what happens if the vote goes against Baiyaan?"

Bok thought carefully before answering.

"You must understand what is at stake before I answer your question," he said, finally. "We are the most powerful individuals in the universe. The Gyeuk is, perhaps, as powerful, but it is not an individual in the commonly understood meaning of the word. Also, as yet, it has shown no interest in interfering significantly in the affairs of what it refers to as the *fleshbound*. We, the T'hn'uuth, have brought peace to the more aggressive species."

"How?"

"Merely by our existence in all but a handful of

instances. Worlds that wage war on each other face our justice, which is simple. We disable their technology, after which it takes generations for them to recover sufficiently to resume their wars. By that time—without fail, up to now—no world, collective, or planet-cluster has had the stomach for it anymore."

"And how does your justice apply to an individual? One of your own?"

Again, Bok waited for the right words before speaking.

"We rarely convene in this way, Seb. Our kind is solitary. We allow each other, if you'll excuse the pun, space. On only one previous occasion have we experienced dissension. The council ruled against the T'hn'uuth in question, and she was returned to her planet of origin. Told never to leave it again. Exiled, if you will. Unfortunately, she ignored the council's instruction in this regard."

The huge dark figure was silent for such a long time, that—if Seb hadn't known from his Manna that it was otherwise—he seemed to have lost the ability to produce sound. When he did speak again, the words themselves seemed heavy and difficult to articulate.

"A T'hn'uuth is too powerful a being to allow to go free. Her intended actions might have led to catastrophic consequences. She was...stopped."

"It was our only option," said Kaani. "Together, we can break the will of another T'hn'uuth, but the result of doing so is, as we discovered, permanent."

"We killed her," said Fypp, cheerfully.

Chapter 10

"You killed a World Walker?" Seb felt a kind of cold horror at his core. He had assumed that beings as advanced as the T'hn'uuth would never kill. The shock he now felt was profound.

"Her death was not the outcome we intended," said Bok. "Our attempt to remove her power was without precedent."

"Seb," said Fypp, "let me give you the skinny." She had adopted a solemn expression which looked too deliberately cute to be genuine. She produced a piece of bubblegum from nowhere and tossed it in her mouth. Her playful nature was completely inappropriate, and yet it was as if she couldn't sound a wrong note, whatever she said or did. Her incredible age was still making Seb's head reel. Her childlike appearance and personality were, he knew, façades beneath which lurked a formidable power. He didn't know how to respond to her, but he was on his guard.

"Go ahead," he said.

"We are all T'hn'uuth," said Fypp. "All of us started as

regular members of our species. But in our formative years —your own experience is an exception—we were seen by other members of our original species as different. Fast learners, picked up languages, outsmarted our parents while our peers were still sucking on their moms' titties."

She laughed then. "I wonder how that particular image translated into your head?" she said. "Never mind. Our carers, parents, guardians, genetic observers, whatever... they didn't know what to do with us. We were using Manna years before we were supposed to. Most of our societies separated us from our fellows, tried to study us. There wasn't much to see for a long time. A very, very long time in my case." Fypp grinned. "My home species doesn't reach adulthood until they are between two hundred and two-hundred-and-fifty years old. We enter our final phase —our old age— at about seven hundred years old.

"It's only in old age that an individual finally develops into a T'hn'uuth. Everything happens more quickly after that. Our relationship with Manna is the major change. Our Manna becomes able to make its own Manna. New, more capable, more adaptable Manna. That Manna goes on to create more powerful Manna still. Manna that can learn, that can develop. In that last stage, we are so far beyond our contemporaries that we are effectively a different species. Then we Walk. Between worlds. Between universes. We change, too. Our physical bodies are just our Manna's memory of what we once were. We are no more fleshbound than the Gyeuk. The difference is, we are still individuals."

"And the World Walker you killed?" said Seb.

"Wow. Same question again. Boring. I was *getting* to that bit. We couldn't take away her power without taking away *her*. No separation. See?"

Seb saw. The communication going on simultaneously

between his Manna and that of the other T'hn'uuth suggested a long, carefully considered and regretful process leading to the demise of the renegade World Walker. He knew that, despite Fypp's outwardly flippant demeanor, it had been an agonizing decision which still troubled her.

"Thing is," said Fypp, pausing while she blew a huge pink bubble, popped it and began chewing again, "you're different. Kaani thinks you can't be T'hn'uuth because Baiyaan cheated when he made you. We voted her down. But you should know your big strong silent hero here bolted T'hn'uuth status onto you without really understanding what might happen. He took a big old risk. Dintcha?"

She looked at Baiyaan, smiling. He made no response. She turned to Bok.

"Tell him, Bok."

Bok considered his words carefully. Too carefully for Kaani, who spoke in his place.

"Your species was evolving too aggressively. Like all species where Manna use is exclusive, kept to a minority, you were heading for a situation where power becomes an end in itself. Yours is a species where, for the most part, individual success is sought and rewarded, often to the detriment of the common good. Galactic harmony does not follow when a species like that develops interstellar drives. The results are never pretty. But Baiyaan selfishly insisted there was something different about your planet. He kept going back. Eventually, he staged some kind of incident big enough to get the attention of your species. He buried enough of his own Manna to draw any Users to its location."

"Roswell?" said Seb. He felt an answering affirmative from Baiyaan's Manna.

"He was convinced humanity was ready for a

T'hn'uuth to evolve. When—if—the appropriate circumstances arose, he wanted to expedite the process by giving the human T'hn'uuth the new Manna. He knew time was short. The Rozzers were on their way to your world."

"To kill us all," said Seb.

"You really take this stuff personally," said Fypp, shaking her head in wonder.

Bok took up the story.

"Baiyaan came to you earlier than he had planned. He admits that. He claims you were the one, the genetic wildcard. Only, you were about to die."

Fypp butted in. "So he weighed up the possible consequences and decided to risk it. How does it feel to be a science experiment, kid?"

Seb shrugged. "I'm still alive."

He felt a sudden craving for coffee. A mugful appeared immediately, and he took a sip.

"It doesn't make sense," he said.

"Which part?" said Fypp.

"Why create me? Why didn't Baiyaan stop the Rozzers himself?"

Fypp scowled at him. "This is getting boring," she said. "Let's vote." She pushed her chair away from the table and swiveled it to face the piano. She began to push random combinations of notes down. Seb noticed, after a few seconds of discordance, that recognizable harmonies were beginning to emerge.

Bok sighed, a sound with such heft that the table rattled, spilling some of Seb's coffee.

"He cannot be expected to vote without all the information."

"He'll never have *all* the information, will he? Just hurry it along. I want to learn how to play this thing." She glanced mischievously over her shoulder while playing the opening notes of Forgotten Blues, a song Seb had written.

"How—?" he said, as she abruptly changed up the melody, morphing it into the Loony Tunes theme. "Never mind." He looked back at Bok. The sound of the piano decreased as if he had turned down the volume. Bok continued speaking.

"Immediately after Baiyaan set in motion your evolution into T'hn'uuth, he Walked to this location and summoned this council."

Seb stared at the chains binding Billy Joe, then looked back at Bok. "*Baiyaan* summoned this council?"

The huge dark head inclined in confirmation.

"A new T'hn'uuth is an event that could never go unnoticed by us. Baiyaan wanted to plead his case before one of us went to investigate the newcomer. We gathered here immediately, then sent for you."

"Immediately?" Seb tried to work out the timeline and failed. "It's been two years."

There was a peal of laughter from Fypp, who had settled into a medley of Beatles songs. "*Two* years? Some of us had much further to come than others. There are only so many games we can play with time and space, Seb."

Seb remembered the sensation of timelessness before he had arrived.

How long did it take me to get here?

When the Rozzers had grabbed him, he had been away for days. Seb remembered the expression on Mee's face that first time when she had walked through the door twelve days after his disappearance to find him playing the piano. She hadn't known if he was ever coming back. He felt a slight twinge of guilt as he realized he'd barely thought of her since arriving. Even now, it was hard to fix on this memory. It felt like something that had happened to someone else. Or something he'd seen on TV. He realized Bok was speaking.

"Baiyaan took a huge risk leaving the fate of humanity in your hands. You might never have become T'hn'uuth. Your power may not have developed fully enough. Your intelligence may have been insufficient to get the better of the Rozzers. But, despite the odds against it, his risk paid off. You prevailed. Humanity survived. Baiyaan has petitioned us to study your species, to see why he believes the established path for the development of intelligent life should be ignored in your planet's case. And, in Baiyaan's opinion, why that path should be avoided in future. He believes your kind should not be moved aside to make room for a species with more potential."

"Why? What's different about us?" said Seb.

Fypp stopped playing and turned to face Seb, standing on the chair. In her left hand, she held a lotus blossom. A string of wooden beads dangled from her right hand.

A rosary? Prayer beads of some kind?

In her saffron robes, with her shaven head and a serene expression on her face, Fypp looked every inch a bodhisattva.

"Religion," she said, jumping lightly down. "Well, not really, more a quality he claims is threaded through the freak show you *call* religion." She walked to the edge of the cabin and motioned Seb to follow, holding out her hand.

"Come on," she said, "I'll show you. But then you have to *promise* me you'll vote."

Chapter 11

When Seb took Fypp's hand and stepped from the wooden floor of the cabin, everything changed. The room behind them disappeared, along with much of the light. He blinked a few times to adjust, then struggled to understand what Fypp was trying to show him.

"I have visited your world," she said. "More than once. I must admit to a certain fascination with it."

They were standing in a room filled with pairs of shoes. Looking behind him, where the cabin had been moments earlier, a courtyard had appeared. The floor was well-trodden hard earth, and there was a fountain in the center, adding moisture to the otherwise dust-dry air. Fypp tugged at his hand, and he followed her into the next room. It was a hall; big, open, its architecture ornate. One wall, in particular, featured a semicircular niche filled with some sort of intricately crafted beaten metal. On the floor, hundreds of men were prostrating themselves in the direction of this niche. Seb realized he was standing in a huge mosque. He remembered a PBS documentary. The niche in the wall was the mihrab, which indicated the position of Mecca, relative to the mosque. He felt slightly awed by the sight of so many people performing the same acts with such fervor and devotion.

Fypp pulled at his hand again, and he followed her through a low door. They were inside a much smaller room now, lit by candles. They followed a group of people wearing white as they left the room, carrying a body. The sky was full of the colors of a stunning sunset. Songs— hymns of some kind in a language Seb did not recognize— were being sung. Rice balls were tucked in around the corpse, and a tearful man in his forties was placing a necklace of wooden beads around the dead woman's neck. Others placed flowers there. The group was heading toward a huge river, where a solitary figure—possibly a priest—waited beside a flaming torch.

Suddenly the scene changed again, and Seb found his footsteps echoing on a hardwood floor as he and Fypp watched a roomful of men chanting, prayer books in their hands, a small black box tied onto one bicep and another onto their foreheads just underneath the edge of their skullcaps.

Seb turned toward the altar and saw a huge ornate crucifix there. In surprise, he turned back to the men, but they were gone, as was the synagogue; replaced by a large church, its worshipers making the sign of the cross as they recited the Nicene Creed. Seb felt the old habits kick in; he could have chanted the words even now, nearly two decades after he last set foot in a church.

Fypp offered no respite, just led him by the hand through a bewildering array of places of worship and their rituals, some of which he recognized, although many were completely unknown to him. He shook his head at this demonstration of his world's religiosity; the intensity, commitment, and diversity. And he asked himself the same question that kept him out of church.

How can any of them seriously claim they are right and everyone else is wrong?

Seb knew he was being slightly unfair, but seeing dozens of religious practices brought it into sharp focus for him - and he'd never had that question answered to his satisfaction.

He turned to Fypp after they left a line of masked Jains, who were sweeping the path before them to ensure they didn't inadvertently tread on an insect.

"Okay, I think I get the point."

"Not yet you don't," she said, and led him through a series of smaller rooms. Some rooms had just one occupant, others a handful, a few, many more. The people in these rooms were incredibly diverse; all races, genders, and ages were represented. The only prevailing commonality was silence. Each room was *full* of silence. Never before had Seb been quite so aware of silence as a presence, as opposed to an absence. He felt an immediate kinship with these people as his own practice of contemplation provided a thread linking all the practices he had seen in the silent spaces.

"Sufi, Buddhist, Christian, Jew, the Order, Atheist, Hindu, Shinto, Jain, Taoism, Shaman, Pagan," said Fypp. "Oh, and there's *her.*"

She tugged at his hand one more time as they walked through door taking them out of a *zazen* hall filled with shaven-headed children who looked like Fypp, out onto a hillside.

It was dawn here, and a thin rain accompanied the mist that rolled gently across the face of the mountain. There was a simple wooden structure with smoke curling out of a chimney. In front of the building, sloping down away from it, was a vegetable garden. Halfway along a row of white-flowering potato drills, a middle-aged woman wearing dirty trainers, jeans, and an old sweater was finishing some planting. She smoothed the earth down over the last seed, then brushed the soil from her hands. She watched the sun for a few minutes, as its light began to make some headway against the mist, the mountains gaining in solidity second by second. Then she stood and walked to the house, where she made coffee and porridge, before bringing mug and bowl out onto the deck and breakfasting there. The silence and stillness were full of sound and movement. Rain bounced off leaves, small birds sang to claim their territory, trees stretched in the breeze, there was a scurrying of tiny animals and insects, and the almost imperceptible movement of growing things. A wooden spoon scraping on the edge of a tin bowl. The woman's breathing.

"That's what Baiyaan wanted us to see," said Fypp. They were back in the clearing outside the cabin. Seb looked at Baiyaan, Bok, and Kaani, still sitting at the table.

"I don't understand," said Seb. "Other worlds, other cultures have religions, don't they?"

"Yeah. Kinda," said Fypp. "Well, no. Actually, not really. You're pretty unusual. Just don't know yet if that makes you outliers or an evolutionary dead end.""

"What do you mean?"

"Well, religion does pop up here and there in other species. It's not entirely unheard of. But it never survives. In the earliest stages of intelligent life, a Creator is some-times posited, but the notion never really gains traction. And, well, once a species starts using Manna and devel-oping technologically, they regard such superstitions as a slightly embarrassing part of growing up. Like body odor. Or excessive masturbation."

Seb laughed at that.

"You're outrageous, Fypp," he said.

"Outrageous?" she said, giggling. "Hardly. You should have met me three and a half million years ago. Well…" She scratched her chin thoughtfully. "Actually, no. Maybe not. Probably best that you didn't."

"We're backward, then? Humanity, I mean. We're clinging onto embarrassing superstitions. So why the fascination with us?"

"Well, remember I'm talking about billions of different species here. Only a few million developed religions, and, of those few million, all religion disappeared over time. *All* religion. The most religious species on record—other than humanity—had six different religions at its zenith."

"Six?" said Seb.

"Six. And you have tens of thousands."

"Why?" said Seb. "What makes us different?"

"That's what Baiyaan was there to find out. He thinks you're onto something."

Seb thought about the whirlwind tour they had just taken. The different dress codes, different rituals, the opposing belief systems. The self-defeating claims of exclusivity. The hostility, not just between proponents of different faiths, but often between those claiming to follow the same tradition. He remembered a homily by a visiting priest during his time in the Catholic orphanage. The old man, his liver-spotted bald head progressively reddening as he spoke, had delivered his conclusions with such absolute certainty, that—had his opinions not been stunningly offensive to anyone with a rudimentary grasp of physics and logic—he might have converted Seb through the power of his righteous conviction alone. Father O'Hanoran had spent the entire service in a state of unusual rigidity and, as the old priest finished up, he muttered a word with just enough volume to be heard by almost everyone in the place: "Bullshit."

"I don't understand," said Seb. "All those different beliefs, all those rituals, the—"

"Oh," said Fypp, grinning at him, "not that. No, that's just the label on the bottle. Baiyaan says there's something inside. And he says if we keep letting the Rozzers control the future of intelligent life, we'll never find out what that is."

"Do you mean God?"

Fypp shook her head at him. "Funny. You said that word, and it just entered my consciousness as a meaningless sound. You may as well have coughed. Or farted. There's nothing that corresponds, no way to translate. Now, I've done a little reading on this, found out about some of the explorers. Buddha, Jesus, Mohammed, Meister Eckhart, Krishnamurti, Shams. That bunch."

"That bunch?" repeated Seb, weakly.

"Yeah. They either used metaphors or refused to define ultimate reality. Buddha even described such definitions and teachings as being like a finger pointing to the moon, not the moon itself. I like that."

"So, let me try to get this straight in my own mind. Billy Joe—Baiyaan—saved my life and made me a World Walker because he hoped I would save humanity. He wanted humanity to survive because he thinks our thousands of religions might, somehow, underneath all the layers of crap, reveal a way of experiencing ultimate reality, the ground of all being?"

Fypp was nodding. "Finger. Moon," she said.

Seb turned to look into the face of the ancient child.

"And what do you think?"

Fypp scowled in thought. "I think it's…" She hesitated, searching for the right word. This was the most earnest and sincere Seb had seen her yet. He wondered what English word he would hear when she finally settled on the best way to express her opinion. Her face cleared and she smiled brightly.

"I think it's probably all bollocks," she said.

⸻

"LET'S VOTE." The voice came from the cabin. Fypp and Seb turned to see Kaani standing at the edge of the room, her long hair blowing around her face despite the fact that there was no wind. Seb supposed this, along with the fact that her eyes had become hard, glittering and unblinking, was supposed to convey impatience and anger. In which case, it was working.

Fypp skipped ahead of him. When she reached Kaani, she leaped up and knocked the pointed hat off the old woman's head, jamming it on her own before running round the cabin laughing. After a few circuits, during which Kaani actively ignored her, she ran head-long into the edge of the table and fell heavily onto the floor.

Seb went to her and gently pulled the hat from her head, only to find another, identical hat, beneath. Removing that one revealed another, then another, and another. After the sixth hat, he stopped and sat back at the table. The hats immediately grew legs—tiny, hairy, muscular legs, he noticed—and sprang up, racing around the cabin before jumping into the grass and heading for the forest. Just as the last hat was about to disappear into the trees, it paused, raised one leg, and—quite deliberately and distinctly—broke wind.

"Can't you take anything seriously?" said Kaani, a new hat now back on her own head.

Fypp joined them at the table, shaking her head at their lack of humor.

"Not so much, these days, Kaani," she said. "I'd have thought you might understand that."

Kaani made an indeterminable sound and looked round at her fellow T'hn'uuth.

"Baiyaan wishes us to call a halt to the Rozzers' creation, and stewardship, of intelligent life in the universe. To this end, he has already intervened unilaterally, breaking all normal ethical boundaries by artificially accelerating the evolution of a T'hn'uuth. In his defense, he cites the possibility of discovering the true nature of reality through spiritual practice, as opposed to using reason to draw valid conclusions from measurable results. And this merits assembling the council."

"Kaani," warned Bok in his deep rumble.

"Well," she continued. Her heavily-lined face and large nose proved able to suggest disdain and contempt without much effort. Her next words emerged as if they pained her to even speak them. "Spiritual practice. We have heard enough."

"Wait," said Seb. "If Baiyaan loses this vote, what happens to Earth?"

"Nothing," said Kaani. "Over time, another species will develop sufficient intelligence to use Manna. I'm sure humans will survive - many evolutionary dead-ends hang on for millions of years."

"Oh, thanks," said Seb, wondering if sarcasm was detectable. Kaani's glare confirmed that it was.

"And Baiyaan?" he said.

"Exiled," said Bok.

There was silence around the table now.

"Those in favor of Baiyaan's actions. Vote."

Baiyaan finally stirred, his long, thin fingers pointing

69

up. Seb raised his hand. He looked around the table. No one else had moved.

After a few seconds, Baiyaan dropped his hand, and Seb did the same.

"Against Baiyaan. Vote."

Kaani's hand went up immediately. Bok, unhurried as always, raised his own giant hand next.

Everyone turned to look at Fypp.

Chapter 12

In the short time Seb had known her, Fypp had proven to be someone who seemed to revel in causing consternation, keen to provoke a reaction. Easily bored, playful, a trickster. Occasional flashes of information hinting at her real age and experience came from Seb's interaction with her Manna, and it was a confusing picture.

After being asked to vote, she turned and stepped out of the cabin so that—so she claimed—she could "have a little think, away from you stiffs." Colorful juggling balls appeared in her hands, and she spent a few minutes struggling to coordinate keeping all three moving. She squealed when she finally achieved it.

Seb heard an odd cracking sound from across the table. Kaani was grinding her teeth.

The surreality of the situation somehow made the importance of the decision for which they were all waiting seem less important. Seb slowly became aware that this was because he was feeling the effects of Fypp's Manna more keenly than that of any of the other T'hn'uuth.

Fypp was a being of such power that Seb was only

able to comprehend a fraction of the information her Manna provided. The sensation reminded Seb of a conversation with a guitarist he'd once listened to in a restaurant in Greece. Seb and Mee had both loved his playing, and had sat in on a couple of numbers, much to the guitarist's pleasure. After the gig, they had spoken for a while in broken French, the only common language they could find, as neither Seb nor Mee spoke any Greek and the guitarist only knew a few English words. The experience had been frustrating and fascinating in equal measure. Seb had finally, triumphantly, turned to Mee and said,

"See? Musicians can communicate in any language. Anatol is just going to fetch a CD by his favorite songwriter for me."

When, a few minutes later, Anatol had returned with a pair of socks and a cheese grater, Mee had laughed so hard, so long and so loudly that the owner of the restaurant had asked them to leave.

Seb wondered if the patchy communication he detected from Fypp was deliberate. How much could a being billions of years old have in common with its fellow T'hn'uuth, let alone him? For all he knew, he could be perceiving just the tiniest fraction of Fypp, the rest of her —dark, impenetrable, impossibly complex—forever beyond his comprehension.

Or she could just be senile, of course.

Fypp had mastered the art of juggling three balls now and was moving on to machetes. Five of them. Then seven. Soon the air was filled with gleaming metal, and Fypp's hands and arms were a blur of speed.

"PLEASE." The shout came from Kaani who was standing now. Fypp paid no attention for a few seconds, then threw each machete higher on her next round of juggling, until all of them were in the air far above her. Then she walked back to the cabin.

Seb watched the machetes fall. The first one hit the ground with a wholly unexpected slapping sound. Seb looked more closely at the silvery object on the floor, which was now jerking and twitching in a strangely familiar way. Within seconds, as all the other machetes hit the ground with a spattering reminiscent of fat raindrops on a tin roof, Seb saw they had turned into fish. Big, silver fish, as long as his arm, wriggling and gasping for a few seconds, then diving into the ground itself, which accepted them like liquid.

Fypp didn't even turn to look at her creations, just jumped lightly into the room and regarded Kaani with a petulant expression.

"Don't rush me," she said. "I'd kinda hoped, during the seven thousand years since I last saw you, you might have learned a little patience."

Kaani didn't reply, just waited for Fypp to announce her decision.

"Well, okay," she said. "But you won't like it."

Kaani half rose from her chair, shaking her head. Fypp winked at her.

"I abstain," she said.

The sound that came from Kaani then was something truly alien and disquieting. Seb looked at the witch and was disturbed to see what could only be described as glitches in her appearance. The effect was similar to early experiments with inserting single frame advertisements into movies - where the word "Thirsty?" would show up for less than a twentieth of a second, followed a few seconds later by the words "Buy a Coke." Only Kaani wasn't promoting soda, she was—Seb guessed— letting glimpses of her true physical nature show.

He saw something that looked like a long purple rope, crackling with energy. Then it was gone, and Kaani's hard, wizened face and body was back. Then it was the rope again, this time seeming to slide in and out of existence, shorter or longer each time. Then Seb felt Bok's Manna interact with Kaani's and she became the wrinkled, pointy-hatted crone again.

"You have been alone too long," said Bok. "You forget yourself. You need to spend time around organic life again, leave your stellar explorations for a while."

"Don't tell me what I should or shouldn't do," said Kaani, but her tone was more controlled, and her eyes were lowered.

Seb was fascinated by the implications of this meeting. Fypp had last seen Kaani seven thousand years ago? What did the T'hn'uuth spend their lives doing? Could a T'hn'uuth die in any other way than at the hands of its peers? How could a being as old as Kaani be so impatient? Could unimaginable longevity lead to a *lack* of empathy, rather than the opposite? Part of him wanted to spend time with these creatures, ask questions, find out where his own life might be heading. But he knew he was only half-accepted by the other T'hn'uuth. They had evolved, he had been created. He wondered if he would ever be able to fill the gaps in his knowledge. If he even wanted to. And, more importantly than any questions he might have, the fate of Baiyaan was hanging in the balance. Seemingly at the whim of Fypp, who, right at this moment, was picking her nose again.

"Fypp," said Bok and his slow, deep, measured tones. If an iceberg could speak, it would sound like Bok. "Please vote."

"I abstained," said Fypp. "I'm not doing it just to make

Kaani mad. Partly, I am, of course, but that's not the only reason."

She sighed, her head shaking slightly. The gesture made her look like an old woman until she tilted her head and blew a kiss at Seb. She came back to the table and sat down.

"I don't want a boring argument about philosophy, theology, metaphysics or any of that crap, okay? Just want to get that straight before I start. Also, don't interrupt. I've had far more intelligent, and surprising, conversations with myself than I'm ever going to get with you four. So shut up for a minute or two."

She looked round the table. No one spoke.

"Good. There are civilizations where religion has flourished beyond the point at which the scientific method becomes prevalent, but they are rare indeed. I can only think of two hundred and thirty-four. Earth is the most fascinating because of the diversity. Somehow, this backwater has managed to spawn tens of thousands of religions. Most are variations on the biggies: Hinduism, Buddhism, Islam, Christianity, Judaism. I've read their texts. Yada yada yada, boring, boring, boring. They write stuff down years after the event, get bits wrong, contradict themselves, then everyone ties themselves in knots trying to make it fit into the same kind of logical framework they see in science. When it won't, everybody gets upset. Predictable, stupid, blinkered. I wouldn't have wasted five minutes on the humans if it weren't for the opening lines of the Tao Te Ching."

Seb spoke before thinking.

"The way that you can name is not the true way," he said. "Or something like that."

"No interruptions," said Fypp, handing him a banana

and crossing her arms. She waited until he started eating it before continuing.

"Still, the toddler is right," she said. "Reality cannot be conceptualized. Only experienced. True, baseline, ground of everything Reality, that is. Not anything that humans, the Rozzers, the Gyeuk or even we, can grasp. If it can be named, it is not The Way.

"If you want to spend a few hundred thousand years pursuing the nature of reality, be my guest. But I can save you the trouble. I've done it. And every path leads to a paradox, a mystery, a riddle. A joke. So you either have to laugh, or go insane."

She broke off for a moment to blow two pink gum bubbles, one out of each nostril. Instead of popping, they deflated rapidly and fell onto her face. Fypp made a loud snorting sound, and the two pink sticky threads disappeared into her nose.

"Or both," she said. "So, here's my problem. I have no desire to shake up the way the universe functions. The Rozzers have acted as creators and midwives for billions of years. Their methods work. Species come and go, but there is no wholesale mutual annihilation any more. Species that might lead us down that road are not allowed to come to maturity. The Rozzers have been doing this before even *I* became T'hn'uuth. I am disinclined to interfere."

Seb could tell that Kaani was itching to speak, but—so far—had managed to stop herself. Fypp had noticed too, and was obviously enjoying Kaani's discomfort.

"However," said Fypp, "I think Baiyaan's onto something here. When you take away the words and the concepts, humanity might, occasionally, be coming face to face with something we have yet to fully encounter. Baiyaan believes what he has seen on Earth will eventually transform the human race in a new way."

Bok raised a hand like a nervous first-grader. Fypp nodded, and he spoke.

"This part of Baiyaan's claims troubles me. It seems nebulous. I find the argument unconvincing. Where is the evidence? We are asked to change the way life develops because of…what? A feeling? An intimation which cannot be adequately expressed in concepts or words? I am sorry, but, despite my sympathy for Baiyaan's undoubted sincerity, I cannot adopt this position. Our decisions must be empirical. I require facts, testing, evidence."

Fypp smiled at this. "That's always been your way, Bok. To be fair, it's always been the way of the T'hn'uuth. We have the luxury of unlimited time in which to formulate opinions. But taking the long view sometimes prevents us seeing what's under our own noses. We are becoming creatures who act in predictable ways, follow predictable patterns of behavior, just like the species from which we broke away when we evolved into T'hn'uuth. Did you know that some Hindu creation stories see reality as a dance?"

Bok shook his huge granite-like head.

"Well, my undoubtedly light-footed friend, there is more than one way to dance. And a dancer—of any ability —who loves their art will tell you that true dancing occurs not when she concentrates on the technical processes involved, but when she empties herself sufficiently that the dance comes into being *through* her. Each time as if it is the first."

"We danced on my planet," said Bok. "Our dances, as I recall, were quite unlike what you are describing."

Seb tried to imagine the giant dancing. It was a struggle. Then he remembered that Bok had referred to his species of origin as water-dwellers. He might take on a very different aspect in his natural element.

"You sound as if your inclination is to vote with Baiyaan," said Bok.

"Don't mistake my research into the issues as bias," said Fypp.

Bok's expression was entirely unreadable, Kaani was outwardly calm, but her knuckles were white. Baiyaan was as enigmatically *there* as he always was, his Manna signature open, trusting. Detached. Seb, by contrast, felt sure his own confusion and fear on behalf of Baiyaan showed on his face, in his body language and was threaded through every Manna interaction he made. He knew this whole conversation was just a macro-level representation of a complex series of exchanges occurring between all of them simultaneously.

He felt a very strong urge for a big glass of neat single malt. Something peaty. Something that tasted of home. Something normal. A glass appeared in front of him. He didn't pick it up.

Fypp spoke again.

"What is it the founders of these religions discovered, that cannot be put into words to enable others to easily follow them? Are they unsolvable puzzles because they are The Way, and The Way that can be named is not the true Way? It's a paradox, a riddle."

Fypp smiled at them. A big, impossible to fake, *ain't this fun?* grin.

"I *like* it," she said. "So how can I vote against Baiyaan?"

Seb found his voice. "Then will you vote *for* him?"

Fypp sat back and, reaching into the depths of her robes, produced a loop of string which she dangled from her fingers. She started to make a cat's cradle. She tried to loop the end of the string over her pinky while grasping three strands in the middle. She stuck her tongue out of

78

the side of her mouth as she concentrated. Suddenly, she pulled her hands apart, displaying what appeared to be, to Seb's eyes at least, a knotted mess.

"How about that?" she said. "Oh, come on. It looks exactly like a Frutmurkle in its robes of office. Really? No one? I'm disappointed."

"Well?" said Kaani.

Fypp bundled up the string and stuffed it up the sleeve of her robes.

"Nope," she said, "I'm still abstaining. But there is a way to settle this."

Chapter 13

As the sun rose and the heat began to beat against the empty landscape, Cley walked in the pitiless, blighted landscape of the Parched Land. He had been walking all night without pausing. He looked neither left nor right, putting one foot in front of the other as he headed in the direction of the Last Mountain. Sopharndi had pointed toward the mountain and gently moved Cley's head until he was looking directly at it, before gently pushing him forward. So that was the direction he walked. It did not enter his mind that this was only time since he had started walking that his mother had allowed him to go somewhere without her. It did not occur to him that the water falling from Sopharndi's eyes and sliding down her dark cheeks meant she was upset. He did not think of her as his mother. He did not think of her at all. He did not think. The Blanks were well named.

Within the first hour of his walk, the kind of vegetation with which Cley had been surrounded all of his life—lush, green and plentiful—had disappeared. Very little grew in its place. Here and there, pathetic-looking patches of gray and yellow scrub—just shades of blue in the light of the moons—provided some contrast with the grit of the dust under his feet.

Thirty minutes brought him to the first blacktree. Towering thirty feet above him, its slender trunk and short stumpy branches offered little shade from the relentless sun. The bark of the tree was smooth and incredibly hard. The People had learned long ago that no cutting edge they had yet devised could make any impression on a blacktree.

A strangled screaming sound came from the top of the tree, and Cley stopped walking for a moment. He looked up toward the sound and—instinctively shading his eyes against the sun—he made out the distinctive blunt head and streamlined body of a lekstrall. It was smoothing its feathers with its orange beak and eyeing Cley with curiosity. The Parched Lands offered little easy sustenance to the lekstralls. The bugs they lived on in the forests were plentiful and easy to find. Out here, their chances of survival were nearly as low as that of one of the People. As if this conclusion had suddenly become clear to the lekstrall, it took one last look at Cley before launching itself from the branch. It spread its wide, brown wings, beating them rapidly at first, then slowing to a soar as it spiraled up within a thermal. When it was no more than a speck in the sky, it turned back toward home and the promise of an easy meal.

Cley watched it go, then resumed his journey. He was able to follow very simple instructions and this one had been simple enough. What he would do when he reached the mountain was unclear, but Cley had no capacity for speculation. He just walked.

Chapter 14

Tradition demanded that the People would gather on the second night after an adolescent left on his or her Journey. Music would be played, wine would be consumed, any challenges would be fought out in front of the fire. Sopharndi saw two long days stretching out in front of her. Two days of moving among those who had been her community for her whole life. Friends, family, rivals, enemies. Two days of sympathy, scorn, or pity. Her strength had limits.

Before dawn, she went to Katela, her Second, a taciturn woman who had watched three children die in infancy before becoming a warrior.

All warriors lived in huts on the outermost fringes of the settlement, forming a protective circle. Each carefully situated hut had another two within sight and earshot. There had been no attack by any other tribe for over a generation, but the warriors knew better than to relax their vigilance. The settlement's location, within a loop of the river, across from Canyon Plains, protected to the West by the Devil's Teeth mountains and to the south by the

Parched Land was an enviable one, and rival tribes would displace them, given the chance. Decades of peace had allowed them to flourish. More than half of the people's children now lived past their first few years, and close proximity to the plains and the forest meant the People's healers could easily find the roots, leaves, herbs and flowers they needed for their poultices and potions.

Sopharndi twitched back the hide hanging across the opening of Katela's hut. Pre-dawn light fell into the interior, revealing her Second already sitting up and reaching for her spear. She squinted at Sopharndi for a moment, then placed the spear back on the hard dirt floor. She prodded a shape under the furs beside her and there was a groan. When there was no other result, she punched the shape, producing a yelp this time, followed by a pouting face.

"Wha—what did you do that for? What's going on? Why are you poking me? What are you pointing at. Who's —oh." The spluttering male stopped talking when he recognized the tribe's First. The Leader held the highest authority among the People, but the First led their warriors, and only a fool would risk incurring her displeasure. He slid out from under the furs and scrabbled around for his cloak before scuttling out. Sopharndi thought she recognized him as one of the fishermen. Warriors had their pick of males, and Katela had always been fond of variety in her sleeping partners.

Sopharndi stepped into the dwelling, tucking the hide doorway open so that they could see each other. It was still as much night or day, but it wouldn't be long before the first gray tendrils of light began to soak into the featureless landscape.

Katela saw the full pouch slung over Sopharndi's shoulder and the long spear in her hand. No one was supposed to hunt unaccompanied, but being First had certain privileges. If Sopharndi wished to hunt alone, she would hunt alone. As long as the People were protected. Katela nodded.

"How long?"

"I will be back at the end of Cley's Journey."

Katela nodded again. She knew Cley must be dead or dying by now. For a Blank to survive into adolescence was unusual, but Cley could neither feed, nor protect, himself. Perhaps it would have been easier on Sopharndi if Cley had met the same fate as Katela's own children. Still, it would be over soon enough, and if Sopharndi could spend the intervening time away from the comments, the sympathy and the stares, she might be better prepared for the gathering, when Cley's death would become official.

"I will place a warrior in your dwelling until you return. The People will be protected."

"I know it, and I thank you." Sopharndi turned to go, but Katela called softly after her.

"The Singer will not let him suffer. It will be quick."

SOPHARNDI WALKED EAST ALL MORNING, following the river, then cut back northwest in the afternoon, heading into Canyon Plains. She knew she needed to grieve, and she knew she needed to be angry. For both, she required solitude. The People required the First to show strength, and Sopharndi had always projected an aura of unshakable, calm confidence. The taunts of Cochta and her cronies could never affect her, but the sympathy from others might find a crack in her demeanor and induce a display of emotion. Which must not happen.

As she walked, she thought about the Singer.

The songs told the story of the People. There were songs describing how the earth cracked open on the first morning and every creature had crawled out, pursued by those who would dominate them. The tribes crawled out last of all because they were greater than all others. The People sang another song which described the way the tribes were divided on that first day, making it clear that the Singer favored the People. There were songs about good hunts and bad hunts. About the dry days without rain, and about the years when good things grew and animals were plentiful. Songs about fishing, songs about drying animal skins and making cloaks. Songs about war, songs about peace, songs about the ancestors and the first Elders. Songs about children, songs about the old. Songs about birth, songs about dying. Songs about the best berries to pick in fall, or the best kind of animal shit to dry for use on fires. All those songs, but none about the Blanks.

The People lived, as did all the tribes, in a hierarchal system that had brought stability to their society. The songs told of a time when the tribes had always been at war, when there were no settlements to live in, just a constant moving on. Life had been shorter, more violent until the Singer had sung her first songs to the first bard.

His name had been Aleiteh.

Before the tribes had learned to speak, before the mountain god had lost her children and wept, creating River, Aleiteh had gone, alone, to the hills west of the forest. He had heard something which seemed to call him, something which could not be ignored. He walked until he dropped to the ground with exhaustion. He slept for three years and, when he woke, a tall woman stood before him, as bright as the sun. He could hardly bear to look at her. She told Aleiteh she had sung to him while he slept, and now he must sing to others. He was the first bard. He must sing these songs to the tribes. Aleiteh returned from the hills and found the first song on his lips, telling of the one he had met - no mortal woman, but the true god above all gods, the Singer. And, of those he met, many were amazed that he was still alive. Then their amazement turned to fear and awe when they found they could hear and understand the words of Aleiteh. They joined the first bard and listened to him sing. Aleiteh sang of the way they should live now. The females had always led, but they listened to this male who had dreamed of God. He told them they would still have authority, for was not the Singer a female herself? There would be Elders to decide, judge and lead warriors to fight, hunters, fishers, and foragers to feed them. The males were to teach the children, make dwellings and prepare food. But some males would become bards - and they would learn the songs, and be given new songs to sing, as the Singer made her wishes known.

The Singer promised Aleiteh's tribe would flourish, that their enemies would fall before them. And so it came to pass. Aleiteh's tribe prevailed in every battle, and they grew in number and strength. All who saw them came to know the power of the Singer and the truth of her songs.

All was well for many generations until the Dark Time, the years of famine, when the People fell to arguing about how it had come to pass that the Singer had deserted them and allowed their children to die. They fought among themselves. The tribe spilled the blood of its own people. The sky darkened, the air turned colder than had ever been known and the world nearly came to an end. Finally, the tribe split into many factions, each establishing settlements far from each other. Slowly, the world recovered and the famine ended.

The final song the bards learned to sing told of the day

the Singer would bring the Last Song and the People would be reunited, making the Land a paradise.

Sopharndi considered how long the People had waited for this new song. So long, that there were those who wondered if it would ever be sung. Such thoughts would never be spoken publicly, of course, but in the privacy of her own dwelling, Sopharndi had heard her own doubts echoed in the quiet conversations of friends. Although she had kept her own counsel on these occasions, she had recognized that her own faith in the Last Song was weak. She had good reason for her lack of faith. She had always honored the Singer and kept her ways, but her reward had been giving birth to a Blank. It was hard to believe in the Singer's justice and mercy after that. Sopharndi had begun to think that the Last Song was no more than a myth.

She thought about the bards she'd known in the settlement. They were very different to the earliest bards revealed in the songs. Those bards were remembered as prophets. They had shaken the People with their revelations, sung to them by the Singer in dreams. Now, it seemed that the correct interpretation of early songs was not straightforward. Many interpretations were only agreed after discussion and analysis over a period of years. Some of the oldest songs contained verses which were still discussed around the fire late into the night. These days, the current bard simply passed on the songs to his chosen apprentice - the boy who had shown the most musical promise. No new songs had been sung by the bards since the Dark Time, generations after Aleiteh's death. It would seem the Singer had nothing more to say to her people. And, although she knew it was heresy, this was something Sopharndi found so bewildering that she had begun to wonder if the Singer had transferred her favor to another tribe.

When she had walked half the morning and the settlement was far, far behind her, Sopharndi stopped, looked around her, laid down her spear, took off her waterskin and pack, and sank to the floor, wailing like a lost child. Startled birds took to the air from the bushes and trees lining the riverbank, and small mammals foraging nearby splashed into the water in surprise, swimming away from the unidentifiable sound.

Sopharndi wept and pummeled the hard-packed dirt with her fists. Next, she beat her own chest with her hands, hard enough to start to bruise the tough skin. Finally, she angled her head upward and yelled defiance at the Singer. At first, her screams were incoherent, then she cursed the god, pouring out the rage she felt at the years of care she had given a child who had never been able to give anything back.

She had tried to harden her heart against her own child when his condition had become obvious, but by then it had been too late. Despite the lack of any response from Cley, somehow she had found herself loving the boy. She had brought him up herself, not trusting the males and old women to give Cley enough time or care, when there were healthy, responsive young to care for. They didn't kill Blanks at birth these days, but that didn't stop almost all of the tribe at best ignoring, at worst, taunting and bullying the defenseless child as he stumbled unknowingly through boyhood into adolescence. Sopharndi knew she had let her stubborn love for him cloud her judgment, even to the extent of going to the Elders, trying to prevent Cley's Journey.

"Where was *his* song?" she demanded of the silent blue sky. "He should have a song. Why is there no song for my son?"

As always, there was no answer.

Chapter 15

Fypp looked at her fellow T'hn'uuth, her eyebrows raised. No one spoke. Seb found the dynamic between them interesting. Baiyaan didn't seem to use language at all, Kaani and Bok had obviously played Fypp's games for long enough to know when there was no point interrupting her.

Fypp sighed theatrically. She turned to Seb, then back to the others.

"The experience they report—the human mystics, I mean—occurs, almost always, within the constraints of their seemingly contradictory religious belief systems. They experience a loss of self. Some traditions embrace the nothingness, the emptiness. Others interpret it through different cultural filters. Julian of Norwich called it being *oned* with God."

"Who's he?" said Seb.

"*She*," corrected Fypp.

"Strange name for a woman."

"Well, on the gaseous swamp-world of Fruvmettlar, *Seb* is the word they use to describe a slug-like creature that feeds on fresh excrement, so you're hardly one to talk."

Seb opened his mouth, then thought better of it.

Fypp turned to her fellow T'hn'uuth.

"You really don't care what's going on? You can't see that this might be important?"

Kaani laughed. "Important? A strong word. Mildly diverting, perhaps. But interesting enough to change the way intelligent life evolves in the universe? You sound convinced by Baiyaan's argument. I'm beginning to wonder why you abstained."

"Because, unlike you, I don't see the need to jump to conclusions. Baiyaan claims the potential danger posed by humans will, ultimately, be nullified and transformed by the mystical thread running through their religions. If we give them long enough. He might even go so far as to say that the threat they pose is worth risking when held up against the potential discoveries they might make."

"We just voted against that," said Kaani.

"Yes. But you may have missed a possible side benefit of allowing Baiyaan his way. It may help us understand the Gyeuk."

Seb was intrigued by the notion that something existed Fypp didn't fully understand.

"We and the Gyeuk follow a policy of mutual respect based on an almost complete lack of understanding. And yet, on the face of it, we are so similar. Both Gyeuk and T'hn'uuth are made up of sentient sub-atomic particles. Ours evolved biologically, the Gyeuk's artificially. The Gyeuk is a hive mind, its consciousness a sea of individuals, groups and fallow regions coexisting in a constant state of change."

That last sentence made Seb's brain hurt. He wondered if that was a sensation produced by his Manna to gently indicate the limits of his intelligence.

"It could be argued that each T'hn'uuth is a smaller,

discrete version of the Gyeuk. We are, in effect, colonies of intelligent nanotech. But our differences are more than just biological. Each T'hn'uuth is a separate, self-suffi-cient, sentient being. I am always Fypp. That identity is coherent, constant and traceable throughout my life. You might argue that the Fypp of a billion years ago is not the Fypp of now, but by most indicators, I am the same person. The Gyeuk has no discrete personalities within it because there never was an individual, only a collective. So the mutual respect between Gyeuk and T'hn'uuth is colored slightly by mutual fear. We don't understand each other."

Seb remembered the ship he had met on Earth, part of the Gyeuk that had carried the Rozzers across space to wipe out humanity and start over.

"H'wan seemed like an individual to me."

"Yes, their ships do present an interesting anomaly. But it's temporary. The ships always return to the swarm, some as quickly as months after forming. Others stay out for years. I've even heard rumors of ships retaining a separate identity for centuries. But, in the end, they can't help them-selves. They always return and are reabsorbed by the Gyeuk. They allow their illusion of selfhood to dissolve in the sentient soup. Weirdos. Still, what I just described sounds surprisingly close to human mystical experiences. "

Bok rumbled a question of his own.

"Please, Fypp. Enough talking. What do you propose?"

Fypp told them. Seb understood approximately one word in every twenty in her rapid explanation.

Kaani stood up and leaned across the table, her voice a low hiss of anger.

"To do what you suggest would mean approaching the Gyeuk, going through their ridiculous protocols, waiting for a response. Even allowing for their skill with the manipulation of quantum time, it would be months before you could even…"

Her voice trailed off suddenly, and her eyes narrowed in anger. Some kind of electrical energy seemed to crackle into life around her and the gray hair visible under her hat began to rise. She looked about as terrifying as it's possible for a witch to look.

Almost as scary as the witch in Disney's Snow White, mused Seb. He still had mental scars from that Sunday afternoon matinee showing.

"You have already consulted the Gyeuk," said Kaani. "You petitioned them. You *have* it here. Don't you?!"

Fypp giggled and clapped her hands at Kaani's display.

"You're just delightful sometimes, Kaani. Yes, of course I do."

"So why not just tell us in the first place? Why this rigmarole of—why bother trying to get us to agree to—why…?" The witch closed her eyes and muttered something. In the far distance, a patch of sky darkened quickly, then became completely black. There was a thunderclap loud enough to make the ground tremble, then a huge flash of lightning which turned the entire scene blindingly white for a split second. The sky cleared instantly, and Kaani retook her seat at the table.

"Ooh," said Fypp, appreciatively, "pretty."

THE ARGUMENT between Fypp and Kaani made so little sense that Seb gave up trying to follow it. When he finally became aware that they were no longer talking, he glanced up and found them all turned toward him. He felt like a fifth grader who had been caught daydreaming. He looked at what Fypp was holding and felt his eyes and his mind slide away from the sight, dismissing it as impossible and—therefore—probably not even there.

"A Gyeuk Egg," said Fypp in answer to Seb's unspoken query. "There is no real equivalent in your human language, no concept that can begin to do justice to its complexity, its depths."

She was holding a dark object, a large oval. It was the first time Seb had seen the ancient child show respect for anything. She handled the Egg reverently, like a holy relic. She had produced it from the air, almost as if she had reached through one plane of existence into another, and pulled it through the skein that separated them. Now she held it toward Seb, and he cupped his hands to receive it.

Seb had expected some weight to the object he'd been handed and was surprised at how light it was. He could feel *something* touching the skin of his hands (no-skin, no-hands) but the sensation was quite unlike anything he'd ever experienced. In one way, it felt like he was holding a ball of cotton, the tiny fibers barely registering on his fingertips. In another way, he felt the *presence* of the thing more solidly than if he was holding a bowling ball. The overriding impression was of something that didn't quite belong, was somehow in his hands, but actually not there at all, a foreign body, something utterly *other*. His Manna was providing no useful information besides a feeling that the object was unreachable. For the first time as a World Walker, he found himself encountering a limit to his power, a line he couldn't cross. It made him a little afraid, but—more than anything—he felt relief. The T'hn'uuth weren't all powerful. At least, he wasn't. And, judging by the way Fypp had handled the object he now held, she was similarly limited.

"But what is a Gyeuk Egg?" said Seb. In answer, Fypp held out a hand, and he gave it back to her. She placed it in the middle of the table. The other T'hn'uuth were silent.

"In the simplest terms possible, it's a simulation," she said.

"Like a computer simulation?"

"Well, like I said, monkey-boy, I'm using the simplest terms possible. A computer simulation is to a Gyeuk Egg as a microbe is to a human being."

Seb was unsure whether "monkey-boy" was intended as an insult or a term of endearment. He decided to let it slide either way.

"So, er...how does it work?"

"You wouldn't understand."

"Try me."

Fypp was right. He didn't understand. Apparently, it had something to do with wormholes, string theory, quantum spinning, and comb-overs. And that was the bit of her explanation that made the most sense. After nearly four minutes of mental pain, he held up a hand and conceded.

"Okay, okay, you're right. But, let me check I've understood the essentials. It *is* a simulation in the sense that it's artificial. But—somehow—the technology they're using allows an entire planet, even a solar system to exist within the simulation at a level of detail that would make it impossible to tell it's a simulation at all. Right?"

Fypp had stretched out on the cabin floor. Her eyes were closed, and she was breathing deeply. She raised a hand and gave Seb the thumbs up before yawning and, seemingly, going back to sleep. He kept talking, trying to make sense of it all.

"So the Gyeuk creates Eggs to run specific scenarios. And it's prepared to make Eggs for others occasionally."

Seb wondered how best to ask the obvious question. Kaani saved him the trouble.

"We would make Eggs if we could," she said, her lip curling in such a clichéd way, that Seb felt sure there must be a picture of her in illustrated dictionaries alongside the entry for *scorn*. "None of us like to admit it, but the Gyeuk has the advantage here. We T'hn'uuth can easily create immensely complex systems using our own Manna, but they are always temporary. We could populate an artificial planet with homunculi, each of which would behave as if it had free will. But it would all collapse back to its component parts within a few days. Our Manna is inextricably linked to our individual consciousness. The Gyeuk, probably due to its non-biological provenance, has no such limitation. And, somehow, it has been able to use wormholes and multiple instances of the multiverse to create Eggs."

Seb was silent for a few moments, taking in the fact that the Gyeuk seemed capable of something possibly beyond even the capacities of a World Walker. Then he remembered that Kaani had artfully avoided answering his question, so he repeated it.

"Okay, it can do something you—*we*—can't. But *why*? Why does it go to all that trouble? What does it get in return?"

Fypp stopped snoring and opened an eye.

"I believe it helps us for two reasons. Firstly, our request feeds its superiority complex. It just *has* to believe it's top of the pile, sentience-wise. But it's not completely sure if we are its equal or inferior. Drives it crazy, I'd bet. So, secondly, I think it makes them for us because every request gives it a chance to add to the information it has about us. By knowing the details of every simulation we run, it learns a little more about us. You play poker, Seb?"

For a moment Seb thought Fypp was suggesting a

game. Just when the surreality of his situation seemed to have peaked, he suddenly imagined playing Texas Hold'em in an imaginary cabin with—as far as he knew—the oldest being in the universe.

"Er, yeah, yes, I do. A little."

"Now that's a game I like. Similar games are played by many millions of species, and the best of them share the same central premise: incomplete information and an element of luck. To win consistently, you have to make guesses about the strength of your opponent's hand based on history, the current situation, psychology, and math. In that order, unless you're playing an Artificial Intelligence. They can cheat by throwing truly random elements into their strategy. Bastards."

She seemed lost in thought for a moment, chuckling at some memory or other.

"Well, that's a story for another time. I once suggested that serious conflicts with the potential to spread beyond, say, the warring parties' solar system, should be settled by poker tournaments - or the equivalent. I still think it's a good idea."

She seemed lost in thought again. Seb cleared his throat.

"The Gyeuk?"

"I was getting to it. I'm not senile, you know. Although, imagine the havoc I could wreak if I did start to lose the plot. Anyway, yes, the Gyeuk. I think of the relationship between the T'hn'uuth and the Gyeuk as one long heads-up game of poker. It finds out a little more about us each time it constructs an Egg, we get some information about it during the negotiations. Naturally, many of the Eggs we request are flim-flam."

"Flim-Flam?"

"Diversions. False trails. We ask it to construct an Egg

based on a very detailed template, engineering a society which will follow certain rules and be confronted with baked-in dilemmas, just to confuse the picture the Gyeuk is building of us. Incomplete information. We suspect the Gyeuk of pursuing its own agenda, and we want its store of knowledge about us to remain as opaque as possible. See?"

Seb had always found the electoral college system confusing. He wasn't about to take on the nuances of inter-species politics. He took a deep breath.

"So what do you want me to do?"

Fypp rubbed her hands together.

"Simple. Get in there and start a religion. If they buy it, you win."

Chapter 16

When he reached the foot of the mountain, it was still light, although the first of the moons was already visible and the sun was painting the sky pink and orange. Cley breathed more deeply as the land lost its flatness and began rising, but he kept his pace steady. When Sopharndi had pointed at the mountain, he had fixed his gaze on a dark spot about two-thirds of the way up. He would stop when he got there.

The Last Mountain was somewhat misleadingly named. It wasn't the only hill in sight, just the nearest. It only rose about four hundred feet above the desert, but, as no other landmarks were visible for miles, it had found itself promoted from a hill to a mountain. On the horizon, far higher peaks could be seen on the clearest days, but— with hundreds of miles of desert lying between the Last Mountain and these distant slopes—only a few adventurers had ever risked making the trek. The People were a pragmatic race. The land on which they lived sustained them. The wasteland to the south showed less vegetation than Cley had passed on his trek to the mountain. Even the hardy blacktrees became less numerous, eventually giving way to a vast dry yellow-gray expanse of nothingness. The only contrast was provided by the occasional piles of bleached white bones belonging to those who had tried, and failed, to satisfy their curiosity about the distant mountains.

Cley's breathing deepened as the incline grew steeper. His lips were dry, and his throat craved the soothing qualities of water, but Sopharndi was not there to provide it. He knew of no other way his thirst could be slaked. Sopharndi had pointed this way, and he had walked. Every day she had given him food and water. Today he had received neither. He would go where he had been told to go. Somewhere in his mind was the certainty that food and drink would be waiting, as would be Sopharndi.

He found the entrance to the cave just as the light of the first and second moons took over illumination duties from the sinking sun. The third moon would only be visible as midnight approached.

As Cley shuffled toward the black mouth of the cave, and finally sat, peering into the darkness, he heard a rustling and hissing as snakes and lizards found new cover away from the intruder. The fact that the moons were in the phase where they were aligned gave every rock crisp, sharp-edged shadows, and plunged the interior of the cave into impenetrable darkness. Cley could make out a few scattered twigs and some darker patches on the ground, but no more. There was a strong animal smell, but part of Cley's brain registered that as familiar; he had often spent hours watching the other children milk the gandreals, feed them, clean out their pens or cut their long, glossy coats when the summer came. The smell in the cave was different to the domestic animals he knew, but similar enough to allow him to settle.

His feet hurt, his legs ached, and his tongue felt furred and thick for lack of water. Cley could see nothing in the cave, so he turned and looked back toward the settlement and home. It was the first time he had looked behind him since setting off the previous night, and everything seemed unfamiliar. He could see the abrupt change in the landscape where, about twenty miles north, the dust of the Parched Lands made way to the greenery of the settlement. The sight made no sense to him. He did not know he was looking at his home. Cley still expected his mother to appear at any moment, and he had no capacity to come up with a plan if she didn't. He waited.

His head was just beginning to nod with sleep when he heard a noise behind him. Cley opened his eyes and listened. The noise came again, a swish of sound as if someone were sweeping the cave. Sopharndi swept their hut every night before sleep. He *knew* this sound. He got to his feet, surprised and confused by the shooting pain in his legs as he stood. He turned and faced the cave mouth.

The moons were higher now, and the third moon was beginning to rise so Cley could see a few feet further into the cave mouth. What he had taken for twigs were revealed to be the discarded bones of lizards and small rodents. The dark patches were dried blood. The animal smell was stronger now.

As the swishing sound came closer, Cley leaned forward, expecting to see Sopharndi sweeping the cave. He had no other association with the sound he was hearing. His life had followed a simple, reliable, repetitive pattern, and his few autonomous actions were triggered by responses to familiar stimuli. Sopharndi was sweeping the cave, so he must go to her.

He stepped forward into the darkness.

As he walked, the smell grew stronger, but the sound

stopped. Cley stopped too, confused. He started humming, then stopped abruptly when he heard something come closer. The smell was almost overpowering now, and was different enough to the familiar gandreal odors that Cley felt suddenly disorientated. He turned and walked back toward the moonlight.

Something moved behind him.

The next *swish* was loud and close. Cley's feet were knocked from under him by something heavy and strong and he fell on his side, grunting with pain. For a second he lay there, then instinct took over and he began to crawl the last few feet to the cave's exit.

He sensed sudden movement near his right foot and drew it rapidly up to his body. He was nearly at the cave mouth now, his eyes adapting to the gloom. The light of the moons was reflected by rows of savage, sharp teeth which closed over the air where—a split second earlier— his foot had been. Cley scrambled out of the cave and got to his feet. Then he stopped for a second, unable to decide what to do next. He did not know where he was, but this was the place his mother had pointed toward. This was where he was supposed to be.

When the skimtail emerged from the cave, it was with such a burst of speed that even a warrior, knife drawn, would have been unlikely to be able to strike in time. As it was, Cley's arms hung by his sides, his knife—an unfamiliar item Sopharndi had attached to his belt the previous day—was still sheathed. Cley took one half-step to the side as the giant lizard sank its barbed teeth into the flesh just above his left wrist.

Had Sopharndi been there, she would, at least, have finally had the satisfaction of knowing that her son could make a noise other than the tuneless humming he was known for. The scream that came from his lips broke through as a high-pitched wail of agony. With an animal instinct for escape from the terrible, searing pain in his arm, Cley did the worst thing he could do under the circumstances, and pulled back against the savage bite of the creature. The foremost teeth of a skimtail are small and hooked, used to grip prey. The more the victim struggles, the further they work themselves on to the initial bite.

When the creature suddenly released him, Cley stared at the ragged mess of blood, skin and bone above his hand. He drew breath for another scream, then stopped, a strange sensation coursing through his body. Had he been able to understand the warnings Sopharndi had given him, he would have known what every child of the People was taught on their parents' laps. The poisonous bite of a skimtail could kill rodents and lizards outright, but it was also potent enough to render a fully grown person unconscious for a few minutes. It was the reason why none of the People ever ventured outside the settlement alone. If you were bitten and there was no one nearby to help you, your only chance was to bury your knife in the thing's throat before the poison took effect. Otherwise, you were as good as dead.

Cley swayed a little, took one faltering step backward, then fell heavily to the floor. The skimtail's long powerful tail coiled around his feet like a giant snake and he was pulled back into the cave, his head bumping across rocks as the last spark of consciousness disappeared.

There was enough meat on an adolescent male like Cley to feed the skimtail's mate and three young for nearly a month.

Chapter 17

Seb looked at the Egg. Although it was on the table, it seemed as if it wasn't there at all. It was physically difficult to look at for long. It was as if the visual information it provided didn't tally in any real sense with the physical *essence* of the thing. Seb reminded himself that nothing around him, including his own body, was "real" in any commonly accepted sense of the word, and yet he had been able to act as if it was. The Egg gave the lie to all of it. It was an impossible object, and his mind couldn't accept its presence in any way that was remotely comfortable. He looked away again. He was beginning to feel as if all this was happening to someone else.

"If you agree, you will enter the simulation, become a part of it." Fypp was, seemingly, being serious and direct now, although it was hard to tell. "It's your decision, Seb. There are dangers."

"Dangers. But, hold on. What? Even if I could, how can starting a religion in a simulation change anything? How will it help Baiyaan?"

"It's simple," said Fypp. "They have a primitive form

of religion already. Go shake them up. Mysticism 101, that's what they need. Prove to us that whatever it is Baiyaan sees in humans can truly change an entire species. Teach them what you know. Then I'll vote for you."

"You need a priest, or a monk, not me. I don't even go to church. I'm the wrong person to do this."

"I think the fact you have stayed away from organized religion makes you a stronger candidate, not a weaker one. You won't ask them to believe that a two thousand-year-old middle-eastern alien is the only one who can save them. Will you?"

"No. I guess not. But even if I agreed to try…it'll take years! And mystical traditions evolve over centuries! I mean, just to get started…I can't, you can't expect me to…"

Bok nodded his huge, dark head. "You have six months. Any shorter would be unfair. Any longer and the risk of losing your identity would be too great."

"Six months? I can't—"

Seb felt like sitting down, before remembering that he was already sitting down. He wondered if sitting on the floor of the cabin itself might make him feel more grounded. Then he reminded himself that the chair, the floor, the cabin itself and everything he could "see" didn't exist in any meaningful sense. After that, he just felt a bit sick.

"Time moves differently inside a Gyeuk Egg," said Fypp. "Try to imagine time happening almost all at once, rather than one event after another. An ocean, not a river. You will have to adjust when you rejoin us here."

"Really? Great. Sounds like a bunch of fun."

They all stared at him. He turned to Fypp.

"Even if I agree, how will you know if what I do has any effect? If I manage to influence a group of people, it might not last. You say they have a primitive form of religion. Is their society pre-technological?"

Fypp nodded. "Pre-almost anything useful, actually. Sorry. No mass-communication. No record-keeping of any kind, either. Oral tradition. Nice and simple."

"Nice and simple? So, unless their oral tradition preserves the essential message of whatever it is I hope to achieve, within a generation or two, no one will even know I was there?"

Kaani leaned forward. "Yes. In which case you will have failed, and we can all go back to our lives."

Seb laughed. "It's impossible."

"Maybe," said Fypp, "maybe not. There's a saying I like from one of your Russian Orthodox saints - Seraphim of Sarov."

Seb started wondering exactly how much time this incredibly old being had spent studying his home. She certainly seemed to have a better knowledge of religious traditions than he did. Which, to be fair, wasn't all that difficult.

"He said, *Acquire the spirit of peace, and a thousand souls around you will be saved.*"

Seb stared at her. That mischievous smile was starting to annoy him.

"I'm starting to think you've got the wrong guy. Maybe Baiyaan got the wrong guy." He turned to Billy Joe. Not for the first time, Seb wondered if Steven Spielberg hadn't had a visit from Baiyaan when he was coming up with *Close Encounters Of The Third Kind.* The resemblance to the aliens at the end of the movie was uncanny. Billy Joe made no response, but his Manna radiated its usual peaceful, calm reassurance. Even that was starting to irritate Seb now.

"Seriously - not only am I not a saint, I'm pretty near the other end of the spectrum. I've screwed around, taken drugs. That whole business about turning the other cheek? I don't do that, I just get pissy and waste hours hoping I'll get my revenge. I'm petty, I'm shallow. Just because I sit down and contemplate twice a day, don't think that makes me holy." Seb realized he had raised his voice, but he couldn't stop himself. He clenched his fist, ready to bang it on the table for emphasis, then saw the Egg—felt the sudden shock from the other T'hn'uuth—and managed to stop himself, waving his hand feebly in the air instead. The gesture was awkward. He suddenly felt like a child having a tantrum in front of elderly, disapproving, and slightly patronizing, relatives. Instead of stopping him short, the feeling made him angrier still.

"I meditate because if I didn't, I would be a complete and utter dick. That's why. *Acquire the spirit of peace*? Are you fucking nuts? Why don't you go? You obviously have some kind of mini-Buddha complex. Or how about Baiyaan? He's the real deal. You see that, right?"

Fypp got up, followed him for a few paces as he stamped around the cabin, then grabbed his hand. He turned, and she reached out for his other hand and took it. He looked down at her, ready to vent some more anger. It felt good—*right,* somehow—to let this frustration show, to rail against the unfairness of the situation in which he found himself. But when he looked at her face, the open, trusting face of a child, even the fact that he knew it wasn't real didn't stop the rage evaporating like rain after a tropical storm. He tried to cling to the remnants of his anger, but they eluded his grasp. His voice, when he finally spoke, was full of fear, loss and plain bewilderment.

"I didn't ask for any of this." His voice shook slightly, and Fypp gently squeezed his hands.

"I know you didn't."

"I'm not even close to being a saint, Fypp. I'll fail. If I try to do this, I'll fail."

She smiled again, but she seemed to allow a little of her true age and experience to inform the expression on her face. "Spoken like a true prophet. If you felt up to the task, if you believed you were capable of leading a single person, let alone a whole society, onto a new spiritual path where they might encounter Reality, you would be—at best —hopelessly deluded. At worst, you would be dangerous. No one ever feels ready when called."

He shook his head. "But I—"

She squeezed his hands again, and he fell silent. "No one," she repeated. "But this is your moment. Yours."

Seb remembered his childhood, reading comics about superheroes, seeing Batman at the local movie theater. He'd always thought of men and women with super powers as being heroic, free - something to aspire to. Now, he realized they were, in a sense, *trapped* by their abilities. Usually, they hadn't asked for their power. Bitten by a spider, escaped from a dying planet, violently orphaned, experimented on by power-crazy scientists. Then they were doomed to spend their lives *reacting* to shit thrown at them, or at others, by the bad guys. They were forever cleaning up the mess. Where was their choice? And where was *his* choice now?

He let himself be led back to the table and sat down. Fypp continued to hold one of his hands.

"You just have to act like you *are* a prophet. Keep acting like it and you might surprise yourself. Plus, you'll have an unfair advantage. You are a T'hn'uuth, after all."

Seb shrugged and tried to be flippant in the face of the relentless monster truck of fate currently bearing down on him. "Well, I guess it's just a simulation," he said. At that, Fypp's smile became broad.

"What's the difference?"

Seb took a deep breath. "Well, I mean, no one really exists there in any meaningful sense, so…" His voice tried off.

"Depends how you define meaningful," said Fypp. Seb knew she was playing with him. She looked him sidelong, her expression sly and knowing.

"Um," said Seb, eloquently expressing his inner thoughts.

"Do you need a biological body to exist in a meaningful sense? That excludes me, you, the Gyeuk and a few thousand species which you aren't yet able to perceive. Don't be such a dimensionalist. Ignorance is no excuse."

"Er," said Seb, expanding his argument somewhat unconvincingly. Fypp pressed her advantage.

"Does consciousness and free will count toward meaningful existence by your definition? Because they experience both where you're going. If you're going. Are you going? You're gonna go, right?"

Fypp's expression changed from *academic lecturer* to *small child pleading* in a millisecond. It was as if she had flicked a switch. She looked crestfallen, her big eyes fixed on his, innocent and imploring in equal measure. Despite the seriousness of the situation, Seb found himself laughing.

"And if I say no? It's still two votes for Baiyaan, two against. What will you do if I refuse?"

Fypp smiled mischievously.

"Well, in that case, I will probably have to vote. We need a decision. And there's only one fair way." She pulled a shiny object out of the folds of her robes. "I'll toss a coin for it."

Seb didn't answer for a few moments. He looked at Baiyaan, whose passivity in the face of the decision Seb was being asked to make on his behalf would have been upsetting, if he hadn't been radiating his usual aura of peaceful acceptance. Bok and Kaani waited for Seb's answer. Fypp made a shooing gesture at Seb with one hand.

"It's a serious decision. I wouldn't expect you to give us an answer right away. That would be cruel. Go for a walk. I'll give you ten minutes."

Chapter 18

Seb walked through the forest, marveling at the detail of the place his subconscious had produced. The slight give of the mulch underfoot in places where sunlight struggled to break through the leafy canopy, the sap bleeding from some of the pines. The spider webs suddenly appearing as they came out of shadow. The smells and the sounds of the forest, the crisp, clean, pure air that never failed to lift his spirits. He remembered his early morning walks back in Los Angeles. The Verdugo slopes at dawn had been a mainstay of his routine when he was at his creative best, writing songs, spending afternoons at the studio. He'd usually walked alone. Sometimes he'd met up with Bob and his dog, Marcie, but Bob—a man of few words at the best of times—had understood the value of silence. Seb missed him.

He walked on. The trees started to thin out. The incline got steeper, and the soft earth gave way to drier, rockier terrain. As he headed for the summit, the sound of birdsong and wind in the trees faded. The growing silence was more intense because the sounds of his body were absent. No cartilage crackles. No breath.

He stopped and sat on a rock, looking back at the clearing, the cabin, and the lake. He thought about Fypp's proposal. Then he turned his thoughts to Earth. More specifically, he thought of Mee and the life he had left behind. The island of Innisfarne, its peace and tranquility. His brother John, whom he'd never had the chance to get to know. A home. Maybe, one day, a family.

Seb knew that his feelings weren't normal. He thought about Mee, the woman he'd loved ever since she'd walked up behind him and pinched his butt at a recording session in London. He could remember the passion, the intensity, the carefree willingness to give up everything just to be able to be with her. To talk with her, kiss her, undress her. But that was the problem - he was *remembering* the passion, the intensity. He could calmly recall the beautiful insanity of love, and that just wasn't right. The distance he felt wasn't just physical. He knew he'd changed. How could it be otherwise? By most standards, surely he wasn't human anymore.

He started walking back to the cabin. He wondered if it was even possible that he could do what Fypp was suggesting if he wasn't fully T'hn'uuth, or fully human. He felt as if he needed time to process what had happened to him since he had sacrificed his biological body to re-engineer the Unmaking Engine and prevent the destruction of his species. His *ex-species*? He felt adrift. Mee had *completed* him in some way beyond the clichés and platitudes associated with romantic love. And yet, he couldn't *make* the feelings come back.

Seb wasn't sure who he was anymore. And this was not the kind of existential crisis that could be sorted out by lying on a couch and talking to a stranger about how you secretly watched your aunt getting changed at the swimming pool when you were ten. This crisis involved sorting out which *species* he belonged to. Maybe it really wasn't the best time to enter some kind of simulation, become someone else and, hopefully, set the future of intelligent life in the entire universe on a new, uncharted course.

On the other hand, who else was gonna do it?

FYPP, naturally, was delighted - a fact she felt compelled to demonstrate by turning cartwheels for five minutes while whooping. Loudly.

When she finally settled down, she stepped back up into the roofless cabin and smiled at the silently calm Baiyaan, the impassive Bok, the simmering Kaani, and the permanently confused Seb.

"Come on, guys, why so serious? It's not life and death, you know. Well, it might be, I suppose." She did her best to look crestfallen and managed it for a split second before grinning again. "Well, it's not life and death for *us*, anyway."

Bok made a noise which Seb's Manna interpreted as clearing his throat. Fypp's brow creased for a moment, then cleared as she glanced around the group and recognized the inaccuracy of her remark.

"Okay, Mr. Pedantic, Seb *could* die, true enough, but it's fairly unlikely, so there's no need for you to bring us all down with your doom and gloom."

Bok ignored her and pointed at Seb.

"Although not significantly high enough to cause great concern, the odds of Seb losing himself and forfeiting his—"

"Oh, don't start with odds, you great baboon. He's not interested in all the boring details, are you, Seb?"

"Well, Fypp, I guess it might be useful to—"

"See?" Fypp took Seb's arm, scooped up the Gyeuk Egg from the table and walked him over to the edge of the lake. The water was lapping gently at the shingle shore. Seb thought briefly of Penn Pond, at Richmond Park, where he'd first met Mee. And where he'd had virtual conversations with Seb2. Then he remembered the beach at Innisfarne. He tried to think of Mee's face and was pleased to find he could picture her perfectly. Next moment, his heart sank when he realized the image he had was *too* perfect. It wasn't the unreliable recall of a lover, with misremembered details and a tendency to airbrush imperfections, it was as perfect as a photograph. And as soulless.

Fypp tugged at his sleeve. Her voice was more gentle than normal.

"Let it go, lover boy." Seb flinched. He wondered how much information his Manna gave away. Perhaps very little was hidden from a creature as ancient as Fypp. The child raised an eyebrow at him. "It'll hurt a little, but it will pass. Some changes, once set in motion, cannot be reversed. You'll learn to accept it. Eventually, those kinds of primitive emotions will seem almost embarrassing. You'll outgrow them."

"And if I don't *want* to outgrow them?"

Fypp shrugged and skipped over to a large, waist-high rock which featured an unnatural indentation perfectly fitted to the Egg's dimensions. She placed it there. Seb noted how gently and carefully Fypp handled the Gyeuk Egg, despite her studied couldn't-care-less demeanor. He walked over and tried, with some difficulty, to look at it again, still in awe at its refusal to settle into an appearance his senses were comfortable with.

Fypp poked him in the side with one finger.

"I asked for a little drama when you first show up," she said, nodding at the Egg. "You'll know it when it happens. Just a little convincer to help you get started."

Seb stopped trying to look at the impossible object.

"Why does someone have to go in there at all?"

Fypp looked at his face and sighed.

"If you had any idea how tedious it is having to explain things at this level...never mind. Fair question, I suppose. Since it's you doing the hard part. Yes, we could request the target species' evolutionary template to favor a certain religiosity. We could even suggest character traits based on what we know of influential religious figures in Earth's history. But what we are searching for is uniquely human, so trying to reproduce that through software, or wetware, however sophisticated the Programming, is impossible. It has to be you, Seb."

Seb sighed. "And when I'm done? When I come back? How will you know if I succeeded? Six months is hardly going to be long enough to change the future of a species."

When Fypp spoke, it was with utter seriousness. He had no idea if she was being sincere or not.

"Don't underestimate yourself. I have faith in you."

Chapter 19

After a cathartic hour of howling her fury and sadness at the uncaring landscape, Sopharndi trekked northwest, doubling back on herself slightly as she headed out into Canyon Plains. She found one of the clumps of plaintrees before dark and clambered high into the canopy of the tallest tree, expertly slinging her cloak under a sturdy branch and curling into it to sleep. After the sustained emotional outburst of the afternoon, her sleep was deep and dreamless, and she awoke with a clear mind, her grief a stone in her belly.

Today she would hunt. Still in her perch high in the tree, she broke her fast with a few strips of dried meat and some water from the skin. Then she surveyed the area, looking for fresh signs of animal movement.

Herds of ha'zek crossed the plains from the northwest every spring, following the river as they went. They had mostly moved on now that summer was here, but small groups of stragglers could be found even now. The skin of the ha'zek was prized for its warmth. Its bladder was often used for waterskins, such as the one Sopharndi now carried. Its meat was unpleasant when fresh, but, smoked and dried, it sweetened, and each summer's bounty was stored, ready to be distributed in the leaner winter months. There were strips of it in the bag tucked next to the knife in Sopharndi's belt. Along with the berries she would find while hunting, she knew she wouldn't go hungry.

She trekked half a day into Canyon Plains, only stopping to eat and take some long swallows of water. She couldn't stray any further and still be able to carry an animal back on her own, and her need for solitude was tempered by her duty to the People. Katela was an extremely able warrior, but Sopharndi was First, and her place was with those she had sworn to protect. She would stay away for one night, no more. She would return for the gathering, Cley's death would be acknowledged, and the tribe would move on. Sopharndi would move on, too, eventually. Cley's life might not be remembered in stories or songs. His memory would never be cherished like the ancestors who had served the People well.

Sopharndi tied the bag back onto her belt. She would never forget Cley. The rage she felt against the harshness of tradition would keep his memory fresh for a good while, but she knew the bitter taste of her sadness and loneliness would surface soon and stay with her far longer.

Before moving on, she thanked the Singer for the food with a few muttered words, followed by touching her fingers to her lips. She thanked the Singer with her words, but not with her heart.

The landscape, like most of the topological features around the settlement, was named unimaginatively, if accurately. Canyon Plains was a mixture of umber canyons and jagged rock formations, surrounded by green-yellow plains, north of the river. To the northwest, the skyline was broken up by a jagged mountain range known as Hell's Teeth. The forest lay south of those forbidding mountains, just patches of trees at their foot, becoming densely wooded closer to the settlement. To the south was the Parched Lands. Walk to the east with the river on your left, and trees, grass and bushes soon gave way to stonier, harder ground as the land started to descend, the water starting to become louder, white-flecked and angry as it made its way downhill, away from the plateau where the People had settled. The river was the only river they knew of, and, longer ago than the first songs, an ancestor ungifted in poetry had named it the River.

She had crossed it at the narrow ford that morning. The ford had been constructed when the People had first abandoned a nomadic existence and chosen this place to become rooted. It was designed to provide a path that was dry for a few months in summer, wet in spring and fall and ankle deep and chilled in winter. It was also designed to be easily defendable. It fell away to deep water either side, and there were breaks at both banks as well as one in the middle, where those crossing—which was only possible in single file—had to jump a four-foot gap to continue. Trees and bushes had been cleared around the ford to make it impossible to approach the crossing without being seen. It was a point of entry into the settlement, but any hostile visitors would be crazy to try such an exposed route.

There was a distinctive rock formation about five hundred yards ahead. The Giant's Fist looked exactly as it sounded - as if a rock giant had tried to punch her way out from below ground and had managed to penetrate the land's skin with one fist before her strength gave out. A song told of her holding her breath underground, waiting for the day another giant would pass that way, recognize her plight and finally pull her free. As Sopharndi silently scaled the rock, she hoped today wouldn't be the day the song came true.

Her careful progress was necessarily slow, as she couldn't afford to make a sound. The Giant's Fist provided the best shelter from the sun for miles. Any ha'zek crossing Canyon Plains would be sure to wait out the worst heat of the day on the far side, where the overhang provided by the Fist's knuckles allowed an area of land to remain relatively cool. The deep shadow made the animals invisible unless you were right on top of them. Which, after twenty patient minutes of climbing, was exactly where Sopharndi was. A breath of wind came from the northwest, bringing a blast of musky, sweaty animal odor, but leaving the beasts themselves ignorant of her presence.

She counted twelve of them, kneeling in the shade, *huffing* in their distinctive fashion, or taking turns to lick the salty, mineral-rich moisture from the rock face. Ha'zek, when fully grown, stood about chest high on a person. Short-haired, with long faces and unfeasibly curled eyelashes above their brown eyes, they were usually born light-gray or white in color, before darkening as they reached maturity. They traveled constantly, their lives following a mysterious, but predictable course the purpose of which was known only to the Singer. The herds began to appear every year on the outermost northwest limits of Canyon Plains as the snows melted on Hell's Teeth far behind them. They grazed along the river until they were about ten miles from the settlement, then peeled away from the water and the danger of the People, heading inland to patchier feeding grounds amongst the rocks of Canyon Plains. Whether they were on their way to somewhere specific, or whether they spent the intervening period wandering, no one knew; but—as sure as bard farts smell like wine—they were always back by mid-fall, heading in the opposite direction.

The group below Sopharndi was late making its trek east. She could see why - eight of the herd were calfs, born too late to make the trip with the main herd. Of the four older animals, Sopharndi set her sights on a female who looked a little past her physical prime. Ha'zek could run like spit in a hurricane, so it was best to target older, or injured beasts. Sopharndi waited until the older animal had separated herself from the others in search of some more of the tough green and purple weeds that somehow managed to thrive in the splits and fissures of the rock itself. A spear thrown from this angle would likely hit the spine - a mass of bone that would deflect even the sharpest blade. The result of that would be a stampede and—more than likely—the loss of her spear. Better to fall onto the animal from her perch above, bring it down hard, breaking one, or both, of its forelegs.

Crouching in preparation, she took a long, steady breath and held it, her eyes fixed on the female.

I will give you a good death.

With a practiced, fluid, motion, she sprang outwards from her position on the rock, twisting in the air so that her feet would hit first. There was a moment in her fall when everything was absolutely quiet. The ha'zek were half-dozing in the shade, their heads down. Sopharndi's sense of time and awareness of anything else around her was now completely gone, as time slowed and the world shrank to just her and the female.

For the space of just under a second, she didn't think of Cley.

Then the soles of her feet hit the shoulder of the ha'zek, driving her into the ground, and the world came back to life in a riot of sound and movement.

The rest of the small herd reacted exactly as Sopharndi knew they would. She had targeted an animal on the edge of the group, so—even as the older female shrieked in surprise and pain—every other ha'zek ran in the opposite direction, away from the threat, abandoning their wounded comrade without any hesitation. As well as being predictable, it was the best course of action to ensure they stood the optimum chance of survival. If Sopharndi had been part of a hunting group, the remaining animals now presented a fast-moving target, much harder to hit.

There was a crack as the older female hit the ground and rolled onto her side. Her scream of agony was cut short and she lay still. It was the best result Sopharndi could have hoped for. Either it had hit its head hard enough to lose consciousness, or the shock had caused it to faint. If it was the latter, as Sopharndi suspected, she didn't have much time to finish the job before the animal woke up.

She took her knife from her belt and knelt by the ha'zek's head. Before slitting its throat, she offered up the traditional prayer of gratitude to the Singer. At that precise moment, the beast opened its eyes, grunted and—with its good foreleg—kicked Sopharndi in the chest. Sopharndi skidded backward and hit the rocks hard enough to hurt. She ran her fingers across her chest and pushed down on the bones underneath. Bruised, not broken.

Sopharndi and the ha'zek got to their feet at the same time and eyed each other. Then the animal took an experimental step forward, decided the injury to her right foreleg wasn't painful enough to stop her, and sprinted away to the north in the same direction as the rest of the group.

Sopharndi growled a few choice curses, then made a grab for her spear, which had fallen a few feet away.

She watched the pace of the animal as it tried to

escape. The impact may not have broken its leg, but it had done enough damage to significantly affect its ability to run. The beast slowed a few times, limping, before looking back and setting off at another sprint, each time a little slower than the last.

Sopharndi pulled the spear back as she ran. She waited until the ha'zek slowed again, then increased her own speed for a few steps - just long enough to give her throw more momentum.

The sharpened tip of the spear glinted in the sun as it flashed into the sky in a low arc. The beast, startled by Sopharndi's sudden burst of speed behind her, stumbled into another run, but her pursuer had allowed for this. The point of the spear, spinning as it fell, pierced the skin at the base of its neck. It emitted a pained scream as it fell, then lay twitching, trying to drag itself back upright, blood spurting onto the sand.

Sopharndi sprinted now, not wanting the animal to suffer more than it had to. As she reached the stricken creature, she drew her knife and buried it into the ha'zek's throat, slicing into its flesh as she pulled it swiftly upward. The scream turned into a wet gargle for a few seconds, then the creature lost consciousness. Its head dropped to the floor, and its death came quickly and quietly.

THE JOURNEY back was tiring and uncomfortable, but Sopharndi welcomed the distraction from her grief. She had hefted the body of the ha'zek onto her shoulders before making the long hike home, and she had only allowed herself two brief rests. Her muscles were beginning to complain now, and she knew she would feel the ache there for the next few days.

First of all, she had to get though the coming night, joining the whole tribe around the fire, while they awaited the return of the one who had made the Journey. Only this time, they all knew there would be no return.

It was late afternoon when she crossed the ford back to the Settlement, nodding at the guard posted there.

She dropped the carcass next to the dwelling of the skinners. Foiyat, an old woman now, but still strong of arm, looked up as Sopharndi approached, but said nothing. The traditional greeting on receiving bounty from the hunt would be, "the Singer blesses you and us," but Foiyat had sense, and decency enough to remain silent. The old woman and her apprentices would skin the animal expertly, passing on the meat to the food preparers and the skin to the men who made clothes, waterskins, and even toys for children from it. No part of the animal would be wasted. To do so would be an insult to the Singer, who used every part of everything, always.

As she made her way back to her own dwelling, Sopharndi saw Cochta and her supporters speaking in low voices. Cochta looked up and saw her. Sopharndi stared back at the female, almost willing her to say something, taunt her again. Her self-control, she realized, was frayed to breaking point. If Cochta pushed her now, her suppressed rage was such that she would certainly kill her. Such an action outside the law would lead inevitably to her own death, but the trade-off seemed an attractive one at that moment.

Cochta half-smiled as Sopharndi passed, then seemed to think better of it, and drew her group of cronies away. Whatever she had seen in Sopharndi's expression had been enough to warn her off, but she would be back. Cochta was far from stupid. It was just a pity that the intelligence she shared with her mother, instead of maturing into wisdom, looked certain to continue as slyness. Where Laak was a mediator and a conciliator, Cochta was a plotter and a manipulator.

Sopharndi threw back the hide at the door to her dwelling and stretched out on her sleeping skins. She was done with weeping. She would carry her grief over Cley like an invisible wound, but none would know her pain.

She would sleep for a while, and face the tribe proud, strong, and in control.

Chapter 20

It was like waking from a dream to find himself in a night-mare. Seb had felt weightless, free and inexpressibly joyful as he had willed his consciousness away from his own body. Bok's instructions had been straightforward enough, and he found himself following them without hesitation.

Just as Bok had warned, it took an effort of will at first to stay focused. The lack of any physical presence gave everything a slightly unreal tinge as he contemplated the new reality being offered to him. In his bodiless state, the artificial nature of the simulation he was entering was obvi-ous, the original fingerprints of the Gyeuk clear on their design. Exactly as the "clockmaker god" deists had posited back on Earth, the Gyeuk had created the perfect condi-tions for life in their simulation, then stepped away and taken no further role in events. The result was an evolving planetary ecosystem, rich with diversity. Seb was aware of hundreds of thousands of species, from the tiniest insect right up to huge plant-eating mammals, placid and grace-ful, grazing in rainforests.

The dominant species had evolved from apelike creatures in a similar way to humanity - that much had been specified by the T'hn'uuth when they had requested this Gyeuk Egg. Seb knew he had to will himself to join the human-like creatures on the planet. For a moment, he felt the temptation to stay as he was. He could feel the presence of this entire world within himself, and it took all of his mental strength to narrow his focus and find the species he had promised to join.

He mourned the loss of his all-embracing consciousness as he narrowed his search and channeled his energy into becoming an individual again. Internally, Seb focused on the name of the creature he was to become, the person he would be in the Gyeuk Egg, the name of the one who he hoped would lead his community into a new way of experiencing reality and—in doing so—might save Baiyaan from exile and allow future species in the universe to develop without the interference of the Rozzers. Seb let the name sound within his mind.

Cley.

At first, there was nothing, and Seb wondered if he had misunderstood in some way, or if his inexperience as a T'hn'uuth meant he wouldn't be able to inhabit the simulation in the way Bok had promised. There was a slight feeling of alarm as he brought his attention back to focus on the name again. This time, he put all his awareness into the simple sounding of the single syllable.

Cley.

He knew something was different immediately. It was far from a pleasant sensation. It was as if he had been standing in a huge open space and had suddenly become aware that the walls around him weren't as distant as he'd first imagined. Not only were they closer, but they were closing in on him at speed. Before he could react, a canyon became a space the size of a concert hall, then a school gym, a large room, a bathroom, a corridor, a coffin.

A terrible pressure began building somewhere inside him, demanding relief. He knew he had to do something, but couldn't find out what, or how, to do it. The pressure became at first uncomfortable, then painful, burning, dangerous. Just as he thought he'd succeeded in doing what Bok had said he must do, Seb felt the real fear of failure and—for the first time in as long as he could remember—the fear of death. The pressure, the pain was intolerable.

Just as he thought he could stand no more, some kind of instinctive muscle memory kicked in. Seb drew a huge breath, his chest heaving and aching.

I have a chest?

He felt oxygen course into his body, filling his lungs, setting his blood singing and his heart thumping.

He was alive. He was *here*. He had a body.

And he was being dragged into a dark cave by a massive lizard with far too many teeth.

ALL SEB KNEW WAS PAIN. A lot of pain. For a while, all-consuming pain. The poison released by the venomous fangs at the front of the skimtail's impressive array of teeth may have stopped signals from Cley's brain traveling to his limbs, but it had done nothing to prevent pain signals going the other way.

Overwhelmed by sheer agony, lost in physical sensations, it took Seb a few seconds—seconds that felt like minutes—to gain enough mental equilibrium to remember who he was. Cley himself had very little sense of identity. His automatic response to hearing his name was due to the way his mother's voice sounded when she said it, not because he associated the word with any sense of self.

Seb's personality stretched tendrils into parts of Cley's brain that he'd never used, and he retreated without resistance or fear. As Cley became Seb, the agony drained away, and Cley returned to his natural state of passive observer.

Seb nullified the effects of the poison and twisted his head to look at the creature whose jaws were locked onto his forearm. They were more than ten yards inside the cave now, and the darkness was almost impenetrable. Even so, Seb realized he could see more than he would have been able to through human eyes. He could make out the outline of the thing as it dragged him and could even see the back of the cave where more creatures waited. As Seb acknowledged this, he enhanced his vision further, and the scene became as clear as if it had been broad daylight. He had time to wonder if this was because his body was already partly, or fully, that of a World Walker again, or if the fact that this was a simulation meant that a physical solution was unnecessary. If all of this were just ones and zeroes in some vast cosmic computer—however sophisticated—then his manipulation of reality was just a case of tweaking the programming.

The existence of such visceral, immediate pain had come as a shock. The pain was still there, but Seb was able to detach himself from it, observe the synapses firing urgent signals, but move them aside while he worked on something else. His body demanded fight or flight, but he knew the answer was neither.

He looked along his arm at the head of the animal attached to the end of it. Cley's memory was perfectly functional despite the fact he'd never been able to use its contents to learn anything. So Seb knew the beast was known as a skimtail, and that it was dangerous, although he'd already reached that conclusion without Cley's help.

The skimtail was shuffling backward, pulling Seb with it. Its head was like a truncated version of a crocodile, with similar bark-like skin and reptilian eyes. The teeth were smaller and sharper than a crocodile's, designed to quickly penetrate the skin of its prey, the fangs releasing poison and the hooked incisors assuring a firm grip should the victim prove slow to succumb. The body reminded Seb of a Komodo dragon's, thickset, strong, low to the ground. He wasn't sure how the skimtail got its name, so he lifted his head in an attempt to get a better look at the rear of the beast. Even as his head moved, the creature's body twisted, and something flicked across the floor of the cave with incredible speed and smashed into the side of Seb's skull, leaving a dent which would certainly have resulted in death in anyone else.

Well, that answers that *question, anyway.*

Seb's eyes failed for a split second while he reacted to the immediate problem of his staved-in skull. As brain tissue moved into place, shards of bone binding and knitting back together, there was a strange sensation as if his ears had popped, then he could see again. He reviewed what had just happened. The tail that had inflicted such damage had been long and sinewy, able to move with great speed and accuracy. It had looked like an anaconda as it propelled itself across the sand, but instead of a head at the end, it had a hardened solid mass, made up of a similar skin to the crocodile-like head. If that hit you, you stayed hit.

Seb decided to keep his head still rather than draw attention to the fact that he was conscious. No need to give the thing a reason to smack him again. He needed time to adjust to the chaos of this new reality and having his skull repeatedly bludgeoned would probably prove to be some-what of a distraction. However, he was going to have to do something fast. He didn't need the evidence of his eyes to know the situation was about to get worse. He could hear and smell the rest of the skimtail's family as they waited for their unexpected meal. They were only a few yards away.

Seb focused on his arm, starting with the cells closest to the point of the creature's vicious teeth. He repaired the damage layer by layer and, as he did so, replaced the yielding flesh with something harder, denser, armored.

From the skimtail's point of view, the result was unprecedented and incomprehensible. The huge creature, top of the predatory pile in the Parched Lands, suddenly found its mouth had lost all grip on its prey. Worse, it couldn't reattach itself. It was like trying to bite a rock. After staring briefly at the impossible sight of Cley's undamaged arm, it tried, savagely and with blinding speed, to repeat its earlier success. After a few failed attempts, it paused and stared at the mysteriously changed limb. After a few seconds, it was joined by its mate and three young. The first skimtail took a few paces back and allowed its family to attack the strange thing he had found. They met with no more success than he had.

The five skimtails looked at each other, then back at what was supposed to be dinner. With the pragmatism inherent in nature, they swung round and used their lethal tails to batter their prey into a ready-tenderized mass of meat.

Only, that wasn't what followed their usually-lethal attack. Tails swished and cracked with the distinctive sound that always sent smaller creatures running for their lives, but they either missed completely, or smacked loudly into the tail of another member of the family. They turned again to look at the result of their actions and found themselves looking at an empty space. There was nothing there. Logic dictated that their prey must—somehow—have escaped, so all five of them made for the mouth of the cave with another surprising lick of speed, considering their mass.

Seb watched them go from his position on the ceiling, four yards above their heads. His fingers and toes had sunk about an inch into the solid rock. He waited until he heard the animals scuttling away before dropping down. He walked to the cave mouth and watched the skimtails searching for him on the slopes below, following his earlier trail. He wasn't sure how keen their sense of smell was, but he'd temporarily disabled his own odor, his scent mimicking that of his immediate surroundings.

When he looked out from his vantage point, he was momentarily shocked into absolute stillness. He knew he was visiting a place that would seem unfamiliar to him, but the psychic shock delivered by what he saw rendered him incapable of coherent thought for almost a minute.

The stars were different, to start with. No familiar constellations. And, due to the lack of light pollution, utterly clear in their alien positions. A large, orange-tinged moon lit the barren land in front of him. Seb looked at the ground, the other-world dirt squeezing up between his toes. His three, sloth-like toes.

I'll think about that later.

As he looked at his feet, Seb's mind sounded a false note, an intimation that something else was completely unfamiliar about what he was seeing. He blinked a few times before he realized what was different. He had a double shadow stretching out from his feet, at about the ten o'clock position on an imaginary clock face. But the moon was in front of him, slightly to the right. Still looking at the floor, he turned and found the shadow behind him.

Then he looked up to his left and confirmed his hypothesis. High in the darkling void, another two moons hung there, yellow, smaller than their single sister opposite.

Seb felt an almost overwhelming rush of loneliness. He tried to picture Mee's face, but it kept losing focus. He tried to remember her smile, her voice, how it had felt to touch her. It was as if he was remembering something that had never really happened. Like remembering a movie. An awful emptiness opened up inside him as he recognized his inability to simply feel the love he had always felt for Mee. Maybe Fypp was right. Maybe he was more T'hn'uuth than human now. Something deep railed against the thought, and he shook his head. He took a few quick deep breaths, allowing the feeling of panic to subside. Even the air was different, tasted different.

On the slopes below him, the sounds of the skimtails became less agitated as they gave up their search. Soon, they'd be heading back to the cave. Seb forced his attention back to what was in front of him here and now. He took a couple of paces back into the cave. He had one last check to make before joining the rest of his new species.

Chapter 21

Back in the cabin, Fypp had left it to Bok to explain—slowly and patiently—the necessity for creating a symbolic link to the reality Seb had left behind.

"Remember, you will be entering a world which is complete in itself," Bok explained, his huge hands cradling the Egg. *"It's an evolved world with eons of real history. If you go in there thinking you will know it to be a simulation, you will underestimate it and may be lost."*

"Lost?"

"It has happened before. Your memories of the real world can seem dreamlike when everything around you points to a different reality. To cling on to what you know to be real, you must keep the connection alive. Otherwise, you will accept what your senses are telling you, and—over time—you will accept the simulation and forget reality."

"And what happens then?" Fypp had told Seb that Bok would fill in the *"boring details"* of his task. Once again, she had proved to be adept at the art of understatement.

"You will be completely immersed in the simulation. You should wake up here if you die there, but not every mind is robust enough to

accept such a shock. Participating in, rather than merely observing, a Gyeuk Egg is rarely attempted for precisely this reason. Insanity is the usual result."

"Wonderful. This just gets better and better. How many people have actually done what I'm about to do?"

"I am personally aware of thirty-seven cases."

"Any of them T'hn'uuth?"

"None."

"Oh. Great. Uncharted territory. Of those thirty-seven, how many of them—how did you put it?—get lost?"

Bok fell silent for a while. After sufficient time passed without him answering, Seb realized it was down to reluctance rather than his customary unhurried approach to dialog.

"How many, Bok?"

"Ah. Thirty-five, I think. No, er, thirty-six."

"Thirty-six?!"

"Correct."

"Right. Thirty-six. Out of thirty-seven. And the thirty-seventh?"

Bok sighed miserably before answering.

"She died," he said.

As Seb stood in the dark cave, he made a conscious effort to disregard the odds against his succeeding and—instead—take practical steps to help make sure he would get through this where everyone else had failed. The big difference in his case was that he was T'hn'uuth, a World Walker. His relationship with reality was already far more fluid than a purely biological being. His consciousness of self was not limited to a lump of brain tissue attempting to make sense of a constant avalanche of sensory input. As far as Seb understood it, every cell in his body now carried an imprint of the whole. When he Walked, when he traveled unimaginable distances, he was unsure of precisely how much of himself actually came along for the ride. He knew it wasn't much. When he'd left Earth, his physical body had, for the most part, dissipated. Only the essential part of him, enough to reconstruct his physicality on arrival, had made the journey. Now, something similar had happened to allow him to enter the Egg. Seb wondered how much of this he would ever fully understand. He guessed a few thousand—or million—years of life might make the task easier, but the thought gave him vertigo.

Bok strapped him into a chair that looked very much like it had been borrowed from a high-tech dental practice. When he sat down, the warm, pliant white surface molded itself to his contours and the whole chair tilted backward. Wires snaked out from hidden orifices and insinuated themselves into his skin at thousands of points across his body. He felt his skin resist, then yield as tiny needles made their way to precise locations. Through clear tubing, Seb could see fluids being drained from his body. Other needles introduced some kind of dark liquid into his system.

"Sometimes it's pretty hard to remember this is all just a metaphor I'm constructing in real time," he said as Bok placed a huge hand on a panel which rose up in front of him. There was a brief hum and a series of small flashes of blue and orange light, then the panel sank back out of sight. Seb kept talking, in part to distract himself from a growing feeling of panic - a feeling which had now become so unfamiliar to him that it took a few seconds to identify it.

"I mean, I'm constructing some kind of futuristic scene for myself, right? It's the closest I can get to interpreting exactly what it is that you're really doing to me. I remember seeing a movie when I was a kid. They shrank this guy and injected him into someone else's body. This feels a bit like that. I know I don't literally have to shrink to get into the Egg, that it's all something to do with chained wormholes and quantum linguine, but, for some reason, that's not making me feel any better about things."

Seb listened to his own voice babbling with an increasing sense of detachment. Was that of his own doing, or the intravenous fluids taking effect? He stopped talking and allowed the chaos of his mind to begin to settle.

Bok had said he could use any words he liked to mark a place where the Gyeuk Egg and the outside world met. Seb's occasional video game binges had provided the perfect inspiration.

"Pause," he said.

For a moment it seemed that nothing had changed, then Seb realized all sound had stopped - even the steady background chirp and whirr of thousands of nocturnal insects had faded to nothing. Even though he had initiated it, he was shocked by the sudden change. He had chosen to use familiar commands from gaming, but watching a scene pause on a monitor was a totally different experience to witnessing a whole world doing the same thing. There was something unnerving about it. Bok had told him the world wouldn't actually pause, it was his own perception of time shifting.

A doorway ascended from the sand and rock floor like an elevator. As it came to a stop, it was revealed as an empty frame. Where the door itself would normally be found, it had a liquid appearance. Despite the fact that it stood in front of him, the sensation Seb felt was as if he was looking down into a pool of water.

He looked at his face for a few moments in the reflection before realizing what was strange about it. It was *him*. A human being. With a start, he looked down at his actual body for a moment and saw tough, dark skin. His hand was long, the palm muscular. Three fingers and a thumb. The pads of the fingers and thumb were like those of a dog - they had tough nails which extended and retracted as Seb flexed his fingers. He brought them up to his face and looked closer. The nails were strong and very sharp. Certainly an evolutionary weapon, possibly for hunting, he speculated. Then he looked at the blade hanging from a belt around his waist. His new species obviously didn't rely completely on their claws.

He glanced away from his unfamiliar new body and back at the reflection in the doorway. A human figure looked back, the hand in the reflection quite definitely belonging to the Seb Varden who was now waving at his new body in the cave.

"Show *Home*."

His reflection disappeared and a scene appeared on the far side of the door, as if the door now led to a new place. Seb felt his stomach lurch a little when he saw it. He knew it was just his subconscious picking the place he had the most powerful associations with, but it shook him, nonetheless.

It was Richmond Park. London.

He was looking through the doorway as if it was at the top of the path leading down to Penn Ponds and the bench where he and Meera had had their first, drunken date. Also, of course, the virtual landscape where he had spent "time" with Seb2, when his personality had split to cope with the change from human to World Walker. He still thought of himself as a World Walker, rather than a T'hn'uuth, partly because it sounded cooler, but mostly because he couldn't pronounce T'hn'uuth.

Seb knew why he was seeing this. It was a way of remembering. Bok had advised him to summon *Home* at least once a month, to remember who he really was, why he was there. If he could remind himself of his true identity, he could protect himself from being lost in the new reality of the Gyeuk Egg. In theory.

He stepped through the door.

The weather was warm, a light breeze causing the leaves in the dense clumps of trees on either side of the path to rustle like subtle, arrhythmic percussion. He walked far enough along the path to see the bench. Two people sat there, their backs toward him. They were passing a bottle between them and laughing.

With a distant, muted pang of recognition, Seb recognized himself and Mee. This wasn't a construct in the same way the Richmond Park where he met Seb2 had been. This version of the London park was a memory, the strongest one he had. The day when he realized Mee felt something for him too. The day he felt life open up to possibilities he had never really considered before. As they had gotten drunk together, he had found his senses sharpening instead of softening, every word they had spoken hooking into his memory, every glance remembered, the smell of every flower, leaf, blade of grass, or Mee's skin and breath, filed away. Every kiss experienced with every sense available.

Halfway down the path, he stopped short, unable to go any closer. Experiencing his own memory this way had done the job it was designed to do. He knew who he was, he knew the Gyeuk Egg was—however real it seemed— just a simulation. But being here was oddly uncomfortable, too. It was the contrast between the intensity of the afternoon that was being replayed in front of him—plus the lingering intensity of the memories associated with it— compared to his current emotional state. He knew he wasn't feeling what he had once felt. He knew he wasn't engaging with this memory in the way he used to. The changes in his body and brain had distanced him from his own emotions. It wasn't just that he had changed. It was that he couldn't quite remember what he once was. Who the boy on that bench was, kissing the laughing girl.

He turned and said, "Resume." The doorway appeared, a shadowed scene beyond it.

As he re-entered the cave, the door slid out of sight behind him.

Seb turned and walked out of the cave. He sat on the narrow ledge, dangling his legs over the precipice. Feeling as alone as he'd ever felt in his life, Seb followed an instinct born of years of habit. He allowed his mind to enter his heart as he turned to his lifelong practice of contemplation. Father O had always warned him that there was no destination in contemplation, no goal, no waypoints, no possibility of success. And yet he had claimed it was worth dedicating his whole life to it. In his mid-teens at the time, Seb had felt let-down by such seemingly vague statements from his normally precise and thoughtful teacher. Years later, he had begun to understand that there was nothing vague about what Father O had said. Just the opposite, in fact. The priest had shown him a hard path and been ruthlessly honest about the difficulties and darkness ahead. Seb still couldn't articulate what it was that drew a resolute non-churchgoer like him back to this seemingly fruitless practice day after day.

Seb wondered what Father O would make of him right now - a short, strong, three-toed, four-fingered bald creature watching its breath in silence. Seb guessed the old priest would probably be delighted.

About twenty minutes passed. Seb watched his thoughts. They crowded into the mental space and denied him peace. All these years of sitting and still his thoughts vied for attention like a roomful of demanding toddlers. No wonder the Desert Fathers and Mothers had referred to their thoughts as demons. Seb stood up, stretched and looked across the land toward the distant firelight of the settlement.

He turned his gaze inward briefly and looked at the jumble of images and memories inside Cley's mind. Nothing added up, it was still confusing and incomplete. But one face stood out, along with a name. Sopharndi. And a label: mother. He would start with her.

Before entering the simulation, Seb, his mind now clouded and slow, looked up to see Bok holding a big, glowing, red button, his massive palm poised about an inch above it. Bok raised his slab-like head and looked at the new World Walker lying on the chair. The first new T'hn'uuth for millennia.

"I voted against Baiyaan," he said, "but such a binary choice does not accurately reflect my thoughts on the issue. I regret we have been forced to convene in this way. I also regret that the onus of putting forward Baiyaan's case has fallen on you. I wish you good luck, Sebastian Varden. Are you ready?"

Seb swallowed. Was he ready? He was about to become part of a different species on a planet that only existed as some kind of simulation. Once there, he had to start a new religion or tweak an existing one to steer an entire civilization in a direction it might never follow, whatever he did. If he failed, Baiyaan was exiled, and the Rozzers would continue directing the course of sentient life. How could he ever be ready for that?

"I'm ready," he said.

Bok pushed the button. Seb felt himself freed from the constraints of his body, floating like a wisp. He felt himself being drawn in a definite direction and he allowed himself to follow. It was time to become someone new.

Seb half-ran, half-leaped down the side of the Last Mountain. He estimated the edge of the desert to be about an eighteen-hour hike. Cley's species—the word in Cley's mind for them was, simply, the People—were shorter in stature than humans, but had greater stamina. Seb started jogging, slowly at first, experimenting with re-routing oxygen intake and adding muscle mass to his legs, lengthening them as he did so. He picked up speed. Soon a small dust cloud followed him, and he smiled, thinking of the Roadrunner cartoons he used to watch.

At this pace, he estimated he would reach the settlement in ninety-eight minutes.

Chapter 22

Sopharndi stood naked in the clearing, a cold fury churning in her stomach. The old scar on her chin began to itch, as it always did when she was angry.

The fire had been lit, the People were assembled. They sat in a rough horseshoe surrounding the fire pit and the hard-packed earth around it. The Elder's meeting circle bisected the bloodspace and Sopharndi stood just a few yards from where her appeal to the Elders had been dismissed. Now her son was dead and her challenger would soon know the force of the anger she felt.

She knew the timing of this challenge was designed to catch her at her weakest, but the fighter now walking from the other edge of the horseshoe into the bloodspace had misjudged Sopharndi. Or—more likely—she had been misinformed. Sopharndi looked over at the group of women who had prepared the challenger. She found Cochta's tall, wiry form and kept looking until the other female's eyes met hers. Then Sopharndi spat deliberately on the hard earth.

Cochta was slippery, unreliable, self-centered. But

clever. *Very* clever. Sending in her strongest lieutenant as challenger was a smart play. Cochta would be able to observe Sopharndi carefully, look for her weaknesses, gage her strength and stamina. Never mind that her comrade would die supplying the information she wanted so badly. Any other challenge was fought with talons sheathed, but a challenge to be First was always fought to the death. Cochta had her eye on the long game and was willing to make sacrifices. No doubt, Sku'ord even believed it was her own idea to take on Sopharndi. Cochta had probably convinced her she would win, told her she would make an excellent First.

Sku'ord was thickset, heavily muscled and almost certainly barren. Firsts often emerged from among those unable to bear children. They channeled their disappointment into training, took the tragedy of a severed bloodline and turned it into focused aggression. By missing the seven months of gestation and subsequent weeks of recovery, they also had additional time to develop their skills as fighters.

Sopharndi had thought herself barren, and it had been as much a shock to her as to everyone else when, a few months after she had become First, she had fattened with child. It was an unprecedented situation, and the Elders ruled that Sopharndi could choose another to take on her duties until she was ready to return as First. Sopharndi had chosen Keku, a young, level-headed, generous-spirited warrior who showed real aptitude for the role. Sopharndi would have considered it an honor to have fallen to the challenge of Keku. Not to tonight's lumbering, ignorant oaf, though. If Keku had lived, she would have been embarrassed to witness this sorry display.

Sku'ord sank to her knees, then prostrated herself, listening to the Singer. Such demonstrative piety was rare among the People. You could hear the song just as easily standing up. Sopharndi imagined it was a deliberate ploy to impress the Elders. She doubted they'd be so easily appeased. They had already made it known they were dismayed by the timing of the challenge, just one night after Cley had taken his Journey. Everyone knew the boy must be dead by now, but by challenging tonight, Sku'ord —or, more accurately, Cochta—hoped to catch Sopharndi at her most vulnerable, her mind undoubtedly circling constantly around the fate of her son.

Getting slowly to her feet, Sku'ord allowed herself a little smirk back at Cochta and her cronies before turning to face her opponent. Her eyes were open wide and bright, her body language exuding absolute confidence. There were those among the People who thought she would win. Everyone knew no one trained harder than Sku'ord, no one punished her body more relentlessly in the pursuit of strength, speed, and stamina.

There were only two of them gathered that night who had no doubts that it would be Sku'ord who would fall. One of them was Sopharndi. The other was Cochta. The younger woman was sacrificing her friend to better know her enemy. She knew brute strength alone could never overcome Sopharndi. Cochta was a cold one, all right.

Sku'ord took two quick steps forward and adopted a fighting stance. Her feet were planted wide apart, her heavily muscled arms were close to her body, ready to strike. Her claws were unsheathed. They glinted in the light of the moons.

Sopharndi stood absolutely still: listening, feeling, sensing, aware of her body and the dirt under her feet. Aware of the stilling of her mind and the breath of the wind. Aware of the unreachable past and the unknowable future.

Laak stepped forward onto the bloodspace, her old

features hidden by the hooded cloak the Elders wore on ceremonial occasions.

"Begin," she said and stepped back into the crowd.

Sopharndi felt the rush of bloodlust like a storm breaking inside her. She placed herself at the silent eye of the storm and nodded at Sku'ord.

"For the Singer," she said, following her words with a whisper. "And for Cley."

The young female moved fast, but her intention to charge was so obviously signposted that Sopharndi had time to consider her options. Should she dodge left, then strike? Dodge right and trip her? Meet the charge with a well-placed kick and knock the knee bone out of its joint? The fight would be as good as over then. Too quickly, though. Cochta thought losing Cley would unbalance her. Let her see the truth.

Sopharndi moved to the left and watched her opponent swipe a clawed hand uselessly through the air at the spot where she had been standing a moment before.

She took a step backward and waited.

Sku'ord recovered fast, using the momentum of her strike to spin her body and face her opponent again. Sopharndi nodded at the unexpected agility of the move, acknowledging a certain level of skill in her opponent. She saw nothing but rage in the other female's expression. Rage was useful, certainly. More than useful - essential. Without it, the fight was often already lost. But a true fighter must be the master of rage, not the other way around. Sku'ord was driven purely by the bloodlust and was relying on her physical advantage to bring victory.

She did, at least, have enough intelligence to change strategy when her first approach failed. Sku'ord came forward more cautiously this time, looking for an opportunity to get in close, where her sheer bulk would give her the upper hand.

"Nothing to say, Sophi?" she whispered as she advanced. 'Sophi' was the contraction Sopharndi had been known by as a child. No one among the People would ever show such little respect. As attempts to goad went, it was fairly lame. Sopharndi said nothing. She started to dance on the balls of her feet, staying out of reach of the powerful arms and looking for indications that her opponent was about to attack.

"Maybe that's where Cley got it from, Sophi. You think so? Maybe you're just too stupid, and Cley couldn't learn from you. You were too old to bond with him. Too old to be a mother."

This was a better approach. If Sopharndi hadn't been watching from the eye of the storm, she might have reacted to personal taunts about her fitness to be a mother. There was some truth in it, after all.

"Either that," whispered Sku'ord, as her shoulder muscles tightened almost—but not quite—imperceptibly, "or the Singer is punishing you for something. I wonder what that could be. Eh, Sophi?"

With that, she feigned a stumble and launched herself at Sopharndi. The tightening of the shoulder muscles indicated she was attempting to grab her opponent by the waist or upper legs and force her to the ground, where her bulk would give her a huge advantage. But her arms closed on air again, as Sopharndi jumped in perfectly-timed anticipation of the move. She landed on top of the younger woman, expelling all the air from her lungs in one painful, *huff*.

Sopharndi thought of Cochta watching.

No more free lessons tonight.

She slashed her unsheathed claws across Sku'ord's legs,

just above the back of her knees. She cut both legs as a kindness. The challenger would be unconscious in three minutes, rather than six. Dead in eight minutes, rather than sixteen.

Sopharndi withdrew to the edge of the bloodspace and waited silently with the rest of the People while Sku'ord's body twitched in its death throes. Then she turned to the Elders and nodded. All three nodded back. Only Laak spoke, as tradition dictated.

"Sopharndi is First," she said. The people raised their right arms and shouted her name as one. "Sopharndi!"

Traditionally, the celebrations should have started immediately, as supporters of both fighters accepted the result and reaffirmed their commitment to the community they loved. This time, as the echoes died away, an unnatural silence descended on the assembled group. Sopharndi, facing the Elders, had her back to the fire. She wondered, for a fraction of a second, if her killing blow had failed. Then she dismissed it as impossible. She looked at the Elders and those around them. They were all staring at something on the far side of the fire. Something that was moving closer.

Sopharndi spun around to face the threat, whatever it was. Sku'ord's corpse still lay on the ground. The fire burned strongly. A figure walked around it and came toward her. A few paces away, it stopped.

It was Cley. And he was *looking* at her. Really *looking*.

He wasn't humming.

"Hello, Mother," said Cley.

Chapter 23

Seb stood at the edge of the clearing, taking long, steady breaths. It felt good to breathe again, even though he knew it wasn't real. He had taken great lungfuls of air as he ran across the Parched Lands, his arms pumping, his legs settling into a kind of lazy-looking loping stride which propelled him across the ground at a rate that turned the surroundings into a moonlit blur. The burn he felt in his muscles put a grin on his face as he ran. If this was a simulation, how did reality stake its claim to being any different? All his senses told him that he was here, wherever *here* was.

Within minutes, the alien body he now inhabited had begun to feel entirely natural to him. By his own estimation, he stood just over four feet tall, his body compact and tightly muscled. His skin was dark and tough, like the skin of an armored avocado. His eyes were closer to those of a cat than a human and sat further apart than a human's on his hairless skull, giving him a bigger field of vision than he had ever experienced. His hearing seemed better too, but it was hard to know if that was just his imagination, as there was no way to measure it. Before he'd started running, he had easily been able to identify the sounds of small animals, snakes, and lizards scuttling around the mountain, as well as similar noises further away. He had a surprisingly accurate mental picture of the precise direction from which the more distant sounds emanated. His ears were fairly humanoid, just a little more prominent and tapered at the bottom as if Mr. Spock had accidentally placed his auditory organs upside down. But the information they sent resonated in some way in the physical skull itself, giving an almost radar-like picture of his surroundings to add to his vision.

He certainly felt gloriously conscious, and wonderfully, physically *alive*.

Mentally, the picture was less clear. At the surface level of consciousness, Seb was completely present, but if he probed deeper, where Cley's memories and unformed personality lay, the picture became more confusing. All of Cley's history was accessible to Seb, and as he had run toward the distant lights of the Settlement, he had begun to tentatively explore them. The sensation was extremely strange, as the memories now belonged to Seb as much as Cley. Seb felt like he was a curious hybrid of some sort. Bok had led him to believe that he would totally dominate the mind of the creature he inhabited. But Seb found that Cley was far from absent. Although the boy—who had never been able to speak—was not present as an inner voice of any kind, his way of seeing the world nevertheless subtly colored the way Seb saw it. Seb knew he was no longer Seb, at least not here. He was one of the People, a tribe of creatures at a pivotal point in their societal development. He would never be able to achieve what he had come here to do, unless he was, in some sense, Cley, son of Sopharndi, the First.

He stood in the clearing, aware that every single eye was on him, and faced the woman who had birthed this body and cared for it for so many years without a single response. As he looked at Sopharndi's face, he saw an expression Cley had never seen before. Shock, for one thing - then happiness and hope mixed with disbelief. Sopharndi had never lowered her guard sufficiently to display such naked emotion. Seb watched her take a few hesitant steps toward him before stopping and simply staring.

He looked at the corpse on the ground, the blood around it reflecting the sparks leaping from the fire. He noted the blood congealing on his mother's claws. He felt a curious calm rather than horror at the scene. This was the traditional way the People settled power struggles. As First, no one came above Sopharndi in the warrior caste. She must have been challenged. She must have prevailed. Even as he accepted the scene as a common one in this society, part of Seb still recoiled at the violence, the waste of life.

Every face was still turned toward him. The Elders had yet to react to the situation. No one had ever expected to see Cley again. To see him now, not only alive and unharmed, but somehow, miraculously able to speak, had silenced everyone.

Laak stepped forward and joined Sopharndi, but came no further. She was Leader. She delivered the law, made judgments. Along with the other Elders, Laak guided her tribe through the seasons, her leadership delivering wisdom, certainty, and continuity. The People lived by their traditions, formed over countless generations, passed on orally through the songs, as well as laws and stories. Every situation could be dealt with according to one tradition or another. Not this situation, though. No song had ever been sung about a Blank finding the power of speech or becoming a functioning member of the tribe. Blanks were pitied, but—these days—they were taken care of. Long gone was the time that they had been left to die, shunned because of their condition. Silmek, the Leader two generations before Laak, had taught that traditions could change. She said the way the People treated the weakest among them was one of the ways they showed they were more than wild beasts. The Singer could be merciful - perhaps the kindness they showed the Blanks would help them earn that mercy. Her edicts had stood from that day until this.

Seb felt the almost unbearable tension grow as he stood opposite Sopharndi and Laak. He knew whatever he said now would never be forgotten by those present. For a moment, he wished he'd spent a little time preparing a speech, rather than running across the desert with a big, stupid grin on his face. Oh, well.

"I have returned from my Journey," he said. Other than the crackle of the fire, there was no sound. He felt the force of the attention focused on him. He turned his head, slowly taking in everyone gathered around the fire, from infants on their mothers' laps, to those who had nearly reached the end of their songs.

"I went into the Parched Lands, where nothing grows but the blacktree. I climbed the Last Mountain. In a cave, I fought a skimtail."

Sopharndi's head twitched at this as she remembered her own Journey. Seb smiled a little.

"I prevailed, but I did not kill it. I spilled no blood on my Journey."

At this, Sopharndi's face clouded, and there were small sounds of confusion from the crowd. How could anyone fight a skimtail without either killing it or dying in the attempt? No one had ever returned from their Journey without spilling another creature's blood. It wasn't that it was a necessary part of the ritual, rather a case of survival. No one took water on the Journey, so the blood of snakes or lizards had to provide vital fluids.

Seb walked to the edge of the circle and gently took an empty waterskin from a wide-eyed child who handed it over without a sound. Every eye followed him as he walked back and knelt on the dry earth.

Time to find out if Bok was right about a T'hn'uuth's abilities inside a Gyeuk Egg. Let's see if a miracle or two can kickstart a religion.

The sensation Seb felt as he reached out with his Manna was, seemingly, identical to that which he felt in the real world. He willed the dusty soil to become water. The physical process now felt almost as natural as reaching out to pick something up. There was a slight change in his state of consciousness, but it happened seamlessly as he moved his attention to the task. It was the same mental state he entered when writing music, a kind of *letting go* in order to allow something to happen. He'd always felt that songs— or, at least, the best phrases in songs—were already out there somewhere, waiting for someone to find them. He just had to train his mind to notice. Manna use was very similar; a letting go of familiar mental processes in order to allow others to become known.

There were gasps of disbelief as a few people noticed what was happening. Seb heard hissed prayers to the Singer as the waterskin swelled. He held up the skin, and the cries of disbelief grew as the water spilled from the opening and ran over his hand and arm, continuing to do so for long enough that it became obvious that more water than the skin could hold had already flowed from it onto the ground. They were witnessing the impossible.

Seb couldn't help smiling to himself. He was not unaware of a certain irony. He still found his own abilities almost as impossible to comprehend as did the tribe watching him. His power felt completely natural, but that only proved it was easy to get used to pretty much anything, given enough time. To him, the appearance of fresh water from thin air was no less magical than it appeared to the People. He might try to explain it by imagining particles in the atmosphere being somehow changed and reassembled into molecules grouped into two parts hydrogen and one part oxygen, but, in truth, it was still a complete and utter mindfuck.

He walked back to the child whose waterskin he had borrowed and returned it. The boy sniffed it cautiously, then—before a nearby male could stop him—upended it and took a long drink. He smiled reassuringly at the adults around him.

Water was held in high regard by the People; in the hot season, the river sometimes dried up to a muddy brown trickle, and the oldest among them remembered their own grandparents' stories of the terrible drought that wiped out half the tribe.

Over the course of the next minute, there was pandemonium as urgent whispers grew into frightened shouts. Some looked scared, or angry, struggling to accept the impossibility of Cley's return, his sudden intelligence and the miracle he had just performed - the like of which had been unknown since the earliest songs. Pockets of almost hysterical laughter broke out around the gathered crowd as members of the tribe tried, and failed, to make sense of what was happening.

The Elders recovered first and stepped forward from the crowd, Laak raising her hands for silence. Such a gesture would normally be instantly obeyed, but this time she was ignored. Laak looked around her in dismay at the excitement and panic building around her. Such a height-ening of emotions could only lead to trouble. Already, scuffles were breaking out as individuals argued over what this could mean. Those who weren't fighting among themselves seemed either frozen with fear, staring at Cley, or overcome with a kind of fervor that left them almost mesmerized.

Laak shouted, "People! Listen!" but she could barely hear herself over the noise. She turned to her fellow Elders. Their eyes betrayed almost as much fear and confusion as the crowd around them. For the first time as Leader, Laak felt her control over the tribe slipping away. She was losing them. She looked to her First, but Sopharndi was stock-still, staring at her son, an unreadable expression on her face.

Laak took a deep breath, preparing to shout with all the authority she could muster, but before she could say a word, the ground beneath her feet began to tremble, then shake.

Seb was reaching out with his Manna just as he would have done outside the Gyeuk Egg, hoping that Bok's promises were correct. Bok had assured him that, as long as he remembered who he really was, he would have limited abilities similar to those he enjoyed outside the simulation.

He wasn't sure he liked the word *limited*, though.

He guessed this must be the "little drama" Fypp had promised, saying it would help his cause at the beginning. She obviously had a talent for understatement.

Around the clearing, the People fell to the ground, scrabbling to hold on to those around them in a desperate attempt to stay upright. Earthquakes were rare, but not completely unknown. Songs told of entire settlements being destroyed by them. The tribe wailed with fear in anticipation of destruction and death.

The noise of the shaking earth was louder than the

screams of the crowd. It was a fearful sound, as if the Land itself was crying out, rock grinding against rock, deep below their feet, as though a giant was grinding its teeth. Great *cracks* were heard as trees split at their roots and fell in the forests. Sparks leaped high from the fire and flew into the sky.

Then, slowly at first, the quake began to subside, the ground no longer feeling as if it were about to break apart, but still rolling and tipping. The roaring sound diminished in volume steadily. After about a minute, it was just a steady rumble, the ground now vibrating rather than shaking.

Seb had watched the response to his return escalate into panic and violence. He knew this moment would be pivotal in his quest to turn Cley's tribe toward a new approach to religion - one that would encompass all aspects of their lives. He had to inspire, not terrify.

Now that he was here, Bok's warnings about losing himself in the simulation seemed almost understated. There was no hint of artificiality about the scene around him, and the emotion of the people was raw, unfeigned and utterly compelling.

"People!"

Seb stretched his arms above his head, just as Laak had done; but this time, everyone turned toward him and listened. He began to lower his arms and, as he did so, the rumbling diminished still further, as did the noise of the crowd. By the time his arms reached his sides, there was silence, broken only by the whimpering of a child.

Seb looked in the direction of the sound, and saw a male cradling a child, trying to soothe it. It was a small female, and Seb could see its arm had been broken during the earthquake. He walked toward the pair, and saw the male's face freeze with confusion and fear as he got closer.

Seb said nothing, but slowly squatted in front of them, keeping his movements slow and unthreatening.

When he reached toward the crying child, the male flinched and held her closer, producing a small scream as the broken bone moved. Seb held his outstretched hand still until the male relaxed a little, then very slowly placed his hand on the damaged limb. The crying ceased immediately and, a few seconds later, the child moved her arm back and forth with an amazed smile on her face. The male, and those around him, saw clearly what had happened, and Seb had no doubt that the story would spread quickly.

He stood and moved back to the center of the clearing, the fire now beginning to subside behind him.

Seb knew that he would be walking a tightrope from this moment on. He had to preserve his sense of who he was internally, but to lead these people, he couldn't be Seb Varden. To bring them along with him, he had to be Cley. But a Cley the People had never imagined possible.

Sopharndi's son took a few steps forward, his face calm, relaxed and peaceful despite the violence of the past few minutes. No one knew whether he had caused the earthquake, but no one was in any doubt that he had quelled it. A Blank who could speak, a Blank who could subdue Nature. Around the clearing, individuals remembered occasions when they had been dismissive, unkind, or even cruel to the youth who now stood before them. They felt fear wriggle into their guts, at the thought of how a being of such power might repay their thoughtless acts.

He smiled, then spoke, in a voice which carried easily, and yet seemed as intimate as a lover's whisper.

"Since the Singer first came to Aleiteh, the People have waited for her to Sing again. Our bards sing the old songs, and we live by the laws inspired by them. Now, our long wait is over."

They looked at Cley's open expression, his eyes soft, his brow unfurrowed by anger, and they dared to hope that he might have forgotten, or even forgiven, their transgressions. All present knew everything had changed. They waited for his final words and—when they had heard them—they returned to their dwellings in shock and confusion, but also with hope and a sense of a larger purpose unfurling within, and around, them.

Cley's words were these:

"The Last Song is begun. I am the Last Song."

Chapter 24

Innisfarne

Seb looked warily at the expression on Mee's face. She was sober. After her first couple of spliffs, Mee had decided Seb's story was too fucked up to listen to stoned.

"How long had you been away for at this point?"

Seb moved over to the window and looked out into the snow. Great fat flakes were still slowly falling, giving the impression that the entire Keep was slowly rising into the sky, drifting upward to some far off land in the clouds.

He tried to answer, but his throat felt constricted. He remembered the moment he had discovered how long he had been away. For a second, he felt the same sense of a spiraling nothingness, a mental retreat from the truth.

Seb turned and looked at Mee and Joni. After traveling unimaginable distances, meeting other World Walkers who had evolved from a variety of alien species, and spending time on a simulated planet constructed by an artificially intelligent hive mind, it was this seemingly commonplace scene of domesticity that was threatening to undo him. The feelings swelling within him were so profound and deep-rooted that he could find no way to even begin to express them.

He raised shaking hands to his face, unsurprised to find tears on his cheeks again.

Mee got up and came to him, taking his hands in hers and looking into his eyes.

"Don't answer that. I want to say something."

Joni stirred behind her.

"Um, do you two need some privacy? Because I could, you know…?"

Mee continued to look into Seb's eyes. Seb Varden, immortal and beyond the limitations of his species, felt utterly powerless when he looked at this woman. He tried to speak, but she put a finger on his lips.

"I've watched you the past few weeks. I've watched you with Joni and, even when you've been with me, there's been a part of me holding back, still watching you."

Seb knew better than to say a word.

"I guess, now that we've been apart for nearly two decades, you think it's going to take a very long time for us to begin to rebuild some kind of relationship, right?"

Seb cautiously raised an eyebrow.

"Permission to nod," said Mee. He nodded.

"Well, it's a funny thing, because that's exactly what I thought, too. But I've realized I was wrong."

She turned to Joni. "And don't you say a sodding word, Jones. I'm still your mother, which gives me a better record on infallibility than the pope. And when it comes to you, I'm *always* right."

"Yes, Mum," said Joni, beaming. This was a side of her mother she'd never seen.

Mee squeezed Seb's hands before continuing.

"Oh, bollocking hell, I can't find the words. I just thought if I let you carry on, tell the whole story, then I forgive you and we start to make a go of things again, it'll always feel—maybe not to you, but to me—as if I had to weigh things up, decide if your reasons for not being here were good enough for me to accept. As if my wanting to be with you was about what you did, or didn't, do, rather than who you are. And the thing is—"

She stopped and took a few quick breaths. Then she giggled. She followed that with a kind of growling sound while stamping her feet. Joni watched, transfixed. Seb knew better than to move an inch.

"Right. Seb. This is what I'm trying to say. I *know* you. Ever since I met you, I knew it was you I wanted to be with for the rest of my life. And listen, Sebby, not for one moment before then did I ever believe in that pile of fairy-tale toss about there being one special somebody. I always thought Prince Charming was a poncey twat. I was fully prepared to go through life meeting a reasonable number of special someones and never getting too serious about any of them. At the very least, it would keep the sex fresh."

"Mum!" protested Joni, but Mee carried on as if she wasn't there.

"But I'm too old to pretend now. So know this, Sebastian Varden. As of *right now*, we are together. And when I say together, I mean in the sense of *forsaking all others* and *'til death do us part* together, okay? Although we might have to have a little talk about exactly what that means in your case, but never mind. What I'm saying is, when Kate gets back from the mainland, you and I are going to go stand in that meditation hall, she can say a few words of our choosing, and that'll be that."

Seb was still looking into her eyes. Joni got up from her chair and stood beside them.

"Did that really just happen?" she said. "Did you just propose?"

Mee didn't look away.

"In a very clumsy way, yeah, I guess I did. But it's not quite a done deal yet. How about it, Seb? Marry me?"

Seb's smile appeared first, then he went to speak, but Mee placed her finger on his lips again.

"Permission to nod," she said.

Seb nodded.

―――

THE SUBSEQUENT KISS WAS–POSSIBLY–NOT the most romantic moment in all of recorded history, but Joni suspected it would easily make the top five. She pretended to find something interesting to look at in the fireplace until they finally broke apart. Then they all hugged for a while, and Joni briefly wondered why—in a species so utterly dependent on language—so many of the most precious moments were beyond the reach of words. If she was going to be a writer, she guessed she was going to have to try harder.

"Okay," she said, when they finally sat down, "just give me a second."

She looked at her mum and dad.

Seb looked at her quizzically.

"You going to…reset?"

"Yup. Well, I'm going to create a *reset point*. I might want to come back and see the expressions on your faces as they are right now one more time at least."

She looked at them for a few more seconds.

"Here goes," she said, and—

Unchapter 25

—smiled broadly at the expression on their faces. They looked exactly like she felt whenever someone asked her to pose for a photograph. Awkward.

"And...relax. That's one for the family album."

Mee broke the slightly charged atmosphere by farting, then blaming the dog.

"We don't have a dog, Mum."

"Who'd have guessed we would have produced such a pedantic child, eh?"

Seb laughed. "It's okay for me," he said. "I don't have to smell your farts unless I choose to."

Mee looked at him in mock-amazement.

"You mean you might *choose* to smell my farts? Now, if that isn't true love, what is?"

Seb hadn't been aware of the huge weight he'd been carrying around until the moment Mee had removed it. He looked at his lover and his daughter with fresh eyes, completely believing, for the first time, that his future with them was real, secure. Well, as secure as anything could be in a world he had come to know as far more mysterious than he'd ever imagined. He could live with that.

"You wanted to know how long," he began. "How long I'd been away by the time I entered the Gyeuk Egg."

"Can we call it something else?" Mee pushed him down into his chair and sat on his lap. Joni rolled her eyes in mock horror.

"What?"

"It's just that you sound like you're clearing your throat every time you say it. I keep wanting to get you a glass of water."

Unsurprised that Mee thought this important enough to address, Seb considered her request.

"Um…"

"Sopharndi's World?" suggested Joni.

"Sounds like a philosophy book," said Mee. "How about Eggville?"

Seb frowned. "Not quite sure it effectively captures the fact that it contains an entire ecosystem, intelligent life, and a solar system."

Mee nodded. "I see your point. Humpty Dumptyland?"

Joni spat out a mouthful of coffee.

Seb gave Mee a look. "I'll just call it the Egg. Okay?"

Mee bit his nose playfully. "Wow. The Egg. *What* an imagination. So, come on. How long were you in this Egg of yours?"

Seb sighed. "This is going to be one of those answers you won't like."

Mee jabbed him in the ribs. "Hey, Walkyboy, I just proposed to you after waiting seventeen years without a postcard, a phone call, a letter. Not even a text."

"No signal on Innisfarne," said Joni, smiling.

"Funny. What I'm trying to tell your father is that I got past the stage where he could piss me off more than I already was about a decade-and-a-half ago. Spill, Sebby."

First *Walkyboy*, now *Sebby*. He had definitely been forgiven.

"I think I was probably inside the Egg for about four months subjectively. Outside the Egg, seconds, minutes - possibly no time at all. Fypp says it's possible to observe any point in the timeline of the simulation. It was only impossible to do that while I was inside."

Mee nodded a few times. "Uh-huh," she said, "yep, right, mmm, got it, okay."

She stopped talking and looked over at Joni. "Well, I haven't got a fucking clue what he's talking about. What about you? You reset the multiverse in your spare time. Any of this sinking in?"

Joni shook her head. "Maybe homeschooling was a mistake after all, Mum."

Seb smiled at that. "You're in good company. I don't understand it either, I just know I wasn't in the Egg for long."

"So," prompted Mee, "the seventeen years..?"

Seb closed his eyes briefly, remembering the moment he had discovered how long he had been away. At the time, he had wondered if he was even mentally equipped to handle the information, and his sanity had teetered on a knife's edge.

"I didn't find out about that until I washed up on the beach near Bamburgh."

Mee held up a hand. "No. You're better off telling this in order. I'm having enough trouble keeping up as it is. Tell us what happened in Humpty Dumpty—in the Egg, first."

Seb picked up his knapsack. He knelt in front of the

open fire, where a sheepskin rug was laid. Carefully, he took the Gyeuk Egg and placed it on the rug. It was wrapped in the same cloth as when he'd shown Joni.

"Mee, I want you to take a look at it. Just for a minute. It would be dangerous to look for too long, I think."

Mee came and knelt alongside him on the rug. She looked questioningly at Joni.

"Seen it before. Gave me the willies."

Seb laughed. Joni was very much her own person, but sometimes her choice of words was so like Mee's, it was uncanny.

He pulled the corners of the cloth, and they fell away from the object beneath.

Mee sniffed dismissively as she leaned forward to get a better look.

"Is that it? I was expecting something more…"

She fell silent as her brain started the attempt to create a manageable object out of the Gyeuk Egg, to reduce it to something able to be held and categorized by a human brain. The attempt failed.

Mee had stood on the edge of the Grand Canyon shortly after first moving to America, and had found herself lost for words for a record three seconds, before finally muttering, "Now that is one big fucking hole." This time, it was all her brain could do to keep her body upright, without diverting precious resources to coming up with a pithy, amusing quip.

Seb watched her reaction, and was ready, after ten seconds, to throw the cloth back over the Egg. Mee's expression had gone through curiosity, incredulity, awe, and fear before heading toward a kind of vacuous acceptance of that which it could never grasp. He shook her gently by the shoulder. It took another three shakes before she responded, followed by two strong cups of tea and a giant spliff before she was ready to speak. When she finally did, it was pure Meera Patel.

"Cockfosters," she said.

Chapter 26

Sopharndi and Cley stood in the Meeting Circle, facing the Elders. Laak, Gron and Hesta had spoken privately for nearly an hour in the dwelling beyond the Circle, while Sopharndi and Cley waited to see what the leaders of their tribe would decide.

The moons lit the scene brightly, casting sharp-edged shadows onto the hard dirt.

Sopharndi was silent for a few minutes, looking at her son. All his life, his body had been in constant motion. Only when sleeping was he still. In every waking moment, whether sitting or standing, he had kept a slight rocking movement going, his head nodding forward and back an inch or two as if he was listening to music no one else could hear. That, and the near-constant humming meant that his presence was obvious to Sopharndi even when she was concentrating on something else, training warriors, exercising, listening to the bards, eating - she always knew he was there. Any absence had been accompanied by a silence and stillness she found distinctly uncomfortable.

Now he was both silent and still, and she couldn't stop the same thought running around her mind.

He's not here. He's not here. He's not here.

The evidence of her senses suggested otherwise. He looked, felt and smelled like Cley. Only now, he spoke. He looked right at her, not off to one side. The tiny, crazy hope she'd always entertained—that there was a mind lost somewhere inside him that might, somehow, be persuaded to emerge—had turned out not to be crazy at all. It had happened. Cley had a mind. There was more to him than anyone had ever suspected.

So why did it feel more like he wasn't here at all?

He's not here. He's not here.

"This must be hard for you."

Sopharndi flinched at the gentle voice that had interrupted her thoughts. Cley was looking at her again, his eyes full of intelligence and concern. She met his eyes briefly and immediately looked away, Taking a long, slow, breath, she forced herself to look back and hold his gaze.

"Cley?"

It was all she could bring herself to say. As a warrior, and now, First, Sopharndi had trained herself to intercept strong emotions and—unless they could be usefully channeled—push them firmly aside. Since early adolescence, she had excelled at this aspect of her training. Where other strong females in her group allowed themselves to be angered, shamed, or distracted by the taunts, insinuations, and insults of their instructors, Sopharndi had let the words fall into ready-made mental slots. She heard them just fine, but, with practice, she found she could absorb them as if they were directed at someone else. Occasionally, she would hear something that might provoke anger. If she felt she could channel that anger without letting it cloud her judgment in a fight, she would do so. If not, she would push it away and bring her focus back to the here and now.

She realized now, as she looked at her son, that she was using the same techniques to avoid dealing with the onslaught of emotion which his return had provoked. He was alive, healthy, intelligent, and able to speak. Not only that, he exuded a charisma stronger than any she had come across before.

He smiled at her, and her heart lurched crazily.

"It's me," he said. "This is hard for you, I know. A Blank cannot speak. A Blank cannot think. A Blank can bring misfortune on a tribe, as well as good luck."

"The People have prospered since your birth," she said, her words seeming to come from far away.

"If they had not, they may have sacrificed me to the Singer in an attempt to appease her."

Sopharndi nodded. Such sacrifices were rare these days, but they still happened. If the dry season was dangerously long, if the animals gave birth to dead, or deformed offspring. If the trees didn't fruit. Animal sacrifices at the edge of the Parched Land had been performed at the change of the seasons since Aleiteh heard the songs, but in more desperate times, the ha'zek, craint, or nuffle whose blood would be spilled to appease the Singer would be replaced by a person. A Blank was always the first choice in these circumstances as they would be the least missed, and they were, most likely in the tribe's view, responsible for the problem in the first place.

"I would not have let them sacrifice you."

Cley smiled at this. "No, you would have fought for me. Your love is strong. You must have loved my father very much."

Love was not a word used much by the People. Sopharndi wondered at Cley's use of it. On the other hand, she had always struggled to name the feelings that kept her so attached to a child many would have given up. Love might be as good a word as any, she supposed.

"Your father was a good man, Cley."

Cley's father was Sharcif. He had been the tribe's bard when Sopharndi met him. Underneath his easy charm, which had made him a popular bedfellow, called to a different dwelling every night, she had found a deep, thoughtful man. He had wooed her relentlessly but told her he would only come to her bed when she was ready for a child. He fathered a child with no one else, and, after fifteen years had passed since he first asked, Sopharndi had called him to her dwelling one night while she was in season. She had spent the previous three nights lying awake, unable to think about anything other than Sharcif, only her pride over his popularity preventing her calling him to her. When she finally gave in, they were together every night for nearly six weeks. She had just begun to show the first signs of pregnancy when she learned he had been killed by a pack of shuks while on a pilgrimage to Hell's Teeth.

Cley nodded. Sopharndi looked in his eyes for the son she had never really had. She could see little of Sharcif in the frank, open expression on Cley's face, but she could see nothing malicious or even slightly duplicitous either. The first songs didn't just speak of the goodness, mercy, and grace of the Singer, or the coming of the Last Song; they also contained verses warning of charming demons who might try to lead the People astray, away from the path of righteousness. Unfortunately, the warnings were vague, and the fact that they had to scan a certain way—and rhyme—made even important messages open to inter-pretation.

Sometimes, Sopharndi wished the Singer had dealt

with some matters by providing a list of instructions rather than songs full of metaphors and confusing allusions. She knew such thoughts were blasphemous, although she suspected others among the People felt the same way.

A few "demons" had been expelled through the traditional method of isolating the "possessed" person, tying them to a post in a dwelling set aside on the limits of the settlement, throwing in food and water once a day and leaving them there for a week. Sopharndi noted a pattern in these exorcisms. Demons seemed most likely to take over children who had recently entered adolescence but not yet taken their Journeys. Children at this point in their development were most likely to challenge authority - either that of their parents or their leaders. Sometimes, even certain songs. Sopharndi suspected a natural period of rebellion was at work, rather than a supernatural intervention. Considering those still possessed knew the next step in their cure would mean their heads being removed by the First, the week of isolation proved to be a completely effective cure in every case since Sopharndi had become First.

Sopharndi was direct. It was her way.

"Are you a demon?"

"No." Again, that openness and calm. Although a demon would hardly have said yes.

"Are you my son?"

"I am." Cley closed his eyes for a moment as if considering something, then opened them again. "And I am more."

She wanted to ask him what he meant, but no words would come.

Then the Elders emerged from the dwelling and took up their positions at the edge of the circle. As always, it was Laak, the Leader, who spoke first.

She beckoned Cley. He stepped forward and stood opposite her, looking up into her age-lined face.

"What happened in the Parched Land, Cley?"

Cley spoke quietly and confidently. Sopharndi may not have been able to see her dead lover in their child's face, but she could hear Sharcif's musical tones in the cadence of Cley's voice.

"I was attacked by a skimtail and badly wounded. I must have hit my head when I fell because I slept. When I slept, I dreamed. The Singer came to me in my dream. When I awoke, the skimtail ran from me. I was healed, I could understand, and I could speak."

Gron stepped forward. "What did the Singer look like?"

Cley spread his hands in a gesture of confusion.

"I do not know. I dreamed of music. Then I started hearing it differently. The music was the same, but I heard the sounds as if they were words. It was the first time I had ever understood anything. She was Singing to me, and I understood. She told me the People had been chosen, of all the tribes, to hear the Last Song. She told me the Last Song was for all the tribes, but the People would learn to listen first, before singing to others."

At this, Laak, Gron, and Host conferred again. Then Hesta spoke up.

"The tribes have been divided since the first songs. The last trading party which approached the Children never returned. The last time we tried to parlay with the Chosen, they impaled the heads of our messengers on spears and placed them on the other side of the river, facing the settlement. They are savages. They will not listen, and I will not put the people in danger by trying to make them."

"In time, they will listen," said Cley, simply. "But it begins with the People, it begins with every individual. It begins with you, Hesta, and you, Gron. It begins with you, Laak, and you, Sopharndi, my mother. We must all learn to listen to the Singer."

Laak and the other Elders eyed each other uneasily. They had seen Cley's demonstration of power, and his words were spoken with conviction, accompanied by the weight of prophecy. Although it had been countless generations since anyone had directly encountered the Singer, they were now confronted with an authority they could never have anticipated, and they did not dare challenge it.

"I must protect my tribe," said Laak.

Seb nodded. "I offer no threat, Laak. You will continue to lead. But it is time for the People to truly become part of the song. Will you allow me to teach them, and you, how?"

Laak did not need to look at her fellow Elders. The return of Cley, and his transformation, was a miracle which would live on in the songs and stories of the People long after they were all dead and gone. Most of the tribe had witnessed the miraculous change in Sopharndi's witless son. Perhaps their god was taking a personal interest in them again, as was sung in the earliest songs. Or, perhaps, other forces were at work here. It was too early to say, but, as Leader, she certainly couldn't be seen to be hostile to such a historic possibility.

"We will allow it," she said.

Chapter 27

Seb woke the next morning in a state of disassociation. It was the first time he'd slept in years, and the experience reminded him of how strange unconsciousness was, once you were used to permanent wakefulness. He had "slept" during many of the nights he had spent on Innisfarne with Mee, but it wasn't natural, necessary human sleep. He had simply trained himself to slow down his mental processes to a crawl while Mee slept beside him. He'd used the time to listen to music - the longer, classical pieces he'd heard in his youth, but never appreciated. He could replay anything he had ever heard at will. Beethoven's late string quartets had become particular favorites. He had once spent an evening at Carnegie Hall half-listening to them, badly hungover. Now, he could recall the concert in its entirety, and had discovered complexities, hints, and numinous moments that never lost their luster.

This was different. Cley's body—and mind—needed sleep. After finally surrendering to it, he awoke confused and scared. It was as if, in entering the Gyeuk Egg, he had opened himself up to two new worlds: the one his every sense told him was real, and that of Cley's unconscious, which lent an extra, subtle credence to this artificially designed existence.

He opened his eyes in darkness, feeling off-kilter, finely poised, balanced between realities. His dreams had been full of Cley's memories interspersed with his own - the most bizarre moment involving a gig he remembered in a New York club. He'd been taking a synth solo when Scrappy—the band's drummer—had suddenly introduced a half-time shuffle feel to the groove, which transformed the feel of the whole song in such an inspired, brilliant way that Seb had burst out laughing. He'd turned around to acknowledge Scrappy, only to find a small, bald, hard-skinned creature attacking the kit with claws, somehow managing to keep the groove going.

He woke dry-skinned, expecting to be drenched in sweat. He jumped out of bed, only to find he was lying on a hard floor, covered in animal skins. Outside, it was still mostly dark, the first hints of light only able to lend a kind of nightmarish substance to his unfamiliar surroundings.

He stumbled toward the nearest wall and put his hand on it. The wall, at least, was reassuringly solid, although when he scratched it, the hard-packed dirt easily flaked away. He looked down at his nails and saw the same three-fingered claw he'd seen on the creature that had replaced Scrappy in his dream. For a moment, he felt a shock as immediate as if he had been suddenly doused with ice-cold water, then his brain seemed to *flip*, and now it was the rest of the dream that was all wrong. Where had he been while he slept? Who were those tall creatures, their heads covered in fur? What about that terrible sound that had come from everywhere all at once? Why was the light constantly changing as if multiple suns were shining? It was unbearable.

He looked around him, his pupils dilating automatically, straining to see some reassuringly familiar details. He looked back at his sleeping place, saw his waterskin beside it. The earth walls were cool to his touch. He frowned at the chunk he'd gouged out of it. He looked again at his hands and saw his claws were still unsheathed. He relaxed, and they eased back into place.

He was Cley. Cley.

I am Seb.

Cley felt another part of him come to full wakefulness, and he swayed in confusion at the sensation.

"Pause." The room darkened almost imperceptibly, and a tiny flying insect, just visible in a shaft of weak sunlight, slowed dramatically, its wings beginning to beat as slowly as if it had been suspended in treacle.

"Show *Home.*"

The doorway slid upward from the floor and Cley, without hesitation or a conscious decision to do so, stepped through it.

Seb looked at the familiar path leading to the ponds, heard the British birdsong that, along with the honking of horns and the unfamiliar European sirens of emergency vehicles, had formed the soundscape for the months he had spent in the city. Alongside the songs of the blackbird, thrush, starling, and robin, he heard the exotic screams of the parrots which had made the park their home, starting life as pets, then breeding in London's royal parks for generations.

For a moment, he felt as incongruous as the exotic birds, part of his consciousness still insisting he was a small, strong, agile alien with three fingers ending in lethal claws.

He shook himself and looked away from the path toward the Royal Oak, the massive tree still fenced off as he remembered it from years ago. It was rumored to be nearly eight hundred years old, possibly the oldest oak tree in Britain. He walked closer, needing the solidity it represented, the link to his own planet and his own kind.

In the distance, he saw joggers and dog walkers, families picnicking, children throwing a frisbee. A game of five-a-side soccer had broken out about three hundred yards north, with a signpost providing one goalpost, a child's stroller the other. Distant shouts were carried across the park by the light breeze.

Seb stood under the canopy of the huge oak and breathed deeply, letting the smells of an early British summer ground him still further.

Bok hadn't been exaggerating. Seb had woken up feeling as much—if not more—Cley than Seb. He wondered if the designers of virtual reality games and entertainment on Earth were aware of the dangers inherent in making the virtual feel a little *too* real. His identity as Seb Varden had still been present but relegated to a small corner of his consciousness. Every single message being picked up by his senses, however tiny, told him the life he was living inside the Gyeuk Egg was real. He was going to have to be careful. Very careful.

He waited a few minutes, allowing the weight of association, memory, and history further ground him as he looked at the ancient oak. Then he headed down the path and watched Mee pass the gin bottle to the earlier version of himself. A sliver of memory brought back something she had said about the ducks in Richmond Park.

"Don't throw bread," she had warned, "they won't touch it if it's not *artisan*. And they'll want to know its provenance. Posh twats, these ducks."

He grinned at the memory.

"Resume," he said.

Back in the dwelling, the insect continued its flight at

normal speed. On the other side of the room, a shape stirred and sat up.

"Cley?" Sopharndi peered toward him in the gloom. He felt suddenly oppressed by the close confines of the small hut.

"I'm going for a walk."

Before his mother could answer, he drew aside the animal skin at the doorway and walked out.

AS CLEY WALKED through the still sleeping settlement, nodding at the sentries, all of whom were too awed to do anything other than watch him pass, Seb established a mental routine to which he knew he would have to adhere rigidly if he were to retain his sanity. He knew now the danger of losing his identity was real, frighteningly so, and he was determined to avoid it. Bok's dire warnings about others failing gave him fresh determination. He had to survive this, for Baiyaan's sake. And, he reminded himself, for Mee.

At dawn, and at dusk, every day, he would pause this simulation and go back to Richmond Park. He would spend enough time there to feel completely *himself* again. He would not be lost.

He had the powers of the T'hn'uuth to keep him safe in the Gyeuk Egg, and he had Richmond Park to keep him sane. He tried to convince himself that he felt confident, and almost succeeded.

To the west of the settlement, past the fire pit and the meeting circle, the ground rose, at first in a shallow incline, then more steeply into an undulating forest which grew densely for many miles before thinning, then finally giving way to the westernmost border of the Parched Lands, where nothing but the blacktree grew.

Cley walked up the nearest hill, then shinnied quickly up the tallest tree he could find. Halfway up, he disturbed a family of yoiks, who shot squeaking from the hollows in the trunk where they nested at night. They looked like squirrels other than their oversized, nocturnal purple eyes and the prehensile tails they used to facilitate their speedy traversing of their habitats. Cley let them go, then shuffled out along one of the highest branches to look back at the settlement.

From his vantage point, it looked tiny. He guessed the People only numbered a few hundred at most, although, to Cley's way of thinking, it contained his whole world. The dwellings were clustered closely together in the center. The Elders, the bards, and those with young families occupied the centermost dwellings. The next ring housed the bards, teachers, farmers, and fisherfolk. Hunters occupied the next ring of huts. There was a gap between the cluster of huts in the center and the ring of dwellings at the perimeter of the settlement. These were occupied by the warriors, the defenders of the People. Sentries made up of a mix of warriors and hunters watched from the perimeter day and night, each within sight of the next, all equipped with a hollowed craint horn, which would be blown in the event of an attack, or a sighting of a particularly bold pack of shuks.

To the north of his perch, the range of mountains known as Hell's Teeth was clearly visible as the sun from the east rose, illuminating the jagged peaks which gave the range its name. Cley knew from the bards' songs that another tribe—the Children— lived at the base of the mountains. He knew of only two other tribes within a few days' walk; the Silent and the Chosen. Both lived to the north. The land of the Silent tribe bordered that of the Children, lying just to its west and—legend had it—the border was a constant source of disagreement and bloody conflict between them. Still further west, and south of the Children, a walk of more than ten days would bring you to the border of the Chosen. Attempts had been made to trade with the Chosen, but, as no trader ever returned, it had been a long time since anyone had volunteered to make the trip.

It's been carefully set up according to Fypp's instructions, Seb reminded himself, wrenching himself away from Cley's memories. *Didn't Mohammed unite warring factions when he brought them the message of Islam? Am I supposed to do the same here?* Even as he thought it, he answered his own question. Taking a new religious message to disparate tribes would be the work of years. There was no way he could stay inside the Egg that long. Even if time outside the Egg was moving at a different rate, as Bok had promised. Even if only seconds had passed since he first entered the simulation. None of that mattered. If he risked staying in this simulation too long, it would be Cley, of the People, who would lead the religious movement. Seb Varden would be a bad dream he'd once had, no more. Until he died, of course, at which time Seb didn't know if he would wake up back with his fellow T'hn'uuth, or Cley would wake up there in his stead. Two other possibilities presented themselves: insanity, or not waking up at all. Neither struck him as particularly desirable.

Whatever Seb was going to achieve in the Egg would have to be finished in months, not years.

Decision made, knowing his time here would be reasonably short, Cley/Seb felt a burst of optimism course through him.

If it turns out I can't do this, it won't be for lack of trying.

Embracing this new body, and this new world, and with an unguarded whoop of pleasure at being alive, fit, and able to think, Cley jumped from the top of the tree, the ground far below yielding like water on impact, then becoming solid as he stood up.

"Right," he said aloud, to no one other than a confused-looking yoik who regarded him from a neighboring tree with a longfruit poised midway to its mouth. "Time to fulfill the old messiah complex."

Chapter 28

Powerful, society-shifting religions had never—as far as Seb knew—been founded by someone deliberately setting out to do just that. Buddha had freed himself and wanted to show others how, so they could do the same. Jesus had looked at his world through eyes that saw reality very differently to his contemporaries and telling them what he saw had led to his death. Mohammed had encountered the angel Gabriel and transcribed Allah's message into Arabic verses so beautiful that they still often induced tears in those reciting it. All three founders were, undeniably, mystics, at least they were according to Seb's understanding of the world. All three encountered reality *directly*, without an intermediary. As a musician, there had been extended periods in Seb's life when he barely encountered reality at all, let alone directly.

Tough gig.

He didn't need to ask if he was a tad under-qualified for the job of starting a spiritual revolution. He *knew* he was. But it was down to him. The template was there - the People had a religion ripe for reinterpretation. The Gyeuk had set it up that way. Psychologically, their makeup was designed to be close to that of humans, so that a human might speak to them in terms they would understand, challenge them in ways to which they might respond.

Seb had a nagging memory of a poem he had studied as a teenager. It had made an impact on him because it spoke of *constructing* a religion, which seemed dangerously close to blasphemy in a Catholic orphanage. All he could remember of it was the poet suggesting the use of water - in rituals and as a metaphor. Water already featured in Christianity, of course, and translations of Taoist texts often used the idea of a river's flow, and how a wise man (it was always a man, natch) would succumb to that flow, rather than try to impose his will upon it. Cley had briefly considered using the expression *going with the flow* but rejected it as too Californian. Seb was still a New Yorker, after all. He had certain standards.

As Cley stood among the trees at dawn, hearing a crowd gathering to hear his words, Seb finally decided to let go of all of his preconceptions and speak from the heart.

If Baiyaan is right, if there really is *something unique underlying the religions of my planet, I'm only going to stand a chance of communicating effectively if I let go. Of everything. Including my self.*

He knew this also meant avoiding conspicuous displays of his T'hn'uuth powers, which were beyond the experience of the People, and could only make him appear as more of an outsider. After creating, then quelling the earthquake, he had almost immediately regretted it. He could not appear to be totally *other*. With luck—and time— his apparent control of the earthquake would be put down to coincidence. The production of water would convince some that the Singer was with him. Others might claim demonic possession. Healing was harder to discredit, though. There was a long tradition of healing in Earth's wisdom traditions, just as there was in the earliest songs of the People.

Mentally, Seb tore up his notes. He allowed himself to become Cley, to let the history and traditions of the People inform his every thought and word.

He walked out of the forest.

No one who was there that morning—and that was everyone other than the dying, the very sick, or infants and the males looking after them—ever forgot what was said, and the impact it had on them. Even much later, when everything had gone wrong, and the message of the miraculous Blank had been discredited, it was impossible to entirely dismiss the force of his words that first day.

For better or for worse, the People would be changed by the Last Song.

━━━

CLEY APPEARED BETWEEN THE TREES, walking toward the meeting circle. With a calmness and the same undeniable aura of authority he had projected the previous night, he approached the crowd which had gathered to listen to Sopharndi's son. When he reached them, he sat quietly for a few minutes. The atmosphere was charged with more fear than hope. Most of the People considered themselves observant of the Singer's edicts; faithful servants, careful to follow the laws laid out in the songs of the bards. They had never expected to be confronted with new information. Their god had spoken eons ago and, since then, had had the decency to remain distant and let them live their lives. The evening's events had been followed by sleepless nights for many. The appearance of Cley, a Blank no longer, and his claim to—somehow—*be* the Last Song, had led to a very rapid examination of the gap between outward obser-vance and inward commitment. Some had found them-selves deficient and regarded the prophet with fear. Others hoped to see his claims exposed as false, so that life could return to normal.

Cley looked out across the crowd, almost all of whom were familiar to him. The expressions with which they now regarded him were far less familiar, betraying a mixture of anxiety, confusion, or plain fear.

A few faces stood out. The first was Laak, her wrinkled features calm and unreadable. Next was Davvi, the Bard, who was rarely seen at public meetings unless he was the focus of attention. His face was clouded and grim, his doubts plain for all to see. Sopharndi, looking down into her lap, had chosen to sit near the front.

The final face that captured Cley's attention that morning belonged to Cochta. Choosing not to sit, she and three of her companions stood at the back, arms folded, heads erect and defiant. A significant faction within the People looked to Cochta for guidance, particularly among the young. Her opinion mattered here, and Cley knew it.

He rose to his feet, and the murmuring crowd grew quickly silent. He chose his words carefully, looking for a way of reaching the old guard, those who looked to the musician priest of their established religion, and those who might be tempted by the certainty and strength of Cochta.

Cley spoke. His message was simple, direct, and revolu-tionary. He tried to reassure the various vested interests represented by Laak, Davvi and Cochta, but, in that—at least for the most part—he failed. He could see it in their faces.

He praised the Law, how it gave a shape to the lives of the People, how it enabled them to live in harmony.

He praised the bards and their songs, the way they had

preserved the message of the Singer for countless generations.

He praised the People for listening to the songs, for following the Law.

Then he told them the Singer wanted to sing to them personally. Each one of them. That She had already been doing so, since they were forming in the wombs of their mothers. That She would continue to do so when they abandoned their bodies and became part of Her eternal song.

He told them the Singer was no more distant than their breath.

He told them they only had to listen.

He told them that listening to the silent song, which was, even now, singing the world into being in every moment, was the simplest thing to do.

He told them all they had to do was to wake up. To pay attention. To *listen*.

He said although it was simple, it wasn't easy. He would teach them how, but only they could decide whether or not to commit to the practice.

He told them that every single one of them was being sung into being right now, that each of them was part of the silent song, without which it would be incomplete.

He asked them to *listen*. Not to him, not to anyone else. Just *listen*.

Then he stopped talking and looked at his audience. There was puzzlement, mistrust, uneasiness. But he also saw curiosity, excitement, and awe. A buzz of intense conversation began.

Laak was speaking quietly to the other Elders.

Davvi was shaking his head, his rejection of what he had just heard obvious to everyone.

Cochta and her companions had gone.

Cley felt like he was emerging from a trance, but his memory of the past half-hour was so vivid, it was almost hyper-real. He raised his hands for quiet. Silence fell immediately. When Cley had raised his hands the previous night, he had stopped an earthquake. If he wanted quiet, those present were certainly going to let him have quiet.

Demon, prophet, or madman, he had made an impression.

"I will be here every morning and every evening. I will teach you how to *listen*. I will not be among you for very long."

With that—briefly wondering if he'd been a touch too pious, *maybe a couple of gags might have broken the ice*—Cley turned and walked back into the forest. After a few seconds, a hubbub of debate broke out behind him. There was no going back now.

As the crowd finally dispersed, in groups of excited, stunned, or angry chatter, Sopharndi stood alone, looking into the woods at the point where her son had disappeared. Her face betrayed no emotion at all. After a few minutes, she was the only member of the tribe still present.

Finally, she turned her back and walked back to the settlement, and her duties as First.

Chapter 29

Three Months Later

The meeting circle's fire had died to embers during the night. With dawn's early light, figures emerged from the gloom and quietly made their way to the west side of the fire pit, sitting close with their backs to it, enjoying the last of the warmth it gave. The atmosphere was quiet and charged with anticipation. A few whispered greetings were the only sounds other than the cracks and pops of the settling embers and the song of the birds greeting another new day. Soon, the members of the tribe present fell into a silent stillness. It was always this way in the hour after dawn. It would be the same at dusk. These were the times Cley, the Last Song, came down from the forests and spent time with the People. They would sit in contemplation together for half an hour, after which he would speak to them and answer questions.

At first, Cley had lived alone, the first member of the tribe ever to do so outside the protected settlement. Now, he was only truly alone in the hour before dawn and the hour before dusk - when he walked further into the forest to be with the Singer. The rest of the time, he was attended by a group of followers of around twenty.

The People numbered over a thousand in the settlement in these days, but fewer than fifty regularly attended the contemplation sessions. Cley's message was undoubtedly powerful, but it was also disconcerting, and he was disseminating it without the official blessing of the Elders, and in the face of increasingly open hostility from their bard, who considered him misguided, or worse.

Cley knew his time was short. He also knew some sort of confrontation was inevitable.

He just hoped he was ready.

━━━

FROM THE MOMENT Cley had returned from his Journey, she had known. Sopharndi had looked into her son's eyes, seeing intelligence there for the first time, and she had known. He *was* Cley, and he *wasn't* Cley. A fighter by trade, strong in mind and body, trained and sworn to protect the People, she felt as if reality had suddenly shifted in a way that she couldn't explain or understand, and she didn't like it.

After that first night, Cley had moved out of their dwelling. He hadn't returned.

She had watched him produce water from the air, witnessed him healing the sick. She had come to his dawn and dusk teaching sessions, had heard him speak of the Singer with conviction. She had closed her eyes along with the rest, but her mind hadn't been *listening*, it had been going round and round, fixating on the same few thoughts.

She and Cley had exchanged greetings every day, but she wouldn't follow him into the forest. She had her duty as First of the People. She was their protector. She couldn't abandon all those that depended on her. Besides, observing her routines, training with her fighters, she could observe the mood of the tribe. She could see divisions start to appear over Cley and his message.

Sometimes, sitting near the fire pit in the sessions Cley had initiated, as those around her focused on *listening*, she would remember Sharcif on their last morning together. She had told him she thought she was carrying his child and he had smiled at her as he dressed.

"I know," he'd said.

She had wondered at his absolute confidence. She had barely begun to show, and it was only the fact that she knew her own body so well that convinced her she was pregnant. Yet, Sharcif seemed unsurprised. Happy, yes, but unsurprised.

"I know you have never felt the Singer's power," he said. "You're even a little embarrassed that, of all the males of the People, it is their bard whom you turn to when you wish to have a child."

Sopharndi said nothing but wondered how he could see through her so easily.

He shrugged. "I am not offended by this. The Singer told me it would be you."

She had flinched a little at that. Her faith in the Singer had never been strong. She believed in the songs, the way they shaped their society, bound them together, taught them there was a judgment of their actions beyond that of the People themselves. She had never, ever, referred to her lack of belief, knowing that her position in the tribe demanded she uphold their traditions. And yet, Sharcif knew her secret. And, knowing it, he had still wanted her to bear a child with him.

"It could only be you," he had said as if he could hear her thoughts. "The Singer came to me in my dreams and sang of our son."

She had sat up then, and begun to pull on her clothes. Again, knowing what she was thinking, Sharcif had flung himself onto the skins next to her and put his head in her lap.

"Don't be haughty, Sophi. I'm not here just because the Singer told me to come." He sat up and slipped a hand between her thighs. "Nowhere else I'd rather be than right here."

She'd giggled despite herself. Sharcif was the only one who'd ever heard her giggle.

In the end, they had got up late that morning, Sopharndi arriving at her briefing slightly breathless, Sharcif waving as he headed off to sing to the hunters.

That had been the last time she had ever seen him.

Now she wondered what dreams Sharcif had had of their son, what future he might have been shown. The last words he had ever said to her, his playful features serious for once as he looked into her eyes, had seemed nonsensical after their son had been born a Blank. It was only since Cley's return as the Last Song that they had been shown to be powerfully prophetic.

"He will change everything, for everyone."

After the initial shock and joy at Cley's return, Sopharndi had kept her distance. It wasn't just the assault on her sense of reality that kept her awake at night, yearning to see him, yet reluctant to do so. From being totally dependent on her for everything, Cley had transformed into someone she struggled to recognize. Finding that her delight at having him back was tempered by an unworthy sadness at not being needed anymore, Sopharndi limited her contact to attending the dawn and dusk sessions and exchanging a few words with him every day. It wasn't that he didn't show a son's natural love and respect, it was more that he showed the same love and respect for *everyone*, regardless of their age or status. That should have made her proud, but Sopharndi knew herself too well. She was ashamed to find more than a little jealousy accompanying her thoughts of Cley, and his adoring followers.

But it wasn't just that. There was something else causing her to hold back from greater contact with him, though she struggled to name it.

So she performed her duties as First, and gradually, in her own slow and considered fashion, examined her own feelings about Cley, and what they might mean. At the same time, she observed the mood of the People, the reaction to this shocking development, this unprecedented intervention by the Singer.

His message might be a peaceful one, but there were those who were unmoved by it. Hostile to it, even. Sopharndi used her network of fighters to relay the gossip about Cley and his followers. As time passed, her fears for him grew.

The most significant danger, she knew, came from Cochta. From the very first morning, Cochta had looked for ways she could use this unforeseeable development to her advantage. She had been noticeably quiet for the first couple of weeks until it became clear that Cley's mission wasn't universally accepted. Then she had begun to make her move. She was careful, circumspect. She could see how disturbed some of the tribe were by Cley's transformation and message. Some were excited, and drawn to his undoubtable charisma. Yet she knew there was a great reluctance among many of the tribe to change, particularly the kind of revolutionary change offered by Cley.

When Davvi had emerged from his dwelling singing old songs that warned of false prophets, of demons who, legend had it, tried to lead the People astray, Cochta had listened, and she'd watched the response of others. It was obvious that Davvi feared his status in the tribe was under threat. Although Cley had claimed to honor the old songs, and the bards who sang them, who would really care about bards if they could listen directly to the Singer? Davvi's son was lined up as the next bard, but what kind of future would there be for him if the People followed Cley?

When he saw that there were those who had some sympathy with his suspicions, Davvi had warmed to his theme. He had spoken more openly, hinting at possible blasphemy. The Singer had always sung her songs directly to the bards. It took training, prayer, and the study of music passed on through generations to be able to understand, play, sing and interpret the songs. Cley didn't even sing the old songs. In fact, he didn't sing at all. He spoke only of listening. He would draw the People away from their god, from all that had brought them to this time of peace. He was leading the People down a very dangerous path. How dare he speak of the Last Song? The bards had long determined the Last Song would be sung by the Singer herself, and it would herald the end of the world.

Although he'd never quite had the courage to say it directly, Davvi had spread the idea that Cley was, in fact, a demon. A Blank now had a personality; was it not possible —likely, even—that he had been possessed by an evil spirit? When Cochta had taken his arm one evening, led him away from the fire and told him she believed his opinion to be not only right but crucial to the survival of the tribe, he immediately abandoned his previous opinion of her. She was no power-hungry, over-aggressive manipulator who only cared about herself. She was a female of rare and deep perspicacity. A future First.

For her part, Cochta and her allies carefully planted the seeds of doubt, fear, and anger among the People.

Then they waited, allowing the inexorable spread of bad news and gossip to do its work.

All of their machinations might have come to nothing, however, if it hadn't been for the attack.

SOPHARNDI STOOD at the dwelling just beyond the meeting circle and banged the flat of her hand on the wall.

Cochta's actions were becoming less subtle and more open by the day. At first, Sopharndi had hoped that Laak would be able to keep her daughter's ambition in check, but it looked increasingly unlikely. Laak was old now and nearing the end of her time as Leader. Age had brought wisdom for Laak, but her otherwise sound judgment was now compromised by a mother's love.

When Laak had called her to the meeting circle alone, Sopharndi knew matters were coming to a head. If Cochta wished to be First, the challenge would be coming soon, and Sopharndi had no doubt she still had the advantage. If Cochta waited another ten years, time would probably have weakened Sopharndi enough to make her vulnerable, but she doubted the young fighter had that kind of patience. Something else was brewing, and Sopharndi didn't like the lack of control she felt, knowing danger was close by, but not knowing exactly how that danger would manifest itself.

The Leader had seen no need to put on a show of strength for a private discussion with her First, and she looked frail. Her body was bent with age and her breath was slightly shallow and labored. Laak's attention drifted occasionally as they spoke, and she leaned on the younger female's arm for support more than once.

"I will step down as Leader when the moons next align," said Laak.

When Sopharndi did not respond immediately, the old woman reached across and took her hand, squeezing it weakly.

"I know you have your doubts about Cochta, "she said. "Her confidence sometimes borders on arrogance. This I concede. But she is strong and intelligent. If the Singer wills it, you must accept her."

Sopharndi was utterly stunned for a moment, her thoughts frozen in shock. She found herself unable to say a word. She held her features carefully immobile, years of training preventing the slightest hint of her disapproval showing. Underneath her studied calmness, her thoughts reeled. After all this time, still she had underestimated Cochta's ambition. Laak's daughter wanted nothing less than the Leadership. She had allowed Sopharndi to believe she had ambitions to become First, but that had merely been a diversionary tactic. Now she had manipulated her mother into giving her the position which would enable her to command Sopharndi's loyalty. If Cochta became Leader, she would be the youngest in the history of the People. And, Sopharndi knew, nothing good could possibly come of it. How could she have missed the signs?

Sopharndi looked at Laak's tired features, the old female's eyes closing as they sat together. She had always shown such wisdom and good judgment. Perhaps she would also be proved right in this, and Sopharndi's anxieties would be exposed as paranoid.

Then Sopharndi recalled Cochta's mocking comments about Cley, and her cynical sacrifice of Sku'ord. Cochta could never be allowed to lead.

She squeezed the older woman's hand back. "As the Singer wills."

She walked away from the meeting circle toward the settlement. Then she stopped, and turned, facing the trees rising up the side of the incline where Cley and his followers lived. She stood still for so long, a few yoiks and nuffles broke cover from the undergrowth and began sniffing around the fire pit, looking for morsels left behind by the tribe.

When she finally moved, the animals scurried back into the shadows with a few surprised squeaks.

Sopharndi returned to the settlement and called softly to Katela, who was patrolling the sentries, making sure the tribe was secure for the night.

Katela knew her First well enough to have shared some of her discomfort over the past months. The internal power struggle would soon become overt, and the fighters would be called upon to keep order. Tensions were high, and the failing health of their aging Leader was doing nothing to settle frayed nerves. The fact that Sopharndi's son seemed to be the catalyst for this unrest was unfortunate. Katela had never been particularly religious - it was common among the fighters to be observant of the Singers rituals, to attend the bard's recitals dutifully, but to maintain a little distance from the truly pious. They might be called on at any moment to fight, or kill, and their minds needed to be focused on that. Which made Cley's involvement awkward. Not that anyone under Sopharndi's command had detected the slightest difference in her unflinching dedication to her duty. They felt the same absolute loyalty to her they always had. They would lay down their lives for her without a moment's hesitation.

"My First." Katela bowed her head slightly in respect.

"Katela, Laak has just told me she will be stepping down as Leader."

Katela looked perturbed at both the information and the fact that Sopharndi had decided to take her into her confidence. The First was a taciturn, self-contained female, who rarely spoke on important matters without long consideration.

"A new Leader will be anointed."

Katela nodded.

"Laak will choose Cochta."

Katela said nothing, but she knew her face had briefly betrayed her shock. She did not yet have the same control over her emotions as Sopharndi.

"But—"

Sopharndi stopped her with a look. "The Leader's decision is final. I believe she may not have the complete support of the Elders, but it is not without precedent for a Leader to choose her successor unilaterally."

Katela's breathing had become shallow. With a visible effort, she brought it back under control.

"The People will not accept her," she said. "It will split the tribe."

"Perhaps," agreed Sopharndi. Both fighters knew that despotic Leaders had been deposed—occasionally violently — in the past. "Leaders like Cochta rarely thrive in times of peace."

It wasn't long before she remembered those words and wondered if she, too, had the gift of prophecy.

"I am going to warn Cley. You have the settlement."

Sopharndi walked back through the dwellings, watching the usual routines being enacted, the children rounded up for bed, the hunters skinning their latest catch, the smell of cooking.

She walked back past the fire pit, the meeting circle and into the forest.

Chapter 30

Cley ate supper with his closest followers. The questions they asked were deeper, and more dangerous, than those asked at the public contemplation sessions. Cley knew, if his message were to spread, if a mystical tradition was to take root among the People, it would be this small group who would provide the flame to start the fire.

They had been with him, living close by, for months.

A few weeks after his return from the Parched Lands, curiosity had won over some of the young, and a group of them had followed him to find out where their teacher spent his nights. They returned with a story which spread among the People like wildfire, mostly because it was too outlandish not to be believed.

The group of adolescents had followed Cley at a distance when he left the settlement, immediately after the dusk silent song. They had thought themselves discovered when, just as he entered the forest, Cley stopped suddenly, standing absolutely still. The group came to a sudden halt. They had chosen an evening when the breeze was a reliable southeasterly, so there was no danger of him picking up their scent. Still, they all held their breaths when he stopped walking, his arms by his sides, his body assuming an unnatural stiffness. For a count of ten, they watched him, beginning to fear he had suffered some sort of affliction, when he relaxed and began to move. Relieved, they followed.

When asked, he had told them that he slept in a tree. Sleeping outside the settlement was considered dangerous, and would only normally be contemplated when on a long hunt. Always, of course, as part of a group. To sleep outside the safety of the tribe *alone* was unheard of. Then, much about Cley was beyond the experience of the People. Sleeping alone, in a tree, was perhaps only to be expected of the first prophet since Aleiteh to whom the Singer had spoken directly.

When Cley had reached the tallest tree in sight—an evergreen akrarn, as were almost all of the mature trees on the hillside— the group had stopped, ducking behind bushes in case he looked behind him.

They needn't have worried. Without pausing, Cley had held out his hand. The lowest branch of the tree swept down toward him. At first, his pursuers assumed it was a trick of the light, but their hypothesis disintegrated within a few seconds. Looking exactly like the arm of a father scooping up a child, the branch lifted Cley about twenty feet into the air, handing him over to another branch which lifted him still higher. Another three handovers and Cley was a distant figure at the very top of the tree, where it looked as if a giant bird had constructed a nest. He jumped lightly over the side and disappeared.

For a few minutes, the young group was reduced to fits of giggles, unable to stop themselves reacting to the impossible sight they had witnessed. None of them could pinpoint why it was so funny, but once one of them had succumbed to laughter, the others were quickly infected. As one of them later commented, it just seemed to fit in perfectly with what they knew of Cley, the prophet. He did the impossible, he *said* the impossible. And they couldn't get enough of him.

The group who followed him, and, soon afterward, began sleeping at the foot of the tree where Cley spent his nights, became the conduit through which his message spread to those of the People who hadn't yet attended his talks and contemplation sessions. His closest followers found their emotions—emotions which were, traditionally, controlled or channeled—came alive and swung wildly when it came to Cley. Sometimes he confused them, occasionally they feared him, sometimes they feared *for* him. But mostly they loved him. They were constantly aware that they were in the presence of someone utterly unlike anyone else they had ever encountered. It wasn't just the miracle of Cley acquiring a personality, and intelligence, it was the nature of that personality, the unique quality of that intelligence. They wanted to be with him all the time, despite the fact that he had taken the unquestioned, firm landscape of their lives and replaced it with a shifting, changing, moving world that he insisted they had to encounter personally.

And so a community had sprung up around the base of the tree where he slept.

Every evening, after the public contemplation session, but before any public meetings around the fire pit, Cley and his followers would wait before returning to the trees. Members of the tribe knew he could be found there, and, as darkness fell, those who needed healing would come to him. Even those who muttered against him in daylight would often have a temporary change of heart when a child ran a dangerous fever, or a hunter was half-killed trying to bring down a shuk - the most dangerous of all the animals, but most prized for its black and red fur.

Cley's customary answer was to fill their water bottles simply by resting his hand against it. When the sick drank from it, they would be healed. Those who made use of this did so circumspectly as time went on, careful not to be seen by their neighbors.

Then, one night, Cley's command of the miraculous failed him for the first time. He took the waterskin of an old woman whose male partner was lame. Placing it between his palms, he cleared his mind and...nothing. It was as if he was trying to finish a sentence and the word he was looking for—an obvious, everyday word, nothing obscure—simply dropped out of his memory. He sat there with the waterskin between his hands and realized he had forgotten what to do.

Then he realized that he had forgotten something far more important.

When had he last paused, when had he last summoned *Home*? He had been doing it every morning and evening until recently, then somehow he had allowed the morning routine to slip. To his shock, he thought it may have been three or four days since he had last called forth the door to Richmond Park.

He stumbled away from the fire pit, apologizing to the old woman, suggesting she came back the following night.

He acknowledged the confused looks from his followers with a nod and a forced smile.

"I must be with the Singer. Alone. I will see you in the forest."

As soon as he entered the cover of the trees, he found a large akrarn and sat out of sight, leaning against the blue-black trunk.

"Pause," he said. His surroundings lost their vibrancy, colors and sounds muted in an instant.

"Show *Home*."

The door slid up from the forest floor, and he crawled through it. He had got this far on instinct, but he could barely remember why or what was supposed to happen next.

As he got to his feet on the path in Richmond Park and looked around at the grass, the summer flowers, the blurred shapes of distant people and the impressive sight of the royal oak, he felt a confused flood of memories judder around the boundaries of consciousness.

He half-closed his eyes against the onslaught of simultaneously comforting, yet jarringly alien, scenes flickering through his lashes. A jumble of images lit up his brain but vanished before he could fully grasp them.

My hands on a piano

A man in black, driving away from a building site in a shining city

A tall, glowing, creature with huge, dark eyes, holding out its hands

A woman, her face wreathed in smoke, saying, "of course I love you, you daft twat."

He stumbled along the path, walking toward the water.

There was a sound in a tree to his left. He looked toward it and saw movement, something racing up the trunk in a streak of red-brown fur.

He moved closer and looked up into the branches, shading his eyes against the sun. Then he saw the creature crawl along a high branch and squat there, eating something.

It was a yoik.

But it wasn't eating a longfruit, it was eating some kind of nut.

He tried to shake off the feeling of horror that seeing the yoik here gave him. His mind was rebelling at the juxtaposition, insisting that either the yoik didn't belong, or the park didn't belong.

His sense of self felt slippery. He turned away from the tree and continued toward the water.

He was Seb, a voice in his head insisted. He wasn't really Cley.

He was Cley. This was a dream.

Cley was a dream of Seb was a dream of Cley.

There was someone on the bench. Two figures. They looked...wrong. The proportions. Too tall. Long limbs.

He sat down on the path and put his head in his hands.

And remembered.

I'm Seb Varden.

Seb Varden.

He sat there until he was calm, until he was confident he knew who he was. And why he was there with the People, in the Gyeuk Egg.

To save Baiyaan. To stop the Rozzers messing with evolution. To find my way back to...

For a second, it had gone.

...Meera. Mee. Meera Patel.

He knew her name. Of course he knew her name. He knew who she was.

But, for a moment, it had gone.

He felt as cold a stab of fear as he'd ever felt in his life.

He vowed to pause, and come here, visit *Home* as often as possible. First thing in the morning, last thing at night.

But he had a sudden, sick feeling he'd made that vow already.

What was happening to him?

He stumbled out of the park, back through the doorway. He was back in the clearing near the forest, the

203

sounds and smells of the settlement drifting up to where he stood, blinking, his claws unsheathing automatically as if he was being attacked.

Drawing a ragged, shaky breath, Seb said the one word that he hoped might stop this rising feeling of panic.

"Show *Exit.*"

THE *EXIT* WAS A DOORWAY, but unlike the *Home* door leading to Richmond Park, there was no hint of what lay beyond the threshold. Seb looked into absolute darkness. It was more intense than the mere absence of light, it was as if the doorway actively sucked away all hint of anything other than blackness, so that what he was staring into would never be anything other than completely impenetrable.

According to Bok, the moment he stepped through the *Exit*, he would trigger the live connection between his "real" body waiting next to the physical representation of the Gyeuk Egg, back in whatever corner of the universe it was where his fellow World Walkers waited. Not that they had waited long. A few minutes may have passed.

If he used the *Exit*, it was all over. He would be back with the T'hn'uuth. Cley would either revert to being a Blank, or die. His followers among the People would be leaderless, either way.

He had already dropped some ambiguous hints to his followers, in the hope that they would be remembered after he'd gone, lending some authority to his message. He had told them he would not be with them long. They just didn't know what that meant. Yet.

The truth was, he still hadn't decided how best to prepare them for the fact that, once he had gone, they might be left with a messiah who hummed all the time, and dribbled. Such an outcome would give Davvi and Cochta more ammunition for their demonic possession theory, which already had traction among some of the People. Seb was aware of the danger, but not yet sure how best to deal with it. He was making it up as he went along, and nothing in his career as a session musician in twenty-first century Los Angeles had prepared him for dealing with political machinations against a nascent religious movement on a simulated alien planet.

He laughed, weakly.

His success so far, he attributed to the fact that he had been able to detach himself from any firm plans, and allow words, and action, to arise naturally, passively. If he got out of his own way, things tended to fall into place.

He looked at the door again.

If he left now, he imagined his youthful, enthusiastic group of immediate followers wouldn't be able to hold on to their new worldview in the teeth of resolute opposition from most of the tribe, which would almost certainly be the general reaction to Cley's reversion to Blank status.

Seb, Cley.

Seb.

He struggled, whether with his conscience, his "true self," Cley's memories, loyalty to Baiyaan - he couldn't say.

He knew he couldn't risk staying much longer. The risk of losing himself was real. Far more real than he had thought when agreeing to Fypp's proposal.

He would have to bring things to a head. And soon.

"Cancel *Exit.*"

The door slid away into nothingness.

THESIS, antithesis, synthesis.

Life, death, rebirth.

Act one, act two, act three.

Headline, set up, punchline.

Father, son, holy ghost.

Say what you're gonna say, say it, say what you said.

Seb walked back to the foot of the tree. His followers fell silent as he approached. They could sense an unnatural tension in him. Something different.

Seb knew about the rule of three. It even worked in songwriting.

Intro, verse, chorus.

He stopped in front of the group and paused before speaking. He felt his *Seb-ness* begin to slide away again, the reality of the world around him insinuating itself back into his consciousness. Cley's memories reinforced everything around him. The human being who had become a T'hn'uuth shrank, becoming a tiny presence in his brain, like a slight, nagging headache that wouldn't go away.

He wouldn't *let it* go away. He would keep it there, call up *Home* as often as it took, until he had finished what he had started, as best he could.

His followers waited, knowing something important was coming.

"My words may have helped you, but even I cannot take that final step with you. The Singer will always be singing, but you must let go of what you think you know if you want to become aware that you are already part of her song."

He stepped forward and smiled at them, raising his hands, claws sheathed, in the People's traditional greeting, the gesture which began every naming ceremony, and every burial.

"You can find her with your will. You can hear her with your being. But you must listen with your heart."

They waited in silence, knowing there was more.

"I will not be with you much longer. It is nearly time for me to join the song."

It sounded pretty portentous, and Cley felt sure his followers were reeling from the import of what he had said. He was still feeling fairly self-congratulatory when he practically walked head-on into Sopharndi.

"I need to talk to you," she said.

Chapter 31

Cley and Sopharndi sat at the foot of one of the few black-trees in the forest. The blacktrees were the only trees capable of growing in the Parched Lands, their dark, hard limbs reaching out toward the sky in defiance of the dusty, lifeless ground which tried to deny them sustenance. The few that flourished beyond the Parched Lands were super-stitiously avoided by the people, who associated them, with death. Other than when taking their Journeys, members of the tribe avoided the lifeless landscape to the south of the settlement.

Cley had chosen the blacktree to prevent them being interrupted. He watched his mother pace around the area for a few minutes, checking for danger, looking for signs of animal activity. She had been First for a long time, and her habitual caution had saved lives on more than one occasion.

Finally, she sat down and was silent for a few minutes. The People were not encouraged to rush to speak, and Sopharndi was more taciturn than most. As Cley waited for her to initiate the conversation, he fell into the same attitude of stillness and listening that he was teaching the tribe. Rather than pre-empt what she might say, or speculate about how he might respond, he simply began to pay attention to everything around, and inside, him.

Listening started with the ears. He heard the far off calls of a pair of lekstrall, hunting nuffles to the north. He heard the fainter sounds of murmuring voices in the settlement as they prepared to sleep. There was no gathering of the People tonight, so the crackle of the fire pit was quiet in comparison to the nights when the tribe met, and the flames rose into the night air, crackling and spitting sparks. Closer, he heard the sounds of his followers, fidgeting as they attempted to be still, igniting their own session of contemplation, their own period of *listening*. Closer still, the slight breeze moving the leaves of the forest around him, the constant tiny sounds of nature - things growing, things unfurling into existence. Things dying.

In his own body, Cley heard his breath as it entered his nostrils and his lungs expanded to use it before expelling it again. Underneath that rhythmic cycle, another regular sound - the beating of his heart. At rest, his heartbeat was much faster than...*than what?* Cley felt a moment's distraction as the comparison he was reaching for eluded him. How could he compare his heartbeat to anything else? It was all he had ever known.

With an ease arrived at through tens of thousands of hours practice, he released the thought and *listened* again. Now, underneath his breath, beyond the pump of his heart, past the thin rush of blood through veins, he found the stillness of the song. The silence that contained everything, from which everything constantly arose and returned. Each moment unfolded from the silence and flowered into emptiness, becoming the silence once again.

Deeper.

Something lodged in the silence, something resisting. Cley couldn't *listen* with his heart while this presence blocked a complete letting go. He allowed his attention to settle on it for a moment. It took on the aspect of a figure, taller than anyone he knew, unfamiliar yet personal. He felt confusion at its presence, then allowed his practice to take over as he let go of the distraction, watching it fall apart and lose substance like bark thrown on a fire.

Cley *listened*.

And, when his mother finally spoke, he knew himself as a note in the song, ephemeral, yet essential.

"Since you returned, it's as if you are someone else entirely."

"I am your son."

"Yes." Sopharndi looked long and hard at Cley. "I know it. I am thankful for every dawn since your Journey. I never thought I would see you again. But I know my son, and you are not Cley. Not...not completely."

Still Cley did not speak. Sopharndi waited for a denial and was glad when one wasn't forthcoming.

"Don't misunderstand me. I know you are no demon, as Davvi might have us believe. I see Cley in you, but I see more than that. I do not fear you, I am not angry with you. Without you, there would be no Cley. I understand that. You speak of the Singer. You speak of the Last Song. I have listened along with the rest. I have seen how the young are drawn to your message. I have heard others talk of healing you have performed. I..."

Here she stopped, uncertain how to continue. Cley leaned forward and placed a hand on her arm. She did not flinch. Whatever her instincts told her, this was still, some-how, her son.

Cley's expression was, as always, open and unguarded.

"You speak a truth I barely understand myself. You are

right. I am not just Cley any more. But I do not fully understand who I am. I cannot speak of what I cannot grasp. I can only ask you to trust me. Because my message is real, what I am teaching is the truth. The Singer has spoken to me, and through me."

"You remember this? You remember the Singer, up there in the mountains on your Journey?"

"No," Cley admitted. "I have no memory of it. The past has clouded over. I remember my childhood, I remember you, my mother. But after setting out on my Journey, the memories are unclear. I have knowledge, I have the teaching to pass on, but I cannot truly tell you where that teaching came from."

Sopharndi placed a hand on top of Cley's.

"I have watched you closely, I have listened to your words and I know you believe the truth of what you say. But—well, it isn't like listening to Davvi sing the songs. He believes in the Singer, and he tells us that just by singing the words, we are pleasing Her. With you it is different. You play with the words. It's as if you don't think they're important. You want us to *listen*, to wake up, but some-times…I don't know. Sometimes what you say makes little sense."

"Labels on bottles," muttered Cley.

"What?"

"I don't know. It just came into my mind. Yes, again, you are right. The words are not important to me. They must lead the listener to silence. If they do not, they have failed."

Sopharndi stood and paced around the small clearing at the base of the blacktree. She did not like to sit for too long, preferring to be active.

"You ask a lot of the People. And you ask a lot of me."

"Yes," Cley admitted, "I do. And I ask you to trust me

now. I know you have never truly *listened*. Some will never truly learn how. It doesn't matter."

"It doesn't matter? I am your mother. How can it not matter that I do not experience what you say is true."

"You will, everyone will experience it, eventually. You must hear the call yourself, no one can, or should, force it upon you. What is far more important is the fact that you trust me despite this. I cannot make you see what I see, hear what I hear. I cannot help you to know that the future of our tribe, and all the tribes, will depend on this. The Last Song must be heard by all, not just the People."

"You tread a dangerous path," said Sopharndi. "Yes, I trust you. I see my child in you, and I know he would never lie to me. But you do not know the danger you are in. Laak will not be Leader for much longer. Cochta will replace her. She will seek to rid the tribe of your influence swiftly, and brutally."

"I can protect myself," said Cley. A small insect bit into the softer flesh at the heel of his claws. He swatted it away. "What of you? She has always seen you as a rival."

"She is mistaken."

Cley stood then and joined his mother as she paced. "Cochta should be pitied. She has become so attached to her envy and ambition that she projects the same character flaws onto everyone else. She never encounters anyone as they truly are, only seeing a distorted version of them. For her, the world is a colorless, small, fearful place."

Sopharndi sighed. "I'd find it easier to pity her if she wasn't such a bitch."

They both laughed. Cley felt a twinge of *something* - a memory? at Sopharndi's crude turn of phrase. Then the feeling passed.

"A change is coming," he said. "Whatever the outcome, this time of uncertainty will pass for the People." He scratched at the insect bite on his hand. "There will be suffering, there will be pain. There will be death. But every moment dies so the next can be born. Every note in the song has its place to be sung. The melody is eternal, there should be no mourning one note, when it is still there, always there in the song."

Sopharndi shrugged. "Do not speak of death, my son."

They hugged then, under the shadow of the cursed blacktree, before Sopharndi turned and headed back to the settlement.

Cley watched her go, absently scratching at his hand. It took him a few minutes to realize something was wrong, a few more before he became aware of what it was.

He looked at the flesh at the base of the claws on his left hand. There was an angry area of swollen skin where the insect had bitten him. He had been bitten by insects before. It wasn't even particularly painful.

So why the rising feeling of alarm?

He experimentally unsheathed his claws, and winced as the skin split and began to bleed.

Then he had it. Since he had returned from his Journey, he had been able to heal. Not just others, himself. It was the same power he used to create the water from nowhere, the miracle that had brought so many to listen to him in those first sessions by the fire pit.

He looked down at the blood. He reached out with his mind, focusing on the wound. Nothing happened. He allowed his thoughts to clear, brought his mind back to the stillness he spent most of his life stepping in and out of.

Nothing. The blood slid down to his wrist, then fell to the floor in fat, purple drops.

He reached into the air to create water.

Nothing. Again.

Something tugged at the corners of his consciousness, an

insistent, panicked flash of warning. As if someone was desperately trying to get his attention, but in a dream where he could no longer hear or see.

Something. Something important. Something he must never forget.

A word.

There was a word. If he said it, he would be able to heal again. And he would be able to bring the People to the Singer.

One word.

If he could just…

His head snapped up.

"Pause," he said.

———

THE COLOR DRAINED OUT of the forest around him, and the sound of the wind faded to nothing. Acting without conscious thought now, but knowing it was right, Cley spoke again.

"*Home.*"

From the forest floor, a doorway rose into view. Cley stumbled through it.

He looked around him. The surface he stood on was different somehow. Harder. He pushed at it with his foot. Unyielding.

At first glance, he thought the trees were different too, but now that he looked properly, he could see that they were familiar to him, Akrarn and blacktrees bordered the path on which he stood.

Cley looked around him wildly. Nothing seemed strange about this place, apart from the fact that he had arrived there through a strange opening in the forest. He looked into the sky. The sun was low, and he could see all three moons, pale in the darkening sky. Everything was how it should be, but somehow that terrified him.

He felt compelled to move then, to head along the path which led down a gentle slope toward water. He felt a rising sense that, if he didn't get to the water, everything would be lost, his life would have been worthless. His heart hammering, he broke into a run.

As he got close to the water, he saw two figures standing there. He felt a flood of relief. That was right! There should be two, a male and a female. Everything would be clear when he saw them properly.

The sun was in his eyes. When he closed to within a few yards of the figures, he cupped one clawed hand over his eyes. Blood dropped onto his face, but he ignored it. He squinted.

One of the figures was his mother. Next to her stood someone so familiar, it took Cley a few seconds to realize who it was.

It was a young male. He was rocking from side to side, spittle at the corner of his mouth. And he was humming.

Cley fell to his knees, feeling blackness closing in on him.

"No," he said, thickly, "no. This is not right. It's not right."

The chaos of his thoughts built in a frenzied crescendo of confusion. Then, nothing at all.

Chapter 32

Sopharndi woke with a start hours before dawn. She knew she had heard something. Around her, there were the sounds of others stirring in nearby dwellings, of frightened whispers. She grabbed her spear and belt, tucking her knife in as she ducked out of the doorway.

The same sound again. Still with a nightmarish quality, made more surreal by the fact that she was awake now. Again. Louder, this time. A huge creaking, cracking, sound. It was coming from the river. She jogged toward the source of the unfamiliar noise.

At the sound of the first screams, Sopharndi broke into a sprint, her claws unsheathing as she ran. She knew every fighter would be doing the same, other than those posted on the perimeter.

Three loud bangs sounded with a couple of seconds of each other, so loud the ground shook slightly. Sopharndi couldn't imagine what she was about to face. If they were under attack, the river—still fast-flowing at this time of the year— was a strong natural defense. Therefore, the most lightly guarded. She put on a fresh burst of speed.

As she ran, she caught sight of Katela among a group of fighters forming a pack just behind her. She slowed momentarily, to let them catch up, then barked orders between snatching breaths.

"Three groups. You go west. Katela, take the east. I will take the center."

There was no more to be said. They parted, and as Sopharndi and her group ran on, other fighters emerged from dwellings to join them.

As they broke through the last line of dwellings at the northern edge of the settlement, they saw the source of the noise. Three of the tallest akrarns on the north bank of the river had been uprooted and pushed forward until they toppled, forming natural bridges across the water. Making their way across the trees were the fighters of the Chosen. They were easy to identify, the skin of their face tattooed with white dots around the eyes, giving their features an animal-like appearance, designed to mimic the dominant predator of their region, the shuk.

No words were necessary now. The People's fighters were trained from childhood in the art of killing. They lived their lives simultaneously hoping they would never be called on to use their skills, and yearning to engage in real combat, where death and honor were at stake. The Challenges around the fire pit were not just a traditional way of ensuring the best fighters got ahead, it was also a safer way of allowing the strongest, most aggressive among them to release some of their bloodlust. Only a Challenge to the First was fought to the death, but even minor Challenges sometimes left a corpse behind.

The fighters lived to fight, their instincts, strength, and minds focused into a deadly knife, spear and claw-wielding beast while they were engaged in combat.

With roars of aggression, they launched themselves fearlessly toward the enemy.

The next few minutes passed in a melange of focused fear and rage. Sopharndi had experienced this before but knew the younger warriors were about to witness the unexpected flexibility that time assumed in a real battle. Moments seemed to pass incredibly slowly, with every detail available to eye, ear, and brain, but—at the same time—it was as if everything was accelerated, every stab, parry, lunge, kick, slash, duck, roll, and recoil occurring with such speed that they seemed virtually simultaneous. Then, disorientated, at the end of the fight, the survivors would look in disbelief at the position of the moons, finding that minutes had passed, rather than hours.

On a purely physical level, Sopharndi accepted, even welcomed the fight. Every minute of training and preparation meant her mind lost all capacity for anything other than the battle. Her body was a blur as she threw herself at the Chosen fighters, cutting two of them down in as many seconds during her initial onslaught. As she fought on, she was always aware of the positions of her group, as they pressed forward as one.

The enemy was making its way across their makeshift bridges as fast as they could, but the very part of their plan which had given them an element of surprise was proving to be their undoing. The Chosen had spent much of the night digging at the roots, cutting through those to the south of each tree, unearthing those to the north, unbalancing each akrarn. They had engineered pivots, using the hard wood of the blacktree, and had levered the giant trees until they fell. The fallen trees bridged the river, but they hadn't reckoned enough on the effect the branches and foliage would have on the speed of their progress across the water.

As Sopharndi fought on, pulling her claws from the throat of one young female, while slashing across the spine of another with her knife, she saw Cochta lead a group through the carnage, making her way to the trees. Her group numbered under a dozen, but they lit up the scene like daylight. Each of them carried four torches, the animal-fat soaked skins wrapped tightly around the top, their light exposing every detail of the bloody scene. Bodies lay everywhere, and those still fighting were grim and bloody. There were no taunts now, no sounds other than the hiss of effort, the clash of weapons or the tearing of flesh. The warriors looked, in the flicker of the torches, like they were performing some kind of macabre dance as they fought, stepping over corpses as they spun and hacked at each other.

Cochta's group split into three, heading for each tree. Four of the group fell as they got closer, cut down by the Chosen fighters. But Cochta had picked her moment well. The Chosen were sending their attack across in waves, and Cochta had seen a gap appear. She reached the central tree while the next enemy fighter was only halfway across, shoving her way through some tangled branches. She looked up at the sight of Cochta's flaming torches, saw the danger and redoubled her efforts to get across. As she broke free of the branches, Cochta set light to the trunk where it had fallen onto the back. As it began to burn, she threw her other torches further onto the akrarn.

It had been just over a week since the last rains, so the leaves and branches were parched and dry. The fire caught quickly, the leaves curling into ash, twigs bursting into flame and, moments later, bigger branches dancing and blackening as orange-white tongues licked them into contortions. The trees to the left and right were also ablaze, and the enemy fighters already on the trunks had turned and were heading back to the far shore, and safety.

The Chosen fighter on Cochta's tree had evidently decided she was too far forward to retreat. With a war whoop full of rage and bloodlust, she ran toward the flames, launching herself forward and to one side, away from the burning trunk, landing ankle deep in the shallows, knife drawn and teeth bared. She advanced quickly, with the practiced economy of movement shared by all experienced fighters.

Cochta, caught up in the triumph of the moment, did not see the danger immediately. When she did see the approaching fighter, she stumbled backward, avoiding the first slash of the knife.

Sopharndi twisted a spear out of the chest of a fallen fighter and hefted it to her shoulder.

Cochta tripped as she backed up, landing squarely on the chest of a headless corpse. The advancing Chosen fighter emitted a triumphant shriek and raised her knife, not realizing that Cochta's fall had saved her life.

Seeing a chance for a clear shot, Sopharndi didn't hesitate, twisting the spear slightly as she released it. A second later, as the enemy warrior's knife began its descent toward Cochta's unprotected throat, the point of the spear entered her chest precisely where Sopharndi had intended. It was a throw of about fifteen yards, so the momentum carried the point and a foot of the shaft through the female and out through her back. She didn't die instantly, but as she fell, the impact of the spear hitting the hard ground caused the shaft to splinter, widening the wound in her chest considerably. Her heart continued to pump blood for nearly a minute, but, as crucial arteries had been crudely severed, most of the dark fluid pooled on the ground beside her while she gasped out her last few breaths.

Cochta got to her knees and looked back at Sopharndi, just as a fallen fighter, regaining consciousness after a blow to the head, sat up behind the First and plunged his knife into her thigh. Sopharndi hissed at the pain and instantly clasped the wrist of the hand on the knife's hilt. As the Chosen fighter's eyes widened, Sopharndi's superior strength allowed her to force the knife back out, and twist his hand so that the blade was facing his gut. Too late, he tried to roll away, but Sopharndi used her weight to fall on him, the knife slicing easily through his flesh. She put her other hand on the hilt and drew the blade across and back, before rolling him onto his front, his guts spilling out around the knife and his bloody hand.

Sopharndi sat up and groaned. The wound on her leg was deep. She pressed a hand on it, staunching the flow of blood. The sounds of the battle were muted as the remaining enemy fighters were engaged, their only exits on fire. Only a few fights were yet to reach their inevitable conclusions. All three trees now blazed above the water. She knew the Chosen raiding party would already have gone, cutting their losses. Such attacks had once been commonplace, but, since the People had settled by the river and established their defenses, other tribes had seemed content to let them be, either because they wished for peace or certainly—in the case of the Chosen—because they could not see a way to guarantee victory. The Chosen were not known for their mercy. Had their raid succeeded, they would have put the village to the torch, sparing only the lives of children, that they might be used as slaves.

Sopharndi got to her feet, wincing, still keeping pressure on the wound. It was over. Bodies littered the ground. In death, it was hard to know which were People, and which Chosen. If this was part of the Singer's song, it was ugly and tuneless.

The near-silence that always accompanied the aftermath of battle now descended. Sopharndi limped around the field of battle, looking for survivors. Katela joined her, stopping her First for a few moments so she could wrap a thin strip of hide tightly around her injury. Sopharndi leaned on her Second's shoulder as they walked, relieved to see the younger woman had come through with only a few cuts and bruises.

"Fifteen dead at least. Maybe more," said Katela in answer to Sopharndi's unspoken question. "Injuries, too. Where is Cley?"

Even those who harbored doubts about Cley's authenticity had no doubt about his gift for healing.

Sopharndi looked around her, beginning to feel the first stirrings of disquiet.

Yes, where *was* Cley?

A shout from one of her fighters brought her and Katela hurrying across to a spot near the water by the westernmost tree. She was standing over someone with terrible injuries, a Chosen spear pinning her to the ground.

"She's alive," said the fighter as they drew close, "but—"

When she crouched down, noting the shallow breaths and the quantity of blood, Sopharndi released the grief wail known by all the People.

The blank eyes looking up at her, seeing nothing, belonged to Laak.

Their Leader was dying.

Chapter 33

As soon as the sounds of fighting started in the settlement below, four of Cley's followers had gone to find him while the rest headed back to their friends and families.

The four headed up the hillside. They found Cley unconscious at the foot of one of the few blacktrees to flourish outside of the Parched Lands. He had hit his head when he had fallen, and the right side of his skull was discolored and slightly swollen.

Easing him into a sitting position, one of his supporters gave him water. They had seen his injury and were shocked by it. Why had he not healed himself?

"Your head," one of them ventured. "You're hurt."

Cley put a hand up to the side of his head and winced when he felt the lump there.

"I—," he began, but stopped when he heard a distant wail. It sounded like Sopharndi. He struggled to his feet, nearly fell, and grabbed the shoulder of one of his young supporters. He took a few breaths, until the rhythmic thumping in his head settled into a more manageable ache.

"What's happening?"

"We think it's an attack. We heard the sounds of fighting. There will be many injuries. You must come."

Cley allowed himself to be led back down the hillside, breaking into a run, despite the flashes of pain each step sent through his skull.

As they entered the outskirts of the settlement, three fighters running in their direction intercepted them. Cley recognized his mother's Second.

"Katela, what's happening?"

"It was the Chosen."

"My mother?"

"Injured, but not badly. We need you. Follow me."

Cley struggled to match the pace Katela set, and was relieved when they stopped at the Elders' dwelling by the Meeting Circle. Katela pulled back the skin at the doorway, but stepped to one side, letting Cley enter.

"Just him," she hissed at the others who tried to follow. One look at Katela's grim expression and they were disinclined to argue.

Inside, two of the Elders stood on one side, Cochta and Sopharndi on the other. Cley saw the way Sopharndi's leg had been bandaged, blood seeping through the wrapped material and running down her leg.

"Mother." He stepped toward her, but she shook her head and motioned toward the pile of animal skins between her and the Elders.

As Cley got closer, he finally registered the smell which had been masked by sweat and blood when he first entered. Everyone in the tribe could identify the scent given off by one close to death. It was as distinctive a smell as that of a hungry infant, an aroused male, or a female giving in to bloodlust. It had a bittersweet quality, a kind of burned sweetness with an underlying note of decay.

He moved closer to the pile of animal skins, finally

seeing the frail body they held. Laak's skin had paled and lost its shine as her body began to shut down. Her breathing was so shallow that Cley could see no movement in her chest at all. Her eyes, when he looked into them, held no hint of the patience, humor, and intelligence that had served her so well in her long tenure as Leader. It was as if she was already looking far beyond the gloomy dwelling to the Beyond, where she would join others waiting to be sung back into existence as a tree, a lekstrall, a shuk, or even one of the People once again. Eventually all creation would join in the same song; disease, pain, and death would end, and the Beyond would merge with the Land.

Cochta bent her head toward Cley as he looked at the dying Leader.

"Heal her."

Cley looked at the Leader's daughter. Her ambition, her schemes and her absolute lack of concern for others had fallen away as she faced the prospect of her mother's death. She wanted power, she had maneuvered herself into a position where the Elders had agreed to her assumption of the leadership, but she had wanted Laak to live on, to see her daughter's strength as she guided the People into their future. Cochta may have allowed personal ambition to trump ethical and moral considerations, but, right now, she was just a daughter terrified of losing her mother.

Cley felt beside the skins, leaned closer to Laak and put his hand gently on her shoulder. He knew the enormity of the opportunity before him. He would heal anyone brought before him, naturally, but winning favor with Cochta in the process would mean she would be forced to acknowledge the validity of his message. Too many witnesses had seen him come here. If Laak lived, Cochta would have to find a way of accommodating the new spiritual direction Cley was teaching. The People would learn to *listen*. A spiritual revolution would be set in motion.

There was just one problem. Cley couldn't remember *how* to heal.

He quieted his mind. That much was instinctive now. His inner practice was so deeply ingrained, he need hardly think about it. He watched himself watching his thoughts, and, as he became aware of moments when he was clinging to them, he let them go, living more and more in the gaps between the thoughts. His breath deepened naturally, and soon it was him, Laak and the others, the sounds, the smells, the feel of the Leader's cooling skin. He reached out...

Cochta broke the silence. "What are you doing? Heal her. Now."

He held up his other hand for quiet, the insect bite red and angry-looking. He felt as if he had forgotten something as obvious as his own name. The next step, the dissolving of barriers between himself and the rest of the world, the exposure of the illusion of separateness...it wasn't happening. It was gone. He continued reaching out, the absence of his power still impossible to acknowledge. Just as fighters who had lost an arm often reached for their spear with the missing limb, he kept flexing muscles that weren't there any longer, sent messages to nerve endings that had disappeared.

After a minute that seemed like an hour, Laak made a sound in her throat that seemed to come from miles away, a harsh, distant scraping. Then the final dim spark of life in her eyes died for ever.

Cley squatted back on his heels, shaking his head, his whole body feeling cold.

"I tried," he began, then stopped, looking up at Cochta. "She's gone."

After a second of absolute silence, Cochta slapped him aside, deliberately allowing her claws to unsheath as she did so. Three wounds opened up on Cley's cheek as he fell backward. Sopharndi grunted in shock and anger, taking half a step toward Cochta, before stopping herself and going to her son, helping him up.

Cochta shouted at Hesta and Gron - the two Elders frozen in shock and disbelief at the death of their Leader.

"Get the traitors out of here, get them out!"

Hesta joined Sopharndi as she squatted beside Cley, who was shaking his head at her.

"I'm all right, Mother."

Hesta put her hand on Sopharndi's shoulder.

"Go. Take him away. She has lost her mother, she does not know what she is saying. We will counsel her tomorrow. We shall speak then."

She walked Sopharndi and Cley to the doorway and watched them limp into the darkness.

⸻

THAT NIGHT, the fire pit was cold and black until dawn, when the People gathered silently to burn the dead. Laak's body was last to be placed upon the pyre. She had been wrapped in the finest skins, and the song of the Beyond was sung for hours. It was a call and response song that induced an almost trancelike state in the singers. The calls were sung by Davvi, the responses by all the People. Each call by the bard offered advice to the dead on how to find the Beyond, to find the place the Singer has made ready, each response encouraged the dead to make their way back to the People after their time in the Beyond.

In the early afternoon, when the fire was burned to ashes, and the bodies reduced to bones, the carers of the dead scraped any remaining flesh from the bones, wrapping them carefully, before carrying them to the burial grounds south of the forest. There, they would be polished before being buried. Laak's bones would be buried last, and nearest to the tree line, where the recently dead would find it easiest to find her, when they came back from the Beyond to guide their fellows to their next destination.

The dead would be remembered. Their names would be added to the song of remembrance, until such time as no one living remained who remembered them.

The meeting was called for that night.

Their new Leader would address them.

It quickly became common knowledge that Cley was back in the Settlement, that he was injured, and that Cochta had ordered his and Sopharndi's dwellings to be guarded before that night's meeting.

There would be no *listening* session led by Cley that evening.

The fire would be lit at dusk, and all were to attend.

Chapter 34

The anointment of Cochta as the new Leader of the People took place while there was still light from the sun, the ceremony concluding just before it sank behind the mountains.

The entire tribe was present other than those still recovering from serious injuries after the attack of the previous night. Infants were cradled in their fathers' arms, the very old were allowed to sit on soft skins rather than the hard ground.

Normally, the anointment of a new Leader would be an occasion for joy and celebration. Leaders handed over the responsibility of guiding the People to their successors at a time of their own choosing, traditionally when they had entered their fifth decade. It was rare indeed for anyone to live past their sixtieth year, so this allowed the departing Leader an old age relieved of responsibility, that they might prepare for their journey to the Beyond.

An anointment following the death of a Leader, particularly a violent death, lent a more somber note to the proceedings. The fact that the new Leader was the daughter of the previous Leader might have caused some controversy, even—particularly given Cochta's arrogance and reputation for intractability—leading to a challenge. But coming, as it did, immediately after the first attack on the tribe for nearly a generation, any potentially dissenting voices were persuaded to remain silent, for the moment. Strong leadership was needed at a time like this, and no one doubted Cochta's resolve. By now, they had all heard how Cochta saved the tribe with her idea to burn the trees.

Cley watched the proceedings in a numb haze of confusion. His mother, sitting next to him, was silent and tense. They had spent the day under guard, with no official word as to what they were accused of, or what might happen to them. Cochta had a sense for the dramatic. Her moment had come, and Cley suspected this night would not be a good one for him or Sopharndi.

He was still fighting an extreme sense of disorientation. It was as if he had mislaid the most important thing in his life, but, not only could he not remember where he had left it, he couldn't even remember what it was. He had sat in contemplation for hours, *listening* but, for the first time since his Journey, hearing nothing. His practice, normally a return to reality, the ground of all experience, today had seemed more like an escape, an attempt to avoid the facts about his life. His failure.

I have failed.

This was the feeling that underpinned all other thoughts flickering through his disturbed mind.

I have failed.

Cley put a hand up to the side of his head. Still tender.

When Cochta addressed the People for the first time as Leader, she began by reinforcing the need for strong leadership at such a dangerous time. She played on the fears of the tribe, emphasizing the differences between the People and other tribes. The People were superior in every way, and such superiority had led others to covet what they had. Weaker voices had sometimes suggested sharing their good fortune, allowing other tribes to settle nearby, in this verdant area that *they*, the People, had discovered. But last night had proved that they were right never to trust the other tribes. They were savages, murderers, heretics. They must never prevail. The People would build up their defenses, increase the patrols around the outer limits of their borders, add to the number of fighters.

It was an effective speech, rousing passions, playing on fears. Cley acknowledged Cochta's skill at manipulating mass emotions. Around him, the majority of the tribe were drumming the backs of their hands on the hard earth in support of Cochta's impassioned references to the greatness of the People, their favored status with the Singer, the relative savagery and ignorance of other tribes. The threat they posed. The way she, Cochta, promised to protect them to her last breath.

She could work a crowd.

Then her voice changed, becoming quieter. There was a regretful tone now, a sadness. Great Leaders had to make hard decisions. Threats to the People did not always come from outside the tribe. The greatest threats of all sometimes came from within. And if these threats were allowed to grow, to flourish unchecked, the rot would spread like a terrible disease, eventually infecting everyone and heralding the end of the People.

Cley's mind cleared a little. He thought he knew where this was heading.

Cochta had the crowd in the palm of her hand now.

"When Cley returned from his Journey transformed, I wept for joy."

Sopharndi's snort of derision was ignored.

"Who else but the Singer could perform such a miracle? Who else could take a Blank, a mistake, an aberration, and give it a voice, intelligence, even the ability to mend broken bones, to work magic and produce water from nowhere? Who but the Singer could do this?"

She paced around the fire, every eye on her. She allowed enough of a pause for those present to find their own answer to her rhetorical question. A few heads turned toward Davvi, sitting with the Elders. He was struggling to look dignified, rather than smug. Cochta pointed at him.

"Our bard warned us. The bards have acted as messengers from the Singer since Aleiteh, the first bard. When Cley returned, many of us strayed from the path, many of us forgot whom the Singer chose to give her a voice among her people. She chose the bards."

She knelt at the edge of the circled crowd, in front of Davvi.

"As Leader, I take this crime against the Singer upon myself, and I swear that it will never happen again. On behalf of the People, I swear our renewed allegiance to the Singer. We will not stray again."

Davvi nodded gravely. He had obviously been told to play his role, and it had been made very clear to him that his was not a speaking part. Cochta rose from her knees and walked as she addressed the People.

"It was Davvi who first saw through the facade. When he recognized Cley for what he was, we did not want to hear it. But now misfortune has fallen on our tribe, we can doubt it any longer. Our Leader is dead. We turned our back on the Singer, choosing instead to listen to a Blank. And we suffered the consequences."

She turned to Cley, pointing him out.

"Laak was alive when this great healer came to her. This prophet who claims the Singer can be heard directly by everyone, who tells us we don't need the bards to know her. She was alive. Alive!"

Cochta let her words echo around the gathered crowd. She let her voice gradually build in volume.

"He placed a hand on her and watched her die. He did *nothing*. He could have saved my mother. He could have saved our Leader. He chose not to. Either that, or his power has left him. Either way, it leaves me with no doubt about who he really is. Cley is no prophet. Cley is a demon."

The drumming on the ground was louder and accompanied by grunts of agreement. Sopharndi's howl of "No!" was the only clear sign of dissent.

Cochta was nearly spitting in passion now, bringing the crowd with her in a crescendo of indignation.

"Cley brought this upon us, but he was not alone. Sopharndi supported him. Sopharndi bore this child who tried to destroy us. Without my intervention, the settlement would have fallen. She failed us."

Cley glanced around him. Katela, about fifteen feet to his right, looked uncomfortable and afraid. The rest of the fighters were immobile, their features betraying no emotions. They were trained to follow their First, but only because she relayed the orders of the Leader. The Leader was their first in command, and they would obey her without question.

Cochta gestured toward Cley and Sopharndi.

"Sopharndi is relieved of her duties. She is no longer First, she is no longer a fighter. Rettyu is First, Johaddo Second."

Out of the corner of his eye, Cley saw Katela flinch as she was demoted.

"Cley."

He looked up. Cochta was standing just a few feet away.

"You should have died on your Journey. Instead, you brought back a demon who inhabits your body. We will settle this in the traditional way of our tribe. If the Singer is truly with you, all will see it now. I challenge you. Stand up."

Sopharndi got to her feet first, shaking with rage and panic.

"You cannot challenge him. A female cannot challenge a male."

There were a few murmurs at this. Females were so much stronger than males that challenges between genders were not permitted.

Cochta spat into the dirt. "I am not challenging a male. Only a coward would do such a thing. I am challenging a demon. Sit down."

With a howl of rage, Sopharndi threw herself at Cochta. The younger female was taken by surprise by the speed and ferocity of the attack. Before she had the chance to take evasive action, Sopharndi's thumb claw had opened up a long gash in her leg. She stumbled, hissing in shock and pain, and a backhander caught her in the face, opening up a cut on her cheek.

The whole attack only lasted a few seconds, before the nearest fighters jumped on Sopharndi and pinned her to the ground.

Cochta breathed heavily for a few moments, looking at her enemy, now prone and unmoving.

"We all know the penalty for attacking the Leader. I should kill you right now."

Sopharndi said nothing but managed to twist her head round so she could fix a look of pure hatred on Cochta.

The new Leader took a knife from one of the fighters

and limped over to the fire. She placed the blade into the flames, watching the blade change color as she spoke.

"A strong Leader can also be merciful. You have brought a demon into our tribe. The attack you failed to prevent led to the death of Laak. But I will not kill you, because you have served the people well for most of your life, and this will not be forgotten."

The blade was white-hot now.

"Hold her head."

She walked back and squatted next to Sopharndi. She whispered the next words.

"No mother should have to see her son die."

With that, she carefully, deliberately pierced Sopharndi's left eyeball with the blade, twisting as she did so, before doing the same to the right.

No one there would ever forget the sound of her screams.

Strong arms held Cley down as he tried to reach his stricken mother, howling his grief and fury.

When the fighters had dragged Sopharndi back to her place in the crowd, Cochta beckoned to Cley.

"Now we will see whom the Singer favors. It's time for you to die, demon."

Cley was pulled to his feet and pushed out to meet Cochta.

Chapter 35

Cley felt the numb cold of shock spread through his body as he looked out across the sea of faces waiting to watch him die. Among those faces he picked out many of the younger members of the tribe who had followed him since the beginning, coming up to live among the trees. Some of them stared at the floor, some looked away. A few had the shiny-eyed glazed expression of true believers, waiting for the next miracle to save their prophet and prove, beyond doubt, in front of the entire tribe, that what he taught was the true path. This last group distressed him most of all. When they had pinned all their hopes to one individual, how would they cope if he was taken away, exposed as mortal just like them?

He must not fail them. Not now.

He turned his back on Cochta and spoke to the People.

"I am neither a demon or a god," he said. "The only demons you'll ever meet, the only gods you will ever know, are inside you. And they are imposters."

He spoke the words, but to Cley, they felt like ashes in his mouth. They were the echo of what he had once believed when he was whole. Now he felt broken. He looked at Sopharndi, her face hideously scarred, the red and black weals where her eyes had been still smoking, the stench of her burned flesh drifting across the clearing. She had lost consciousness. For that, he was glad.

"No more words, demon. No more blasphemy. Now you die."

He turned to face Cochta. Her face was bleeding, and she was favoring her left leg. It would make no difference to the inevitable outcome. She could kill him with both legs broken and one arm tied behind her back. Females were taller, bigger, stronger, more heavily muscled and naturally far more aggressive than males. In a knife fight, rare males who displayed an aptitude for fighting had been known to best females, using speed and lack of bulk to their advantage, often favoring a longer blade to compensate for their lack of reach.

There would be no knives in this fight, not that Cley knew how to use one anyway. This was a Challenge, to be fought with claws alone. Cochta wasted no time, unsheathing her claws and rushing him. Cley ducked to one side and rolled, but she slashed across his right shoulder, and he cried out in pain. Coming out of his roll, he immediately got up and backed away.

Cochta advanced more slowly this time. He tried to keep just out of range, but with a sudden burst of speed, she leaned in and slashed again, opening up a long cut across his ribs.

Cochta, her back to the crowd, smiled at Cley and he knew, with a kind of tired, sick feeling of resignation, that she meant to make his death long and painful.

She advanced on him again.

As the fight continued, and she opened up more wounds, Cochta sheathed her claws and began sadistically punching him directly on the gaping bloody injuries she had already inflicted. Cley found his mind retreating, his world shrinking, returning to that time before the Journey, when there was no knowledge, no understanding, no god, and no pain. He thought maybe he *had* heard the song back then. He had tried to sing along with it all his life, hadn't he?

A heavy blow to the side of his face sent Cley reeling, twisting as he lost his footing, coming down heavily on his right side, the already tender flesh on his head hitting the ground hard.

For a moment, he saw nothing at all. Then he saw the orange-red dance of the flames. He couldn't bring the fire into focus. He blinked a few times. There was blood in his eyes. He closed them again. Maybe she would just come and slash his throat, end it now.

"Get up," howled Cochta, the bloodlust thickening her voice. "Get up!"

She saw him, and she loved him.

He heard Cochta as if she spoke from miles away, but he was ready to obey her. Ready for it all to be over. Ready to die.

She wanted to get to him, but she couldn't. She was calling him but he didn't understand the words.

Cley opened his eyes slowly. He looked at the fire. But he didn't see it. He saw *her.*

My name is Seb. Seb Varden. I was born in New York City. Now, I live on a tiny island off the northeast coast of Britain. With Meera. Mee.

He saw a shock of wild black hair and deep eyes that saw *all* of him. Gray eyes. His own eyes, but not his own.

Next a wave of love hit him like nothing he had ever even dreamed was possible. Not romantic love, not compassionate empathy with your fellow beings love. It was raw, visceral, messy, unstoppable, full/empty/full, eternally temporary love. It was like nothing—

—*and he* knew—

—nothing he had ever known, he had no name for it, it was just—

—*he* knew—

—just as if he had been living in two dimensions his whole life and someone had pushed him through a door into a three-dimensional world, he couldn't—

—a *child*—

—couldn't comprehend what was happening, but neither—

—a *child* that, somehow, knew him, *saw* him, across the impossible gulf—

—neither could he deny the reality of it; time, space, distance, they all just dissolved like a drop of rain in an ocean and—

—who was it? who was he looking at?—

—he knew, he knew, he knew.

Who had called him, come to him, brought him back to who he was? He smiled at the apparition in stunned disbelief and love as she vanished and the flames once again rose from the fire pit.

He stood up. Cochta was facing the crowd. She had subdued the demon and was preparing herself to deliver the killing blow. When the crowd suddenly hushed, she turned to face Cley.

And saw Seb.

Only Cochta knew the difference. Every other member of the tribe watched in awe as Sopharndi's son got to his feet, his wounds healing as he rose. He faced the Leader, and the cuts on his body closed, the swollen and bruised flesh smoothing over. Within seconds, he was whole again.

With a scream of rage, Cochta sprang at him. Seb

moved to one side and her claws closed on air. She reacted quickly and swung her legs under his, to sweep him off his feet. He stepped over them with ease and backed up. She got up again.

"The demon has emerged," she shouted to the crowd. There were shouts of encouragements and cries of fear, but not every voice was raised in her support.

She rushed him again, throwing every last technique into the attack, feinting, parrying, slashing and stabbing, punching and kicking.

The flurry of blows lasted only a few seconds, Cochta's limbs a blur of highly-trained and deadly movements. Not a single blow landed. Her eyes widened as, for the first time, the possibility of defeat entered her mind.

As if he could see her thoughts, Seb raised a hand.

"No more," he said.

Cochta shook her head at his words, hardly believing he would dare to address her this way. She tensed her muscles, preparing to launch another attack, when she found she could not move at all. Her limbs refused to obey her commands. Her legs were locked in place. She tried to speak, but could not even do that.

Seb looked at her, and she felt a tightening on her leg and her face. The pain from her injuries disappeared, and she knew he had healed her. She felt herself fill with impotent rage.

Seb turned to the crowd for the last time. He repeated the words Cley had found, adding some of his own.

"I am neither a demon or a god," he said. "The only demons you'll ever meet, the only gods you will ever know, are inside you. And they are imposters. Treat them as such. Learn to *listen*."

He took one last look at Sopharndi. She was still unconscious, but she would live. And, whatever happened

240

next, she would not have to endure the rest of her life with the whole tribe believing she had brought a demon among them.

Seb turned to face the fire. He reached out with his mind and felt the subtle, lingering traces of the love that had found him over unimaginable distances in time and space.

He didn't want to know the whys and hows of it all.

He just wanted to go home. He was *needed*. Seb had never known a mother or father, but the connection he had felt with the presence in the flames had been close to that he'd used to imagine as a child, in the orphanage, dreaming of parents he'd never met.

He walked forward and, as the crowd behind him rose to their feet, shouting, he walked into the flames.

He remembered those gray eyes. He remembered Mee Patel and a million tiny shared moments.

The flames rose up around him but he felt no heat, although he was aware of his body burning up.

He felt the pull of everything he had left behind.

He reached the center of the fire pit.

And was gone.

Unchapter 36

Innisfarne

Joni cried for ten minutes solid after learning that she was the cause of her father's return to Earth. She hugged her dad first, then her mum, as they all struggled to comprehend the enormity of what had happened that day when she'd fallen from the oak. The first time she had *reset* the multiverse.

After her sobs subsided, Seb listened to the story of what had happened on her ninth birthday; the vision she had seen when she had lost her grip on a high branch, plunged to the forest floor and broken her neck. Moments from death, she had *reset* and the day had continued as if nothing untoward had happened. She had never really considered it out of the ordinary. She'd just assumed it was something everyone could do. Then, over time, it had been smudged into other childhood memories, dreams and stories.

The Unnamed Way

It was late afternoon now, and the snow, which had fallen steadily throughout the day, had settled into a pure white blanket which gave Innisfarne a fairytale appearance. Seb looked at his and Joni's reflections, superimposed, ghostlike, floating above the cold, white ground, flickering with the light of the fire. He rubbed Joni's back, still marveling at the fact that he was a father now. He had a family.

Mee joined them at the window.

"Joni was nine when she saw you - when you saw each other. And you came straight back."

Seb could see her making the same calculation he had already made.

"When you left here, when you Walked - how long did it seem to you?"

Seb thought about his answer before replying.

"It's like falling asleep in the afternoon, watching a movie. Your head drops forward, and you jerk and wake up. Time distorts. In that first instant, when you open your eyes, you feel like you've been asleep for hours. Then the rest of your brain kicks in and you realize it's only been seconds. It was like that. As if I was deeply asleep, but only for a few seconds. There was no sensation of time passing at all."

"But if the time you spent with the other World Walkers was, actually, short—hours, days maybe—then the Walk itself must have taken…"

"Over nine and a half years," said Joni. "You were pregnant with me when Dad left. But the Walk back was shorter."

"About seven and a half years," said Mee.

"I was in a hurry that time," said Seb.

"If that's supposed to be a joke, it's lame."

"It's the best I've got. It wasn't funny at the time."

243

Mee put her arms around his waist. "What happened when you got back here? Why the whole charade, living out in the cottage, looking like Moses?"

"Two reasons. I needed time to try to be human again, time to think, to contemplate, to *remember.*"

"And the second reason?"

"It was seventeen years, Mee. I was supposed to think you'd waited for me? That seemed a little too much to expect. And even if you had, or if you were single now, how could I assume you'd even want to see me? You must have thought I'd deserted you."

"Twat," said Mee, kissing his neck.

"Then I remembered the Odyssey. Father O read it to us at the orphanage. When Odysseus finally makes it back home after twenty years, he disguises himself as an old beggar until he has had a chance to see what's happening, whether his wife still wants him."

"Hold on," said Joni, remembering her own reading of the story. "Wasn't she about to marry someone else?"

"Well, possibly, yeah. There were a hundred suitors. But she said she would only marry the one who could use Odysseus's old bow to send an arrow through twelve axe heads. And, of course, when she saw the old beggar do it, she knew it was her husband."

"All very well, but didn't he then kill all the other suitors?"

Mee gave Seb a look. "Good job I hadn't got myself a fella, then, you psycho."

"I'd forgotten that bit," admitted Seb.

"One more question."

"Shoot."

"How did you know Joni was in danger that day? How did you know to come and save her?"

Seb sighed heavily.

"I've been thinking about this. When Joni fell from the tree, she connected with me somehow. But it happened at the moment when I was in danger too. I was about to die. The point is, the connection was made when both of us were close to death. But Joni told me she nearly died on the beach here, and in London. *Would* have died if she hadn't *reset*. There was no connection either of those times. The same when Adam finally made his move here. I felt nothing."

Mee waited for Seb to wrestle with his emotions before continuing.

"If I had been braver when I came back…if I had come to you earlier, John would still be alive. I let my brother die. Then I nearly let my daughter die."

"Seb." Mee folded her arms and waited for him to look at her. "Stop it. And I mean, stop it for good. Without you, John wouldn't have had a life at all. You didn't even know Joni existed until you saved her. Yes I know, I know—"

She waved her hands to stop Seb interrupting.

"You knew *someone* had called to you. But you didn't know who that was. You had no idea. When you got back to the island, you took this cottage so you could get your shit together before coming to me. I get that. I'm amazed you can even feed yourself or take a dump without help after what you've been through. But listen, don't you dare beat yourself up about what happened. You knew John was here, healthy and happy. You knew I was around because I took a pair of binoculars and spied on you. You gonna tell me you didn't know I was watching you?"

Seb smiled a little at the memory.

"It was the first contact with you," he said. "I could feel you out there, but I didn't dare show you that I knew you were watching me. I wasn't ready. But I was prepared to walk up and down that beach all day just as long as you were there."

Mee smiled too.

"Just so you know, Sebby, you start agonizing over what you should, or could, have done when that evil murderous shitbag showed up, and we are going to fall out. You did everything you could, okay? Drop it."

Seb knew the sound of Mee making up her mind.

Joni coughed.

"Sorry. It's just…well. You still didn't say how you knew to come and save me."

"You're right. You can thank Sym. I heard a plane flying low, and when I went to investigate, I saw a guy jump out into the sea, swim to shore and run toward the woods at about forty miles an hour. I followed him."

"Wow," said Joni. "I would thank him again, but it'll have to wait until I get onto the mainland. Sym is kind of an uncle too, you know? An uncle without a body who started life as a few lines of alien nanotechnology code. This is some weird family."

No one was willing to argue with that conclusion.

Mee took charge.

"Right. In summary, a whole lot of shite has happened which will probably take years to process fully. But we are here, we love each other, and we have a life together. Agreed?"

Neither Seb nor Joni disagreed.

"Fine. More tea, then."

Seb was beginning to wonder if the British approach to dealing with adversity, or a profound shock, by consuming tea, might have something to recommend it after all. On the face of it, pouring boiling water into a mug containing dried leaves from bushes grown on Indian hillsides, seemed an odd approach to ameliorating the effects of trauma.

Mee's ritual of tea making had little in common with the almost balletic dignity of the Japanese ceremony, but it followed a certain pattern, including the precise amount of time a teabag should be left in the cup, and the opaque logic of leaving the teabag to "rest" on the side of the sink for a few minutes before disposing of it in the trash. And there was no denying the efficacy of the ritual. Seb was sure that, given the choice between giving up marijuana or English breakfast tea, Mee would sacrifice the dope.

While Mee began the precise dunking technique, Seb sat next to Joni.

"What did *you* think happened that night? When I was inside the Egg. When I saw you."

Joni leaned against his shoulder. "I was hoping you might be able to answer that one."

Seb spread his hands. "Honey, I have no idea. Even Fypp thought it was impossible."

Joni smiled sadly. "Uncle John used to call me honey," she said.

"Wait." Mee had flung herself onto the sofa. "You've seen Fypp *since*? I mean, I thought you came home when you walked into the fire."

"I did. Well, I ended up on the mainland first."

"But Fypp came *here*? To Earth?"

"Yeah. She followed me. She was on the beach a few minutes after I woke up there. I was just getting to that part."

Mee wasn't quite ready to drop it. "And she's gone now? She's sodded off back to Planet Walky and she's going to leave us alone, right?"

Seb hesitated.

"Oh, for fuck's sake," said Mee. "Where is she? I've had enough of this. I'll kick her bony Buddhist arse back to where-the-fuck-ever she crawled out from."

It was almost worth making Mee angry to see her like this. Seb had forgotten how anger could light her up, especially when she was angry on behalf of others. It was a pretty wonderful sight.

"She wants the Egg. I told her she could have it when I had talked to you, told you where I'd been. I needed you to see it, Mee."

"Well, great, I've seen it. Now she can piss off."

Seb stood up.

"She's at the cottage. She wants me to observe what's happened in the Egg since I left. Since Cley died."

Mee went to the door and took a big winter coat from the back of it. She lifted another coat and tossed it to Joni.

"Right, then. I'm not leaving you alone with that weirdo for a second. We're all going. She can show the three of us what's in the Egg."

Chapter 37

Bamburgh Beach - Three Months Earlier

Sergeant Toby Lark was the only human witness to Seb Varden's return to earth. A pair of frolicking seals in the waves just off Bamburgh beach were the first to detect the sudden, strange change in the atmosphere, and they wisely decided to take their games a mile further south.

It started with the sky. Sergeant Lark was an early riser. Always had been. At least twice a week, somebody, convinced they were the first to come up with an original piece of wit, would comment on his morning habits, referring to the phrase "you're up with the lark, then." He had long since given up responding to such remarks, finding that a curt nod of the head generally discouraged any further inane conversation. Sergeant Lark was most definitely not what is commonly referred to as a people person.

A long time insomniac, this was Sergeant Lark's

favorite part of the day, or night; he had never really decided which part of the solar cycle this half-lit scenario belonged to. Not that he cared much, so long as it kept its reliably unpopulated properties. It wasn't just the lack of people, it was the blurred outlines, the lack of definition of otherwise familiar landmarks, the hushed, almost reverential feel to buildings, trees and paths that would be drab, uninspiring and depressingly concrete once daylight took over.

Still, there was always a backdrop of birdsong as he walked east, the castle at his back, toward the hiss of the North Sea. That was what struck him first that morning. The relative quiet that he enjoyed so much on his predawn walks had suddenly turned to absolute silence. He stopped for a moment and listened. Over the course of the previous ten seconds or so, the nightingales, blackbirds, starlings, song thrushes, even the robins, dunnocks, and sparrows had all stopped singing. The resulting vacuum was unnerving. It was as if nature was listening for something —something that was about to happen. Sergeant Lark did not like the feeling of being unnerved. He was a solid, dependable man. He enjoyed fishing, doing the Times crossword, and listening to the musical stylings of the James Last Orchestra. He attended church on Sunday and slept in a pew at the back throughout every sermon. He thought a website was where one might find a spider. He was just over a year away from retirement and was looking forward to the uninterrupted tedium that giving up work would bring.

He stopped and listened along with the birds. He stood quietly for a minute or two. Reassured by the distant roar of the sea, he rolled himself a cigarette, lit up, and continued on his way.

The sky, when he noticed it, didn't worry him unduly at

first. Sergeant Lark was not a particularly imaginative man, and a sky that rapidly turned from blue-gray to absolute blackness, with flashes and sparks and some kind of roiling tornado in its center provoked no more than a raised eyebrow and a muttered, "bloody weather."

The unusual meteorological phenomena did attract his eye, though, and he couldn't help but keep glancing up at it as he neared the beach. Then, as an unnaturally deep sound caused the ground to tremble slightly and the fillings in his teeth to buzz uncomfortably, he found he was unable to look away.

The cigarette in his mouth dangled from his lower lip as he gaped upward, burning a hole in his beard that took another six months to grow back fully. Sergeant Lark didn't notice it in the slightest. All his attention was focused on the figure which had just fallen from the sky.

It was undoubtedly human. Sergeant Lark had once watched a suicide jump from a building and knew what a falling body looked like. This was different. Whereas the jumper had changed his mind a second after committing to his fatal leap, his arms flailing around and a thin scream reaching every onlooker, this body was slack, unconscious. There was no movement at all other than the effect of air currents plucking at the unresisting limbs.

The sky suddenly cleared, returning to its more usual pre-dawn gray, seconds before the falling body hit the beach, with a loud, wet *smack*. Sergeant Lark turned away just before the moment of impact, remembering the awful sound and sight of the suicide victim as the frailty of skin muscle and bone met the unyielding solidity of set concrete. Hard-packed sand was unlikely to be more forgiving, especially considering the half mile he had watched the body fall.

Lark finally became aware of the lit cigarette burning

his beard, swore and flipped it away. He started walking toward the distant crater in the sand, knowing it was his responsibility to report the incident and save some unsuspecting dog walker the horror of happening across the grim scene.

He took a few preparatory deep breaths. No point in rushing anything. Whatever was left of the body on the sand, it certainly wouldn't be going anywhere in the next few minutes. Police training had emphasized the importance of not making assumptions, but Lark felt fairly confident about this one. Overconfident, as it turned out.

The next few minutes were certainly the most unexpectedly bizarre of the sergeant's life, even allowing for the Christmas party incident when Constable Molly Glenpike had abruptly admitted to harboring unprofessional feelings toward him, and had made certain lewd remarks about his truncheon. He had never been good with the ladies, but occasionally wondered if he had missed somewhat of an opportunity that night. Still, spilled milk and all that.

Briefly, Lark wondered if this memory of Constable Glenpike was merely a way of his brain avoiding the facts that had just begun to unfold in front of him.

If he'd had a cell phone on his person, he could have notified the County Constabulary immediately. Lark eschewed modern technology, however. He had to wear a radio while on duty, he didn't see why he would want to make himself equally accessible to everyone during his leisure time.

Even if he had been in possession of a mobile communication device, he wasn't entirely sure what form his verbal report might have taken.

I was proceeding in an easterly direction when a single storm cloud appeared, from which a falling body emerged. It hit the beach at terminal velocity, producing a sizable crater. Just as I decided to approach the scene, the corpse began to behave in a suspicious manner. Rather than, as is customary in a fall from thousands of feet, breaking apart at the moment of impact and spreading itself outwards in a puddle of liquefied organs, it took the unexpected action of standing up, looking around, and spitting out mouthfuls of sand. The body appeared to be that of a man in his thirties, wearing a pale T-shirt, blue denim legwear, and training shoes. He had a rucksack about his person, which he opened once, looking inside.

As I was about to approach, a second figure appeared on the beach, seeming to walk out of the air about a foot above the sand, and step down onto it. I could not have been mistaken about the impossible way in which she appeared, as I was looking at the male at that point, and she appeared approximately three feet to his left. She was a female child aged between seven and nine. She had a shaven head and was wearing orange and red robes.

I decided to remain where I was and observe. It was possible that I was witnessing some sort of criminal meeting. Drug smuggling is not unknown on this stretch of the coast, although using people who fall out the sky and magical children would represent quite a departure for the criminal gangs, who generally employ adults in boats for their nefarious activities.

The female child spoke to the adult male for a few minutes, after which the male took a step toward the sea and vanished. The child sat on the beach for another few minutes, making sandcastles. Then she stood up, stretched and also vanished.

Lark was a stickler for doing things by the book, but he could feel the first seeds of doubt enter his mind as he walked toward the spot from which the two individuals had disappeared. When he got close enough, the sun had lent enough light to the scene to allow him to see clearly the results of the child's construction attempts.

They weren't sandcastles. It was just one, big sandcastle.

He was looking at a perfect scale model of Bamburgh

castle, down to the details of the cannons facing the sea. As he bent down to see more closely, Lark could make out tiny figures walking the battlements. There was even someone licking a minuscule ice-cream. Three birds—pigeons by the look of them—were flying across the castle toward the café. Lark leaned in still further. The pigeons were perfect in every detail, undoubtedly made of sand. They were hanging, unsupported, in mid-air.

Sergeant Lark took off his shoes and socks and sat down, scrunching the tide-wet sand between dry, talcum-powdered toes. If he made a report, there would be an investigation. No evidence other than the crater and the sandcastle was left on the beach, and the tide would take care of that before anyone else arrived. Someone would be sure to leak any report he made, and then he would be a laughing stock. They might even force him to retire early, thereby reducing his pension. The tax-free lump sum he was due to receive would be smaller, meaning he would have to give up his dream of a bungalow nearer the allot-ment, where he could do the crossword every morning among his broad beans, chard, potatoes, and herbs.

He took a quick look around him, then—satisfied that he was still alone—carefully kicked over every trace of the impossibly elaborate sandcastle. After brushing the sand from his feet, he put his socks and shoes back on and turned his back on the beach.

No need for a report.

▭

SEB OPENED HIS EYES. There was no light at all. He felt

pressure around his face and an oddly familiar taste in his mouth. He sniffed experimentally. No air. His nostrils were completely blocked. Unsure which way was up, or even if there was any gravity at all, he tried moving his limbs. Everything seemed to be functioning normally. A light breeze lifted the hair on the back of his head.

His brain did the math. He was lying face down.

Seb stood up and brought his hands to his face. He was covered in soil. No, not soil, sand. That was why it had tasted familiar. Every picnic Mee had ever taken him on involving a British beach had ended with food covered with sand. Or wasps and ants. Or all three. When, once, he had voiced his bewilderment at the idea of trying to consume food on a cold, windy day surrounded by trillions of tiny particles made up of dead fish, rocks, glass, and shit, she had passed him a gin bottle and said, "Drink up, you fussy Yank ponce. It's *traditional*, innit."

He bent over and spat sand onto the beach and rubbed at his eyes, squinting at his surroundings. Then, as if remembering what he was, he closed his eyes again. All the sand on his body was instantly repelled from every square inch of his skin. His clothes returned to his default sneakers, jeans, and T-shirt. There was a backpack at his feet. He picked it up and looked inside, knowing before he did so what he would find there. It was the Gyeuk Egg. Sopharndi, Cochta, Laak, the Elders, the People, the Settlement, the meeting circle, the fire pit, the Parched Lands, the river, Canyon Plains, the entire planet with its three moons and its hot sun, its entire history and future, it was all here. In his backpack.

He knew which planet he was on. At some semi-automated level in his consciousness, he was already picking up the chatter of the internet. For some reason, he took this moment to confirm something he had always suspected: someone, somewhere, is always watching *Seinfeld*. With enhanced vision, he scanned the pre-dawn darkness. He saw Sergeant Lark gaping at him, but his attention was captured by the sight of Bamburgh Castle. Which meant... he turned and looked southeast, out to sea, quickly identifying the dark silhouette of Innisfarne.

He *felt* Fypp arrive, his Manna alerting him to her presence just before the ancient child stepped out of nowhere onto the sand beside him. She stared up at him inquisitively for a moment.

"How? How did you do that?"

Even her arrival couldn't detract from how alive he felt. He was Seb Varden again, and he wanted nothing other than to get back to Mee and find out what had woken him from his dream of another existence. Baiyaan's fate had taken on a secondary importance for the moment. He would think about that once he had seen Mee. He grinned at the absurdity of prioritizing seeing a foul-mouthed, talented, pot-smoking, tough, beautiful East London singer over the fate of one of a handful of godlike aliens and the future of all intelligent species in the universe. It was fucked up, all right. He was definitely feeling more like himself.

"Tell me. How?" Fypp had her hands on her hips and her voice sounded childishly petulant, but Seb's Manna picked up a genuine puzzlement in her inquiry.

"What do you mean?"

"You were in the Gyeuk Egg. I looked in on you a couple of times."

"You *what*?"

"How am I supposed to make up my mind otherwise? I couldn't interfere, I wasn't really there. Just like..." she searched for a helpful analogy and must have found one in Seb's Manna. "Like television. You seemed to be doing fine."

"Fine? I had forgotten who I was. I was completely lost in there. I could have died, or gone insane like Bok warned me. I was lucky to get out at all. How did you find me here?"

"Hmm." Fypp rolled her eyes. "For the strong, silent type, Bok can be quite the chatterbox, can't he?" She jabbed a finger into Seb's midriff. "Never mind that. The body you left behind disintegrated, and the Egg vanished. This was the first place I tried, couldn't think of anywhere else you might go. But I used the open route. You didn't. *How*?"

"What open route?"

"The one we made when we called you. You can't Walk that distance the same way you can from one planet to the next in the same galaxy. It takes planning, some lining up of wormholes. I left the route open so you could come home. But you didn't use it. You came straight here. How?"

Seb looked at the tiny face, with its furious, frustrated expression.

"I don't know."

"Argh! I *knew* you were going to say that."

Seb thought of the face he had seen in the flames. He detected nothing other than curiosity from Fypp.

"I saw something while I was in the Gyeuk Egg. A human face. Connected to me, somehow. Needing me. I followed it."

"You *followed* it? You just…*followed* it?"

Seb thought for a moment.

"It was a little like when you called me, I guess. I was

on Innisfarne then, and it felt as if I was leaving a piece at a time. As if the island, and the people on it, were becoming less real. But that took weeks. This time, it was minutes. And I was in control, I had more of a choice."

"I gave you a choice, too. You could have said no."

Seb thought back to those weeks.

"That's not true."

Fypp stuck her lower lip out. "Oh, boohoo," she said, but Seb could sense genuine regret for her actions behind the flippant facade. She had called him in exactly the same way as the other T'hn'uuth, forgetting, or not properly considering, the fact that Seb had only just become T'hn'uuth. He was a puzzle to her. Her demonstrable lack of empathy for him and his situation, however much of an enigma he represented, was now causing her some discomfort.

"Well, whatever," she said. "The thing is, you just did the impossible. And here you are again on this tiny planet. Maybe Baiyaan is right after all. Maybe. We'll know better when we check the Egg."

"Check it? But I failed. The People rejected me. They watched Cochta cut me to pieces."

"We won't know whether you failed, or succeeded, for certain until we observe what happens in the years following your intervention."

"Years?"

"Yes. Years. We can observe any point in history we choose to. We can see the result of your messiah schtick."

"No."

"No?"

"I'm going home first. I may have been gone weeks. Mee will be worried. We can check the Gyeuk Egg once I've seen her."

"Ah." Fypp's face didn't change, but Seb began picking

up some kind of shielding in her Manna, as if she was withholding access to something.

"What are you hiding, Fypp?"

As if trying to compensate for her previous lack of empathy, Fypp seemed determined to be more careful this time.

"Well, I know you think of time differently. When you're billions of years old, it seems far more fluid. Shorter periods of time seem almost inconsequential. Do you see?"

"No."

"Well, take the route I opened for you, for instance. It covered quite a distance. When a T'hn'uuth Walks a significant distance, she cannot break the laws of physics, just manipulate existing laws and her own mental processes. Hmm?"

"What are you trying to say?"

"A Walk across vast distances requires you to slow your conscious and unconscious routines significantly enough to give the illusion of instantaneous travel. In reality, of course, no such thing is possible."

Seb had become very quiet and still.

"How long?"

"And, of course, you made the trip both ways." Fypp was babbling now. She never babbled. "The time you spent with us, and the time you spent in the simulation, were just hours in your timeline, but the journey, well—"

"How long? Months? Longer?" Seb didn't raise his voice, but Fypp knew she had to answer him.

"Seventeen years, three months," she said.

———

FYPP DECIDED to make the sandcastle while maintaining a Zen-like mental state, focusing only on the intricacies of the task in front of her, moving each grain of sand into place one by one, building a perfect replica of the castle a few miles behind her back. She deliberately slowed her progress to allow herself time to settle back into her customary mindset. She knew individual consciousness to be illusory; she had lived so many lifetimes that she barely recognized the person she was a thousand years ago, let alone a million. And yet the flash of pain from Seb Varden before he Walked had wounded her as well. She was unsettled. The monkey-descended upstart had barely lived long enough to begin to comprehend the merest hint of the beginnings of a partial understanding of the most basic concepts that might allow even a half-baked guess at the structures, real, imaginary and real/imaginary, that governed simultaneously his primitive flickering consciousness and the known and suspected dimensions of the multiverse. But try telling *him* that.

"Kids," she muttered, aware that her attempt at returning to now-consciousness had failed. She completed the castle and stood, stretching like a cat.

She knew where Seb had gone, of course. In the same way that many animals sniffed their own shit, humanity was a species which actively sought out pain - particularly emotional pain. Seb had gone in search of his most recent sexual partner.

Fypp looked out across the sea, wondering how long to give him before she brought him back. Her fascination with humanity and the nub of ultimate reality they may have butted up against was fairly evenly balanced with the disdain she felt regarding the mess they constantly made of something as simple as sexual relationships. Even a cursory study of humans showed them to have an ambivalent relationship to mating, often weighing down the simple act of propagating the species with metaphysical notions regarding love. Love was an ill-defined term, and, bizarrely, that seemed to be how they liked it. Despite the fact that confusion about love's meaning, how it should be dealt with, and to what extent it should be allowed to excuse otherwise incomprehensible behavior caused a great deal of unnecessary misery.

Fypp's species of origin had not recognized the existence of love at all. Their evolution to Manna-using sentience had been swift, as only the most intelligent were permitted to mate. A few thousand years after her transformation into T'hn'uuth, Fypp had gained enough knowledge and insight to be able to look at her own species objectively, and wonder if such a calculated process of evolution was, in fact, optimal. Her own personality had changed significantly once she had freed herself of the societal constraints she'd barely been aware she was still carrying, and she had experimented with various relationships, some of which had evoked an emotional response akin to love. But the way love could hold an entire species like humanity in thrall, despite its manifest problems, was still a puzzle to her. She suspected a connection with the religious impulse, but the debate around it was so muddied by centuries of bickering that it was hard to find any clear, satisfying theory.

She looked out in the direction of Innisfarne. She had Walked there first, emerging on the beach where she had originally opened the route to bring Seb to his fellow T'hn'uuth. That he had arrived within a few miles of the same spot without the use of her route was almost beyond comprehension.

Seb was still an unknown quantity. He was either more powerful than she or any of her fellows had suspected, or he had somehow been helped when he made the Walk home. Fypp could detect the presence of no other

T'hn'uuth nearby, but she had been around long enough to know that the universe was still capable of throwing up surprises.

There was an immediate, practical problem that would have to be confronted here. Mentally, emotionally, Seb was immature. He was still attached to the mortal creatures who made up his species of origin. He was yet to disconnect from humanity and accept his new status. The love he imagined he still felt could only ever be akin to the fondness humans themselves showed to animals they kept as pets. Until he managed to distance himself, he was vulnerable. For his own sake, it would be better not to watch those he loved grow old and die while he grew stronger and more powerful. It would only hold him back.

Fypp shook her head. Baiyaan had always been the compassionate one, but what he had done to this young human was surely going to lead to misery. He may have saved his life, but he had condemned Seb to a torturous lesson in the inevitability of impermanence. It was possible the shock Seb had received finding he'd been absent for nearly two decades would be sufficient to affect his sanity. She doubted it - he had certainly proven to be surprisingly resourceful so far. But…well, the risk was there.

She realized that the damage was done, that she was responsible as much as Baiyaan, and that the best course of action would be to leave him alone to find his own way through. If he could.

She sighed. She had never liked following "the best course of action," preferring instead to consider other options until she could come up with a far more exciting course of action, usually with the potential for disaster. But, in this case, she elected to do the right thing, however boring that might be.

On the bright side, she hadn't spent much time on Earth. She could be a tourist.

She decided to start with a few days at the bottom of the Pacific ocean. She'd heard it was fun there this time of year.

She Walked.

38

Unchapter 38

Innisfarne - Present Day

The moon that reflected on the pure white snow meant their walk to the north of the island was as well lit as it would have been during the day, the only difference being the blue, white, gray, and black tones that lent the familiar landscape a slightly dreamlike quality. As they rounded the final bend and the crofter's cottage came into view, Seb turned to Mee and Joni, shrugging off the backpack and placing it on the ground.

"I'll leave this with you. Just give me a minute."

Mee raised an eyebrow. "That alien tosser took you away from me once before. I won't let her do it again. We should go together."

"She won't do it again. She's billions of years old, Mee, she had no idea such a short period of time away—as far as she understands time, at least—could cause us such pain. But I need to speak to her alone."

Mee looked unconvinced. An unconvinced Mee was a dangerous thing. Seb took her hands in his.

"Trust me. Please."

Finally, Mee nodded. "If you're not back in five minutes, we're coming in. And I'm going to give her a piece of my mind. Arsing alien shitburger."

She was still mumbling obscenities when Seb disappeared into the cottage.

━━━

TO HIS SURPRISE, Seb found Fypp sitting calmly in front of a blazing fire, her legs folded under her in the lotus position. She didn't acknowledge his return immediately, so he sat on the hard wooden chair by the window and watched her.

"I thought I'd give it a try," she said, without opening her eyes. "Not sure it works for a T'hn'uuth. I learned to control my mind during the first few thousand years. So, no unbidden thoughts to distract me while I meditate. But no chance of encountering my true self, or no-self, either. I have tried on personalities like you might try on shoes. Some I've kept, and still wear now and again. Others have been discarded. 'Fypp' is just an arbitrary sound. Your method of communication couldn't even say my original name. 'Say' is the wrong word, of course, but you don't have the frame of reference to understand the difference."

She got to her feet and looked at Seb. At times, her guise as a child failed to conceal her unimaginable age. Or maybe she just wasn't trying to hide it. Whatever the reason, it made it hard for Seb to return her look.

"It's possible that I'm not doing it properly. Self-sabotaging. Maybe because if I face myself as I truly am, I'll know it's time to let go. I know the allure, the beauty, of death. But I've avoided that final release, so far. I have my reasons. I sometimes wonder if those reasons are really good enough."

She took out a yo-yo from the sleeve of her robe.

"I thought you'd be back sooner. I was in a funnier mood earlier."

Seb was momentarily disorientated by the switch to practical considerations.

"I wanted to tell them where I had been, why I had been missing so long. About trying to help Baiyaan, about my time with the People."

"Them?"

"Excuse me?"

"You said *them*. You wanted to tell *them*. Who?"

She stared back at the fire again, while sending the yo-yo up toward the ceiling and back in slow-motion. Seb felt a wave of anger and regret. Not as powerful as the feelings which had threatened to overwhelm him daily since his return, but enough that Fypp would certainly pick it up in his Manna.

"I have a daughter, Fypp. She's nearly seventeen years old. I've missed her entire life."

Fypp considered this. "Not yet, you haven't."

Seb felt a flash of rage rise up and instantly recede as his Manna interaction with Fypp's told him that she wasn't trying to make an inappropriate joke. She was just being logical.

"Everything has changed, Fypp. I failed the People, and I failed Baiyaan. Now I've come home to find I've failed as a father and a lover. I have to make things right from now on. With Mee, and with Joni. This is where I need to be. This is who I am."

Seb felt Fypp partially block some of her Manna feed.

He was getting better at reading the nuances within the constant stream of communication between them.

"You think I'm wrong, that I don't belong here anymore. Don't you?"

Fypp looked at him again, and he managed to meet those frighteningly ancient eyes.

"I don't *think* you're wrong, T'hn'uuth. I know it."

At that moment, the door opened.

"Right, you, sling your hook. You lot love the final frontier, right? Well, boldly bugger off back to it."

"You must be Mee," said Fypp. She flicked the yo-yo back up her sleeve and held out her hand. Mee looked at it, slightly thrown by the polite gesture. Then, after a brief, but obvious, internal struggle between her feelings and her upbringing, her upbringing won. She shook the tiny hand, scowling.

"I'm Joni." Fypp repeated the handshaking procedure. Seb had never seen Fypp act in such a polite, normal manner. It was perplexing.

Fypp stared at Joni for a few seconds. Seb was aware of Fypp's Manna flowing around his daughter, probing, looking for information, but getting very little.

"Oh," said Fypp, "this is what I felt when you were getting close a few minutes ago. Now, that's *very* interesting. Maybe that starts to explain how Seb got back here."

Mee stepped forward.

"Right, here's your sodding Egg. Show us what you want to show us. But don't take all day about it, we've got some more catching up to do."

Seb knew Mee's attitude was mostly bluster to cover how profoundly unsettled she was by meeting Fypp. It was one thing to be told about an alien older than your solar system, but it was quite another to actually meet her and feel the truth of it.

Fypp continued her unusual display of politeness and consideration.

"If I could have the Gyeuk Egg, please?"

Mee handed over the backpack, and they watched as Fypp took out its contents and slowly unwrapped the object, placing it carefully on the table.

"Wait," she said. She closed her eyes briefly. Seb felt a burst of incredibly intricate Manna flow from Fypp to the Egg and return. The process lasted a few seconds before she opened her eyes again.

"Okay," she said. "Are you ready?"

"Do we all have to join hands and chant?" said Mee.

"No." Fypp showed absolutely no sign of rising to the bait. "Although you might want to sit down. It can be a little discombobulating."

Joni and Seb sat on the sofa while Fypp reassumed the lotus position. Mee remained standing and rolled her eyes.

"Discombollocks. I think I'll stand, thank you very much. I'm perfectly capable of SH—"

⬛

"—IT!"

They stood on the edge of the meeting circle. Seb guessed it was very early morning, as only one of the moons was still partially visible, sinking slowly behind Hell's Teeth. Seb turned to see Fypp, Mee, and Joni alongside him, looking utterly out of place. He felt unexpectedly upset, as if they were intruding disrespectfully where they did not belong. He looked down at himself. Seeing his customary T-shirt and jeans, he winced.

The fire pit was cold, the ash old. There had been no meeting the previous night. Looking toward the settlement, Seb could see little difference from when he had left.

He turned to Fypp. "How long since I left?"

His voice sounded odd, but the musician in him recognized why immediately. Out of doors, in an open area, natural speech sounds a certain way - inside, the dimensions of the room subtly colors the sound, as reflections of the speaker's voice come back in waves. A sound engineer would have spotted it immediately, and Seb only took a couple of seconds to figure out what was happening. His voice sounded exactly as it would sound back in the cottage. He was hearing himself back there.

As if reading his mind, Fypp winked at him.

"We're not really here. Not like you were."

The Elders' meeting place, a slightly larger dwelling than those used for sleeping, was—unusually for this time of day—occupied. The animal skin across the opening had been secured from inside. Normally, the dwelling would only be used for meetings. The only time tradition dictated that a Leader might sleep there was when she was approaching death. As Seb watched, the skin was pulled aside, and two figures emerged, walking slowly, straight toward them. Seb did not recognize either one, although the strips of shuk skin on their belts marked them as Elders. They stopped and spoke in low voices.

Joni was looking around her excitedly, staring at the fire pit, then at the meeting circle and the forest to the west.

"This is it! They look just like the creatures I saw - the ones I thought were demons. This is where I saw you in my vision, my dream. This is where you were figh—" She stopped suddenly, clapping a hand over her mouth when she realized how loudly she was speaking. When she saw that the Elders had paid no attention to her, she slowly lowered her hand.

"They can't hear, or see, you," said Fypp. "Fortunately."

Seb moved closer to the Elders to try to listen on their conversation. As he got close enough to hear, he marveled at how much taller he was. They were perhaps four and a half feet tall, bald, wiry, with tough, gray skin. Tightly muscled bodies and lined faces with eyes that looked like they belonged to a predatory cat.

No wonder Joni thought they were demons. They look like something out of Tolkien.

They spoke to each other in low, hushed tones and Seb could only make out a few words. Of those few, there was only one he recognized: "Sopharndi."

Joni had followed Seb and now moved in front of the Elders, blocking their path. She closed her eyes.

"Joni, what are you doin—"

Seb watched as the Elders walked through Joni as if she wasn't there. She opened her eyes again and smiled at Seb.

"I had to try it." She nodded toward Fypp. "She's like one of the Ghosts in *A Christmas Carol.*"

Fypp looked over at them. Seb doubted she'd understand the reference, but he'd misjudged her again.

"Exactly. They can't see us, or hear us. We are looking *at* this scene, but we are not part of it."

"So which ghost are you? Past, present, or future?"

"That's actually a better question than I'd expect from such a primitive brain. Although you do appear to be a special case."

Joni wasn't sure if she'd just been complimented or insulted, so she didn't respond. Fypp started to walk toward the dwelling as she spoke. They followed her.

"We are all ghosts of Christmas past. More than three thousand years have passed in this world since Seb was here, but this moment is only about twenty years after his time here."

270

Seb put a hand up and stopped Fypp just as they reached the dwelling.

"Three thousand years? So you know the outcome." It wasn't a question.

"Yes," said Fypp, simply, and stepped through the solid wall of the dwelling. The three of them looked at each other for a moment, then Mee shrugged and followed, only flinching slightly. Seb and Joni walked through together.

It was dark inside, but not pitch black, as a small fire glowed in the middle of the dwelling. By its light, Seb could make out some details. The ceremonial Leader's robe hanging on the wall, a small pot containing some sort of broth uneaten near the fire. A pile of sleeping skins with an emaciated body propped up on top, the face lost in the shadows.

When the figure spoke, they all jumped, even Fypp.

"I knew you would come back."

Seb took a step toward the shadowy figure. Even cracked with age, the voice sounded familiar, but he wanted to be sure.

"I keep the fire burning so that the Elders can see," the voice continued. "It's been a long time since I was able to see anything." The thin voice stopped and gave way to a wheezing cough, followed by a few rough, shallow breaths. The next sentence was no louder than a whisper.

"I know you're here, Cley."

Seb was close enough to see the old, lined face now, the familiar strong jaw, a thin scar running along the underside of the chin. Where the eyes should have been there were only sockets, long since healed over with dense, fibrous connective tissue.

"Sopharndi?" His voice still sounded like it was back in the crofter's cottage.

"She can't hear you." Fypp was playing with the yo-yo

again, looking at the old female with frank curiosity. "Then again, there's no way she can possibly be aware of us. So who knows?"

Sopharndi, didn't respond, and when Seb moved closer, her head didn't turn toward him, her sightless eye sockets still looking straight ahead.

"I have learned much in the years since you left us, Cley. I have also unlearned much. Dying will teach me a little more, I think. There will always be mysteries. You, for instance. You are Cley, and yet you are not Cley. This is one secret I have kept from the People. Whatever you were, whatever you are, you helped show me that what I thought to be real may not be so. You were with us, but not of us. Of course, the same may apply to what *you* think to be real."

"Smart cookie," said Fypp, although her casual manner seemed a little forced.

"Cochta called you a demon. She left us believing you to be an angel. Can you believe that?"

A dry rattling sound came from the dying female. She was laughing.

"That was when the People finally chose to become Listeners. When Cochta saw past her anger and bitterness for one moment and became free of them. It was not I, nor even you, who changed the course of the People. It was Cochta. When she lost her firstborn, she sought me out in the mountains, secretly. By then, a few hundred of the People had joined me in exile, learning to Listen, as you had taught them.

"She sought me out because I had turned away from my own anger and she could not understand how that was possible. She had blinded me, killed my only child. She expected madness, hatred, fury. I came close to that, but the path you had spoken of called me. It called so softly that I barely heard it, such was my pain. But hear it I did. It promised no relief, no easy comfort. It offered no answers. What it did offer was an encounter with what was real, and when I finally began to Listen, to let go of that inside me which imprisoned me, I found joy. Not happiness. I found that acceptance was not something passive, but was a channel through which life could begin to flow, unblocked, joyful, full of power.

"For me, the process was slow. Like a rock in the river being worn smooth by the water. For Cochta, it happened in an instant. As if she was trying to fight an enemy, only to suddenly discover it was her own reflection in a pool of water."

Sopharndi fell silent for a few minutes. Seb could see the barely discernible rise and fall of her chest.

"She led us back to the settlement. A year later she made me Leader. She died at the hand of one of her former supporters. Death is one of those mysteries I shall know more of soon. You died and yet you did not die. You are Cley, and yet you are not Cley. Perhaps I am not Sopharndi. Soon, I shall know."

She leaned forward a little, turning her head as if looking at the dwelling and its three invisible visitors.

"It's strange, Cley. Even as you taught the People how to listen to the Singer, even as you led us to a new path, I always felt you were still looking for your own answers. I hope you find them, along with some new questions. Remember this: when you were with us, it was as if you belonged elsewhere. To you, we were a story you helped tell. How can you be sure someone else is not telling your own story? Now. The sun is dawning on my last day. I knew you would come. Now I want to prepare. As if anyone can."

She laughed again and sank back, exhausted, whispering the last words.

"Go, son. Whatever you are, you are still my child."

She went quiet then, her head turned back to stare sightlessly upward.

39

Unchapter 39

The fire in the center of the dwelling flared up and became the fire in the crofter's cottage on Innisfarne.

They sat in silence for a while. Mee, the only one standing, steadied herself against the table before finally breaking the silence.

"Well," she said, "if that was your mum, you must get your good looks from your dad."

Seb looked at Fypp but found it hard to find the right words. He had been shocked to find Sopharndi still alive, even more shocked to discover she had become Leader. The fact that she had been aware of him was, as Fypp had suggested, supposed to be impossible. And the force of her wisdom had been almost physical in its power. It was not only that she had been totally unsurprised by his return, but that she had seemed to be waiting for him. So that she could tell him what he wanted to know.

Fypp was doing tricks with two yo-yos now, using her feet.

"Can a simulated being become aware of the fact that she exists in a simulation? Or, as she put it, a story? Yes, it happens a lot, although it is only speculation as it cannot be proved. Is it interesting? No. Here's what's interesting."

———

JONI, Mee, Seb, and Fypp stood on a grassy plain, dotted with trees.

"What's this?" said Mee. "Where are we now?"

Seb slowly turned in a full circle, looking at the forest nearby, and the distant mountains. When he began walking, the others followed. After a few minutes, they arrived at the banks of a fast-flowing river. He turned and looked back.

"It's the settlement."

Fypp nodded.

"When?" he asked.

"Over two and a half thousand years since we were last here."

There wasn't much anyone could say after that revelation. Mee and Joni looked at the landscape and pieced together the missing details, imagining where the dwelling they had just visited must have stood. Judging from the lack of physical evidence, it had been many hundreds of years since any kind of civilization had last left its mark.

Eventually, Seb spoke.

"Was it war? Disease? Famine?" He could hear a pair of lekstralls calling to each other in the forest, and, looking back across the river to Canyon Plains beyond, herds of ha'zek kicked up clouds of dust as they moved. Animal life was thriving, but where were the People?

"None of the above." Fypp had an odd expression on her face. If Seb hadn't known her better, he would have guessed that Fypp was confused.

"I checked the Egg in the cottage," she said. "I've been

reviewing the data. The People did the opposite of what almost every species does as it grows and matures. They became nomadic. They went to the other tribes. After a few hundred years of population increase, numbers leveled off. Technologically, they advanced to the equivalent of the Iron Age on Earth, no further."

"So where are they?" said Mee.

Fypp shrugged. "I don't know." She started to giggle, then stopped abruptly. "Been a while since I've said that. I have my suspicions, of course, but…"

"But what?" said Seb.

"But I can't prove anything. There's a missing period I couldn't access, then, suddenly, this. Along with what happened to you, it all points to something. But I could be wrong. I must be wrong. It wouldn't. Not after all this time. Not when it still fears us."

"Who?" "What?" "Stop talking in fucking riddles, Grasshopper." Seb, Joni, and Mee spoke simultaneously.

━━

FYPP BLINKED, and they were back in the cottage. She knelt, her back to the fire. Seb paced the small room. Mee flopped onto the sofa next to Joni.

"The Gyeuk," said Fypp. She turned to Seb. "Tell me again what happened at the end of your time in there. When you lost yourself."

Seb told her what he remembered of that time. The way he had kept his sense of identity in a version of Richmond Park, and how that had become corrupted, leaving him with no anchor, no way to remember who he was.

Fypp was uncharacteristically silent. No yo-yos.

"It's almost as if…" She stopped talking.

"For fuck's sake," said Mee. "Spit it out, will you?"

Fypp looked at her as if she couldn't see her at all.

"Almost as if the Egg wasn't fully constructed. As if it was designed to only go so far before it had fulfilled its purpose."

Seb realized he had never really thought of the world inside the Gyeuk Egg as a simulation. They were as real to him as anyone else he had ever met, and the disappearance of their entire species filled him with horror.

"The People? What about them?"

Fypp continued staring into nothingness.

"What happened in the environment you selected as *Home*, the corruption of the scene there…it could only have been possible if there was a flaw in the programming. If there was a mistake. But the Gyeuk doesn't make mistakes."

"What are you saying?" Seb thought of the eerie atmosphere of the landscape they had just left. "That the Gyeuk did it deliberately?"

"If so," said Fypp, slowly, "it was to ensure you failed. Your failure would see Baiyaan exiled and the Rozzers given the freedom to continue their manipulation of intelligent species."

"I thought the Gyeuk was above getting its hands dirty."

Fypp still had that distant look in her eye. Finally, she shook her head.

"No," she said. "No, it's not possible. The Gyeuk would never move so openly against us. Even if it secretly planned to take on the T'hn'uuth, it would know there was too great a risk. We are as powerful, perhaps more so. It doesn't make any sense. The Gyeuk is ruthlessly logical if nothing else. And yet…"

The ensuing silence stretched to a few minutes before

Mee opened her mouth. Seb glanced at her, and she grudgingly closed it again.

"Your Walk here, your escape from the Egg could not have been foreseen by the Gyeuk. It is possible that we are on the brink of open conflict."

"The People!" Seb did not want to accept what Fypp was saying. He clenched his fists reflexively. "And don't tell me they're not real, that they're just a simulation."

Fypp snapped out of her reverie and looked at him with an expression that equally mixed surprise and sorrow.

"Don't misunderstand me. All instances of life within a simulation are accorded the same rights as every other sentient being in the universe. Every species that reaches the technological stage of being able to build sophisticated simulations agrees to abide by this rule. After all, it is extremely likely that we exist in an Egg—or its equivalent—ourselves. The very existence of T'hn'uuth certainly points to that conclusion."

She got up, blithely unaware of any consternation her last remark may have provoked.

"I must warn the rest. Baiyaan will be freed. I no longer abstain. I vote with Baiyaan, and with you, Seb."

Seb tried to take in the enormity of what she was saying, and the speed in which this was all happening. Billy Joe—Baiyaan—had won. But the People had been lost.

Fypp walked to the table and rewrapped the Egg before picking it up. Demonstrating her uncanny ability to guess the direction of Seb's thoughts, she took his hand and looked at him, her ancient eyes as unreadable as ever.

"Nothing is ever lost. The 'I' I believed to be 'me' has died, over and over again. A billion such deaths brought me here, but I am not the Fypp of even ten years ago. Physical death is the same, of course. Planets, solar systems, civilizations come and go, yet the universe does not gain, or lose, a single particle. Patterns emerge and disappear, and those of us who are bound—or who have chosen to be bound—by time, experience a sense of loss. The sense of loss is real, but the loss itself is an illusion."

She released his hand.

"I am still not completely certain about what has happened here. I will confront the Gyeuk. Whatever its motives now, it has always been peaceable."

Fypp walked out of the door. Seb turned to Mee and Joni. Mee stood up and pulled Joni to her feet.

"Come on, Jones," she said. "Let's see the alien off the premises. Then I'll make you a sandwich."

Outside, the moon was bright, and everything was cold and still.

"I'll leave the route open," said Fypp.

Seb shook his head. "I won't use it. I'm staying here."

Fypp gave him an unreadable look. "You might change your mind at some point in the next hundred years or so."

She looked over at Mee and Joni in the cottage doorway, then back at Seb who was still shaking his head. She gave him one last trademark wink.

"I'll be back to check out the mystical traditions again. I intended to stay around this time, but work calls."

Without another word, she turned and stepped into nothingness, leaving the yard, Innisfarne, and the planet behind.

40

Unchapter 40

Mee spoke first. "Correct me if I'm wrong. We're all probably living in a simulation, right? And within this simulation, other simulations are created."

Seb nodded. He looked tired. Mee thought he looked almost as old as her. She suspected him of deliberately adding a wrinkle here, a laughter line there over the last couple of weeks, but she hadn't confronted him about it. More accurately, she'd pretty much decided she wouldn't confront him about it.

"Okay. So it's equally likely that the so-called 'reality' above ours, the one in which this simulation—our universe —was created, is also a simulation. Right?"

"Right."

Joni's forehead creased as she tried to grasp the implications.

"So how many layers do you have to go up before you get to base reality?"

That's my girl.

"Maybe you don't. I mean maybe you can't." Seb was struggling to find the right words. Mee dived in.

"There's a new theory in town about the start of the universe. A lot of physicists love it. There was no Big Bang at all. It's all always been here."

Joni groaned. "Brain hurts. Need coffee."

Mee rubbed her back. "I don't know. There's something liberating about trying to grasp the ungraspable. And if the universe has always been here, why does there have to be a base reality? Why not infinite Eggs nested inside each other? It might help explain that 'resetting the entire universe' trick you do."

Silence greeted this observation as the three of them breathed the cold air, heard the sound of snow creaking and birds and small animals foraging and hunting. No one had anything to say for a while.

"Shit in a slipper," said Mee, "now my brain hurts, too."

When the change came, Mee noticed it before anyone else did. She'd always been sensitive to atmospheric conditions. As a child, Mee's announcement that it, "smelled like rain" was always followed by the whole family grabbing coats and umbrellas. On one memorable school trip in central London, Mee had been the butt of a few jokes when everyone apart from her had worn shorts and T-shirts. She hadn't been able to prevent a smile spreading across her face when an almost cloudless sky suddenly unleashed a hailstorm. Mee had watched her classmates slipping, sliding and swearing as teachers and children alike scrambled for the coach. She had strolled slowly behind, warm and dry in her mac underneath her umbrella.

This was no hailstorm. This was something much, much bigger.

It was only a few minutes after Fypp had Walked. The huge moon still hung above them unperturbed, the snow lay deep and smooth, the only falling flakes floating from the branches of trees when a breath of wind lifted them. The scene was a picture postcard: the moon, a wispy cloud or two, a barn owl hunting among the trees, the crofter's cottage, smoke curling from its brick chimney.

Mee sniffed. A storm, definitely. A big one. She sniffed again, and the sensation had doubled in intensity. Something was seriously wrong. No storm arrived this quickly.

Seb had stepped further into the yard in front of the cottage. As she watched him turn toward her, every hackle rose, every sense screamed *danger*.

Mee pulled Joni close to her and called to Seb.

"Come inside," she said. "Quickly! Something's wrong. Something's—"

Seb heard the edge in her voice and started to move, when there was a sudden crackle of sound behind him, accompanied by a burst of purple-white light. The elm nearest the cottage burst briefly into flames. The burst of heat was so intense, Mee felt it like midday sunlight on her face. Her grip on Joni's shoulder got tighter.

As quickly as the elm had caught fire, it burned out again, leaving a blackened, smoking husk.

Standing next to it was a witch. Mee rubbed her eyes disbelievingly, like a cartoon character doubting its own senses. Nope, she had been right the first time. Definitely a witch.

"It was a pity Baiyaan had to drag you into this," said the witch. She even *sounded* like a witch, with a grating, rasping tone that had all the appeal of a fork scraped across a china plate. Lifting the hem of a long, dark green dress, she stepped down from the edge of the trees and into the yard.

Finally, Mee's brain re-engaged, allowing her to put together what she was seeing in front of her now, with the story Seb had told them earlier. All the details matched.

Long green dress, wooden staff, pointy hat, a face lined like a walnut with carrot shaped nose a snowman would be proud of.

"Kaani," she and Joni whispered at the same time.

Seb turned toward the approaching figure.

"Kaani," he said. "I didn't expect to see you here."

The witch laughed. No, it was definitely more of a cackle than a laugh. Mee wondered if it was okay to stereotype like this, or if she was being witchist. Then she realized she might be experiencing mild shock.

"Well, that's one of the two key elements of a surprise attack," said the witch. "Surprise!"

She cackled again. It really was a very unpleasant sound.

Seb stood his ground as the witch approached. She stopped about six feet in front of him.

"Attack?" he said. "Why would you attack me?"

"Nothing personal," said the witch. "If you're looking for someone to blame, try Baiyaan. He dares to suggest changing the way the universe is run, he claims to want so-called *natural* evolution, yet he can't resist tinkering with a backward race like yours, making his own pet T'hn'uuth."

Despite this insult to Seb, which would normally provoke an almost Pavlovian response from her, Mee's mouth had gone dry. Her usual instinct to heckle had withered away. The storm she had sensed was still growing, and an almost primal sense of fear had locked her limbs. She had often wondered why rabbits sometimes froze when danger was extremely close, now she knew. It was some kind of instinctual reaction to unavoidable peril. Her breaths were fast and shallow. She wanted to go to Seb, but she couldn't move.

Seb was silent, but Mee recognized the determined look on his face. Her eyes flicked between her lover and the witch. Kaani was much older, surely much more powerful. How could he defend himself against that?

"We voted, Kaani. You agreed to honor that."

Kaani smirked.

"Fypp has no honor. She plays her games and expects us to come when she whistles for us. She is so sure that she is the most powerful being in the universe, that lately, she has started to behave like a god. Yet, neither she or you even knew I was here. Perhaps this little god isn't omniscient after all."

"You have no Manna," said Seb, simply. "What happened to you?"

"You're as arrogant as she is. You cannot detect my Manna because the Gyeuk helped find a way to cloak it."

Mee watched Seb's face change as he pieced things together.

"*You* sabotaged the Egg. You killed the People."

"They never existed," said Kaani. "So how can they die?"

Mee noticed that Seb was doing the unconscious fist-clenching thing he did on the rare occasions when he got angry.

"I was supposed to die in there too, wasn't I?"

Kaani nodded.

"Of course. Neat trick you pulled, but it only delayed the inevitable."

"Why? Why work with the Gyeuk? Why betray your species?"

"Species?" Kaani's cackling laugh had no humor in it. "The T'hn'uuth are not a species. Each one of us stands alone, Seb Varden. The Gyeuk needed an ally. Its technology and my power make for an unstoppable force."

"Fypp might disagree."

"Yes, I'm sure she would. But the Gyeuk and I altered

her route home slightly. She's trapped in an infinite loop of linked wormholes. She will Walk forever."

Mee's brain continued to provide ammunition that her body wouldn't allow her to vocalize. About now, she was wondering why villains always felt the need to talk through their motivations, or actions, with their enemies. She had always thought it was down to bad scriptwriting in the movies, but now she wondered if, perhaps, it was due to some undeniable psychological imperative. Either way, it didn't matter, as it seemed Kaani was now, demonstrably, done with talking.

The witch changed. It was as if she had vanished and been replaced with some kind of neon-purple, twisting rope, crackling with force, like an electric storm condensed to a column of power. Somehow, Mee knew that it wasn't the witch's form that had changed, it was her own perception of what was there. She watched, horrified, as a sparking tendril snaked out from the column and caught hold of Seb, lifting him from the ground.

As the tendril made contact with Seb, he screamed, and a wave of force lifted Joni and Mee, slamming them into the cottage wall behind them. Mee felt something snap in her back on impact with the bricks, and when they fell to the floor, a cold numbness spreading rapidly from her kidneys, reaching her arms and legs. She had landed in a sitting position. She found she could still move her head. She looked at Joni, who been wrenched out of her grasp and had landed in the doorway. There was blood on her face and in her hair. Her eyes were open, but she looked stunned.

Oh, God, Joni.

Mee heard a shout then and looked back into the yard. Seb was trying to fight back, she could see it in his eyes as he stared at the obscene creature that was trying to kill him. Mee blinked back tears as she saw the agony in his expression. She focused on his face, willing him to fight, to survive.

Another tendril shot out, then another and another. Seb's entire body went rigid. There was an awful, unforgettable sound, only just audible among the sizzles, crackles, and explosions of raw electrical energy. It was a tearing sound, a sound made by flesh and bone put under unimaginable, and irresistible, duress.

It only lasted a few seconds. A few seconds which Mee doubted she had the mental strength to survive unscathed. She found herself unable to do anything other than watch.

Seb's body was pulled in every direction, simultaneously, by unimaginable forces. For a moment, he still resembled a human being, albeit one drawn by an abstract artist, a vague shape hanging in space. Then, with a *crack* of energy that lit the sky for miles, even that was gone.

Mee felt an animal howl gathering at the very core of her being. As it rose, she wondered if she would ever be able to stop screaming, if she allowed it to emerge. Then it dried in her throat, as she became horribly aware that the creature that had just murdered the only man she'd ever loved, had now turned its attention to her and her daughter.

It was the witch, rather than the alien energy being, that walked toward the cottage. Mee forced herself to look at her, the pain, grief, and hate twisting her features.

The witch didn't even glance at her. She was looking at Joni.

"No," whispered Mee. It was, suddenly, the only sound she was capable of making. "No."

Joni looked back. Her eyes looked more focused now. Mee willed her to wake up fully. To react.

Come on, Joni. Come on.

"Interesting," said the witch. "What *are* you?" She put her head on one side. Mee knew she was using Manna to try to probe Joni. Then the witch shook her head, as if coming to a decision.

She raised a hand. Mee felt the energy begin to grow again.

"No," she whispered.

Joni looked at the witch, a dark, determined fury in her eyes that made Mee proud.

Yes.

Joni *reset*.

Chapter 41

She was back in the Keep. It was the moment after her parents had kissed. Just after they had pretty much announced their wedding. That would explain why she was grinning.

Joni felt her face drop. She had just seen her mother's back broken and her father killed by a rogue World Walker who was half witch, half rope-shaped lightning storm. It was impossible to conceal her emotions.

She saw her mum catch the expression on her face. She turned away quickly and walked across the room.

Mee wasn't fooled.

"Jones. What's wrong?"

Joni looked back over her shoulder with what she hoped was a convincing smile.

"Nothing. Just felt a little faint. Must be all the excitement. I'll sit down for a minute."

Joni saw Mee give Seb a look. She started toward Joni, a concerned look on her face.

"Mum." Joni held up a hand. "I'm fine. Honestly. Just give a me a minute."

As Mee hesitated, Joni sat down, angling her face slightly away from her, thinking fast. She was as scared as she'd ever been in her life. She'd used her ability to escape a psychopath, but in the end he'd caught up with her. If it hadn't been for her father's reappearance, she'd be dead. Now she had a few hours to work out how to stop someone, some*thing* more powerful even than Seb. And if she failed, everything was over. The family that had found itself after seventeen years would be ripped apart before it began. If she didn't come up with a plan, if she didn't get this right, they'd all die today.

Mee walked over. Joni stood up and started pacing in front of the fire.

"You just *reset*, didn't you? What happened? I mean, what's *going* to happen? Nothing good, right? Talk to me, Jones."

Joni shook her head.

"You're going to have to trust me."

"You need to give me a little more than that. Last time you decided to sort something out on your own, you almost got killed by that psycho."

Hearing her own fears confirmed was far from comforting. But there was something in what her mum had just said that sparked the beginnings of an idea.

"Mum…"

Mee spoke over her.

"Whatever it is, things are different now, Jones. Your dad is here. Trust me, if he can't deal with it, no one can."

Joni went even whiter. Seb stood up too and went over to her.

"Please, Joni, let me help."

She shook her head again, then smiled at him. Joni was pitching for a reassuring, airy, *everything's peachy, honestly* smile, but from the expression on her parents' faces, she'd missed it by a country mile. She held up her hand again.

"Right, the pair of you, just shut up for five minutes. *Please.* I have to think."

Mee and Seb looked at each other. They shut up.

Joni knew Seb was completely outgunned by Kaani. If he faced her alone, he would die. Maybe the best thing would be to tell him, so they could all decide together what to do differently. The problem was, if they did *anything* differently, there was no predicting how events might play out. Right now, Joni knew where and when Kaani would appear, and how it was all going to go down. The witch was waiting to trap Fypp before attacking Seb. If Joni risked changing anything significantly, she might be the first to die. Then they were all—how would her mum put it?—deeply, and completely, fucked.

She took a couple of deep breaths. She knew what she was going to do. It meant taking the responsibility herself. It was a hell of a risk, but she couldn't see any other way.

Joni turned to her parents. She didn't bother with the fake smile.

"Dad, Mum. It's okay. It's going to be okay. Yes, I *reset.* Yes, there's a problem. And I will tell you about it. But it'll have to wait until tomorrow. Today, you're going to have to trust me and not ask any more questions. Dad, you need to finish your story. But you'll only be telling Mum. I heard it already."

Seb took a moment to process this.

"Anyway," said Joni, "it's not over yet. Mum, you need to stay here and listen."

They both looked at her, torn by the overwhelming urge to protect her, but knowing her unique ability to *reset* the multiverse meant she knew something they didn't. If she could tell them, Mee knew she would.

Mee frowned. "Swear to me you're not in danger."

Joni didn't hesitate. Lying to save someone's life turned out to be relatively easy. "I'm not. I swear."

Mee sighed heavily.

"Okay. Okay. I trust you, Jones. If this is the only way…?"

"It is."

"Then do what you have to do."

Seb looked up sharply. "But…you haven't heard the rest. I need to tell you the rest. Especially about the fire because I think that was—"

"I know. I don't need to hear every gory detail again. I know the whole story."

"All of it?"

"All of it."

"But I—"

"Dad. Please." She paused a moment. She was deliberately calling him Dad as much as possible. She could see he loved hearing her say it, but for her, after the day she had just *reset*, it carried even more of an emotional heft than he or Mum could possibly imagine. She felt suddenly dizzy. She hung onto the door handle, trying to look as if she were thinking. After a few seconds, she recovered enough to find her voice.

"Dad? Is there…" She hesitated, trying to think of the right way to ask. "Is there….*someone* at the cottage right now?"

Seb hesitated for a moment.

"Yes," he said. Mee shot him a curious look.

"Okay," she said. "I'll be back before dark."

Joni could see that her mother was still undecided about letting her go. She needed to appear more confident about what she was doing. Before the door closed fully, she stopped it with one hand and popped her head back into the room.

"And no hankypanky until after the wedding."

The door shut. Mee and Seb looked at each other.

"Lame joke," said Mee. "Normally she's funnier."

Chapter 42

Joni's first meeting with Fypp went on far too long, was incredibly frustrating and eventually ended with an offer from Fypp to teach her how to do cartwheels without touching the floor. Joni resisted the urge to burst into tears, instead opting to *reset*. Considering the way her dad had described Fypp's maddeningly inconsistent ways of communicating, Joni braced herself for a series of *resets*, assuming it might take a number of tries to get the alien to take her seriously. It came as quite a surprise when she succeeded on the second attempt.

She came back to the *reset point* she'd created about hundred yards away from the crofter's cottage.

Armed with more information after her first visit, she picked up her pace.

As Joni got closer to the cottage, she felt a strange sensation - neither purely physical or mental, but something bizarrely in-between. It was as if a stiff breeze blew up against her - suddenly, with no warning. And the breeze seemed to push against her mind, rather than her body.

The feeling continued as she reached the cottage. She had felt the same thing before *resetting*, and, in another version of the multiverse, she had felt it later on in the day she was currently reliving. Her unique ability often led to a slightly confusing relationship with time.

When Joni pushed open the door and saw Batman hanging upside down from the rafters, she hesitated for a moment, one foot poised above the lintel. Then she swallowed hard and walked in.

The inverted superhero was snoring loudly. A line of drool descended from the corner of his mouth and made a track across his square, unshaven chin before making a small pool on the floorboards.

Joni folded her arms and tried to mentally prepare herself for the upcoming encounter. It was impossible. How did anyone prepare themselves to meet a billions of years old being who was currently posing as Batman?

Although I already will have met her twice.

Resetting made a real mess of tenses in the English language.

"Fypp," she said. As there was no response other than a slight deepening of the snores, she stepped forward and pulled the hanging cape.

"Fypp!"

"Wassup?" The figure's eyes opened and fixed on Joni, before comically widening in an over-acted expression of surprise.

The dark, caped figure dropped to the floor and landed on its head.

"Ow."

As the body hit the floor, it turned into a viscous liquid, black, oil-like, which formed a pool about three feet across. Joni skipped backward to avoid touching it. It formed a perfect circle. Joni realized it was highly reflective, showing the wooden beams of the ceiling above. She leaned over cautiously and looked at her reflection.

Instead of her own face, she saw that of a child—Thai, perhaps, or Vietnamese—with a shaved head.

"Boo!" said the apparition.

Joni couldn't stop herself shrieking a little. She'd known what to expect, but that didn't stop her being freaked out.

Joni, Seb, and Mee had already spent a few hours with Fypp, but as that was later, in a universe which had either branched away separately or collapsed into non-existence ever since Joni *reset*. She'd also seen all of this twenty minutes previously. Joni had slightly more of an advantage than the T'hn'uuth staring up at her from the oily puddle could possibly know.

The pool began to move then, shifting and writhing like a living shadow. After a few seconds, it began to solidify and grow upward from the old, split floorboards, taking on the form Seb had described.

A few seconds later, the small, Zen nun-like child in saffron robes stood in front of Joni, looking up at her with an expression of frank puzzlement.

"Yes," she said, "I'm Fypp. You seem to have the advantage of me, which is, in all practical terms, impossible."

Again, Joni felt the strange sensation of something pushing against her. She knew it was coming from Fypp, as she had tried it at their other meetings. It reminded her of the time she was sick as a child. Manna had been used to try to help her, but her body had rejected it. This was a very similar sensation. Her body was throwing Manna back at its source. Whatever was trying to get through to her was being met with a firm, impregnable resistance.

"Well…" Fypp, for a moment, seemed to struggle to express what she was feeling. If Joni had known it was the first time in over eleven million years that anything like this had happened, she might have been more convinced by Fypp's air of puzzlement. She was about to speak when the diminutive child stamped her foot.

"Shh! Let me just…" Again, the sensation of being pushed, even more insistent this time. Again, her body's automatic resistance.

"Astonishing," murmured Fypp. "What *are* you?"

Joni decided the occasion called for short, factual answers and absolute honesty. She needed this alien to focus. She needed her help. So she simply repeated the words Fypp had told her to say once she had *reset* and was meeting her again for the first time.

"I'm Joni, Seb's daughter. I was conceived when his body was still partly human. This may account, in part, for the fact that I am protected from all Manna - whether the intent behind it is good or bad. We've had this conversation already. I am the only being you've ever met who could reset the multiverse. You once encountered a species which could detect points at which the multiverse was about to branch off significantly. They used their knowledge to avoid danger and to help them in trade and political negotiations, but that planet is long since gone. When you last visited, you assumed their ability must have finally failed them, as their world had, apparently, been eaten by some sort of trans-dimensional space-snake. At least, that's how you described it to me."

"When did I describe it to you?" Fypp was utterly unused to being surprised. The grin that had appeared on her face suggested she was rather enjoying it.

"When I first met you."

"Which was when, precisely?"

"Now. And twenty minutes ago. Which was also now."

Fypp took a moment to process this.

"Oh," she said. "Oh. This is going to be fun, isn't it?"

"Fun? Not really," said Joni, "no."

Chapter 43

Joni, Seb, and Mee walked from the Keep to the cottage. Joni had timed her return to the Keep to match, as closely as she could remember, the moment when the three of them had visited Fypp first time around. The enormity of what was about to unfold weighed heavily on Joni's mind, but she tried to keep her features neutral and her voice level as they made the trip through the snow.

The last time Joni had made this journey with them, it had ended with her dad dead, her mum crippled and she herself about to die at the hands of some kind of space witch. And, if Joni and Fypp's plans proved not to be up to the task, it would all happen again. Joni's last *reset* had been made just after leaving Fypp and coming back to the Keep. In theory, assuming she didn't get fried by Kaani, she could come back and try again, and again, and again, but each window of opportunity would get smaller, and the time she would have to make changes would get tighter and tighter. And, of course, if Kaani killed her first, there would be no more opportunities.

In her gut, Joni knew that this was their best, possibly only, chance. She felt sick.

As they rounded the final bend and the crofter's cottage came into view, Seb stopped walking. He turned to Mee and Joni, shrugging off the backpack and placing it on the ground.

"I'll leave this with you. Just give me a minute."

Mee raised an eyebrow. "That alien twonk took you away from me once before. I won't let her do it again. We should go together."

Joni let the scene play out exactly as it had before. She listened to her dad, careful not to allow her face to betray any of the fear flooding her body. She was very glad that Manna couldn't uncover any of her secrets.

"She won't do it again," said Seb. "She's billions of years old, Mee, she had no idea such a short period of time away—as far as she understands time, at least—could cause us such pain. But I need to speak to her alone."

Mee looked unconvinced. An unconvinced Mee was a dangerous thing. Seb took her hands in his.

"Trust me. Please."

Finally, Mee nodded. "If you're not back in five minutes, we're coming in. And I'm going to give her a piece of my mind. Arsing alien shitburger."

Joni fought the urge to tell her mother how much she loved her.

We're going to get through this, we're going to get through this.

Seb disappeared into the cottage.

Four and a half minutes' later, Mee grabbed Joni's hand and they walked down the slight slope, across the yard, and into the cottage.

"Right, you, sling your hook. You lot love the final frontier, right? Well, boldly bugger off back to it."

Mee wasted no time, fixing Fypp with her scariest look.

Brave men had felt their testicles spontaneously shrink under the weight of that glare, but Fypp seemed not even to notice it.

"You must be Mee," said the alien. She flicked the yo-yo back up her sleeve and held out her hand. Mee looked at it, slightly thrown by the polite gesture. Then, after a brief, but obvious, internal struggle between her feelings and her upbringing, her upbringing won. She shook the tiny hand, scowling.

"Hi, Joni." Fypp repeated the handshaking procedure, giving Joni a nod.

Mee couldn't hold it in any longer.

"Are you two going to tell us what's going on, now, or will I have—"

Fypp held up a hand, and Mee's voice vanished. She was still speaking—shouting, if her demeanor was anything to go by—but no sound at all came out.

Seb looked at Fypp. "What are you doing?"

"Shh." Fypp held a finger up to Mee. "You 'shh' too."

After a couple of expletives which even a novice lip-reader would have blushed at, Mee stopped speaking.

"No more, please," said Fypp. "I know Joni has asked you to trust her. I assume you said you would. I am telling you now that you *must*. Whatever happens from now on has to happen as if Joni has been with you all afternoon. Remember, I'm not asking you to trust me, I'm asking you to trust Joni. Right?"

Joni nodded. "Please, Mum. Dad."

Mee's shoulders slumped, and she nodded. Fypp pointed again.

"Got it," said Mee. "Sorry, Jones." She closed her eyes for a moment as if settling herself, then opened them again. She stepped forward.

"Right, here's your sodding Egg. Show us what you

want to show us. But don't take all day about it, we've got some more catching up to do."

Chapter 44

Joni and Mee watched Seb talk to Fypp in the yard. Their voices were low, and Joni could only assume Fypp was trying to repeat what she would have said if she had hadn't been aware that a traitorous World Walker was hidden close by, waiting for her to Walk. And knowing that if she Walked where she originally intended, she would never arrive.

Fypp looked over at Mee and Joni in the cottage door-way, then back at Seb, who was shaking his head. Over Seb's shoulder, she gave Joni one last trademark wink.

"I'll be back sometime - this planet is just too interesting to stay away from."

Joni unconsciously gritted her teeth at the slight change in what Fypp had said. She just couldn't be sure how each tiny alteration in what they did or said might alter the outcome.

Without another word, Fypp turned and stepped into nothingness, leaving the yard, Innisfarne, and the planet behind.

The silence that followed Fypp's departure seemed to

last longer than Joni remembered. She had been as specific as she could about timings. If Kaani didn't come at the same time...she felt the beginnings of panic, a hard lump in her stomach. Then Mee pulled her closer and called to Seb.

"Come inside," she said. "Quickly! Something's wrong. Something's—"

The elm burst into flame.

When the tree was reduced to a blackened silhouette, and her eyes had recovered from the burst of light, Joni was slightly surprised to discover the witch was just as terrifying the second time around.

Kaani's short conversation with Seb may not have been word-for-word the same, but Joni wasn't sure she noticed any difference. It was hard to focus as she was counting in her head.

sixty-four, sixty-five, sixty-six

This was the crucial part, and it was all down to how well she had remembered this scene. She had helped Mum work with some of the domestic abuse sufferers who had come to Innisfarne for counseling, so she knew that extreme duress could mess with someone's perception of time.

seventy-nine, eighty, eighty-one

Watching your father being murdered by a witch must count as pretty extreme duress. Kaani was moving forward now. Fypp had said their best chance was to wait until she was at her most vulnerable, which would be the moment she attacked Dad. Too early, and she might escape. Too late, and Dad died.

hundred and six, hundred and seven, hundred and eight

Joni had guessed it had been just over two minutes between Kaani's appearance and her attack on Dad. She had gone over the scene again and again in her mind until she was confident her guess was as accurate as she could make it.

That afternoon, she had been sure it was a pretty accurate guess.

Fairly sure.

But it was still a guess.

a hundred and fourteen, a hundre—

Kaani changed into the crackling purple lightning-rope, the atmosphere in the yard changing, getting hot, buzzing with unnatural, powerful energy.

Joni and Mee were slammed back against the cottage wall.

no

Joni fought through a wave of nausea. Her vision was blurred, and her hearing was muffled. She knew she was only stunned, and she fought to bring the scene into focus.

too early, she's attacking too early

Her father's scream was a distant sound, her head full of cotton.

she's killing him

The distant screaming suddenly stopped, and there was a thud as Seb's body hit the snow.

Joni made a huge effort and managed to push herself up onto her hands and knees before looking into the yard, blinking her vision back into focus.

Fypp was back. And she was formidable. She stood, arms by her sides, her expression serene and peaceful - completely at odds with the devastation she was wreaking. Her tiny body was surrounded by a corona of energy, the snowy forest scene behind her looking distorted and surreal.

Kaani's rope-like form was blackened in places, and there was a smell like the aftermath of an electrical fire. A powerful hum was not only audible but could be felt through the ground and in Joni's body as the vibrations rose and fell in intensity.

Joni looked back to where Seb had fallen.

oh God, is he dead?

Her father's body lay on the ground. Intact, but covered in raw, bleeding lacerations as if his body had stretched and split, every visible patch of skin marked by terrible wounds. He wasn't moving. This wasn't how it ended the first time, but Joni knew it was all for nothing if he died anyway.

She looked over at her mother. Mee had already turned toward her, desperately checking that Joni was unhurt. Her expression filled with relief when she saw Joni's face. Joni looked back at her, deliberately avoiding making the mistake she had made at this point the first time: that of looking at her mother's twisted, mangled and broken back, horribly twisted and useless.

Mee must have seen something in her peripheral vision, because she turned abruptly away from Joni, looking back toward the battle in the yard.

The witch had been forced to turn her attack toward the last being she had expected to see. Standing next to the fire-scorched elm, Fypp was throwing everything she had at the renegade T'hn'uuth. Fypp still kept the appearance of the child nun, but there was a confusion to her presence, the space occupied by her physical body also seeming to hold another entity. Joni's human senses could make little sense of it - her brain interpreted it as a constant rolling, coiling movement of green-blue streams constantly moving in and around each other like liquid snakes. At the same time, the child's saffron and red robes whipped around her rigid humanoid body as if she were caught in a gale. Her features looked utterly calm, yet the energies that filled the air between the warring World Walkers were causing some kind of disruption that spread over an area far larger than the yard, as if Innisfarne was flying through the biggest electrical storm in history.

Joni looked back at Kaani and wondered if the darker patches were injuries. It was impossible to work out who had the upper hand in the struggle. At first, Joni had been sure that Kaani was being defeated, but the light around her twisting, rope-like body, having dimmed in the first seconds, was now visibly brightening. Conversely, the area around Fypp's fluctuating form was darkening now, and Joni could see torn patches of skin on her face. There was no blood, just an absence of anything resembling flesh, or any kind of matter. Fypp was losing coherence. The Gyeuk had obviously helped Kaani in more ways than just allowing her to cloak her Manna signature.

There was no doubt about it now. Fypp was losing this fight. Kaani was pressing her advantage, hitting her opponent with a barrage of incredible energy. Farmers on the mainland talked for weeks afterward about the panicked herds of cows and flocks of sheep, who had been so frightened that night that they had stampeded out of their fields, breaking gates, tearing up hedges and causing havoc on the roads as they ran away from the coast.

Kaani's attack was reaching a peak. Joni could feel it. She prepared herself to *reset* again, a terrible sense of the inevitability of this awful fate settling on her like a cold, wet blanket of fog.

Fypp's eyes blazed with the light of every star she'd seen die in her billions of years of life. And yet it was possible to look into that light and not be blinded. It felt as if her defenses were being stripped away one by one. Joni struggled to look away until she heard her mother gasp beside her.

She looked back at her father's body. It was glowing.

Even as she watched, his face began to heal, his eyes losing their frightening, blank, dead stare, the light of intelligence filling them again.

He didn't get to his feet, he rose from the ground like an avenging angel, his remade body pulsing with energy. He hovered about ten feet from the surface of the snow, facing Kaani.

Seb didn't waste any time with words, he just held out his hands in front of his face as if cupped around an invisible ball. Then he slowly pushed that invisible ball outward, away from him. Toward Kaani.

At first, it seemed that his action would have no effect. Then there was a strange flicker in Kaani's form, like a screen with a bad connection. The flicker became more pronounced, then the attack on Fypp stopped, and she turned her attention back to Seb. Five tendrils of crackling energy whipped toward him, pouring horrific pulses of destructive power into his body, which twisted as, once again, he fought to repel them.

He held out for three, four, five seconds. It was enough.

During those few precious seconds of respite, Fypp the child had disappeared, absorbed into a ball of pure white light. The light wasn't just present in the yard, it stretched behind her and up into the clear night sky, as if someone had taken a paintbrush and, with one long stroke, had sketched a blinding white line reaching clear out of Earth's atmosphere.

Riding that white line, arriving through the ball of white light, which opened up like a lotus blossom, something emerged in the yard of the Innisfarne crofter's cottage, something that so patently didn't belong in that place, that human senses simply could find no way to acknowledge its presence.

Joni closed her eyes and turned away as that unearthly

energy flowed into the yard. If she had tried to look directly at what was happening, she felt sure the image that would burn itself onto her retinas might be the last sight her eyes would ever see.

There was an odd sound, indescribable, so unlike anything Joni had ever heard that her brain—searching for a way of categorizing it—abandoned the attempt within a second and turned its attention instead to pretending it had never heard it in the first place.

After a few more seconds had passed, Joni heard the song of one of the robins which had nested in the log store behind the cottage. It was such a reassuringly normal sound that she burst into tears. Cautiously, and blinking rapidly to clear her vision, she opened her eyes.

Kaani was gone. Gone as if she had never been there at all. So comprehensively obliterated that no trace of even one particle of her unique Manna remained to give any hint of what she had once been.

Seb, his body healed, his clothes still smoking slightly, drifted slowly back to the ground, settling as lightly as fallen snow.

Mee shouted up into the sky.

"Yeah. And don't come back, you pointy-hatted bitch."

Joni laughed, and groaned almost immediately as her head sent a burst of pain to remind her that she'd hit it pretty hard. She looked up to see her dad standing over her, smiling.

Mee coughed. "I would have kicked her arse myself, but my back's fucked."

Seb sat between them and held their hands. Joni shook her head as she felt her body repel his Manna.

"It's just a headache, Dad. I'll be fine. Take care of Mum."

She leaned forward and looked at Mee, who was

smiling broadly. Getting to her feet, her mother stretched, twisting her freshly remade back in every direction.

"That's better. Thank you."

She bent forward, keeping her legs straight.

"Still can't touch my toes, though."

"Well, if you want me to sort that out, you only have to—"

"No. I'll just stay as I am, if it's all the same to you."

"The way you are seems pretty good to me. More than good, actually."

He reached up and pulled her down onto his lap, kissing her deeply.

"Oh please," said Joni. "You wanna get a room?"

Chapter 45

"Where's the bald kid?"

"She has a name, Mee."

"Yeah, but it sounds daft. I feel stupid saying it."

"This from a woman who has a personal pronoun instead of a name."

"Seriously, Varden, if this is your idea of foreplay, we need to talk."

"Have you two finished?"

Joni was pointing to the far side of the yard, where Fypp had been standing. A three-foot circle of snow had melted around the spot, and a strange kind of heat haze blurred the view beyond.

Seb, Mee, and Joni walked over, but there was no sign of the missing T'hn'uuth.

"You don't suppose..?" began Mee.

"I don't know," said Seb. His body may have been remade, but his mind carried the memory of the incredible power unleashed against him by Kaani. His defenses had been brushed aside frighteningly quickly. A few seconds and he would have had nothing left.

"Joni?"

She looked up at him, her face pale. "I know what you want to ask, Dad. Please don't. I don't want to have to think about it."

"Okay. Okay. But I…?"

She nodded. Seb smiled, not knowing she would never be able to forget the sound of his body being ripped apart as he died. Despite the accepted wisdom offered by psychotherapists, Joni's future held a lifetime of *not* talking about it.

Seb supposed he should be unsurprised that a T'hn'uuth much older and more experienced than himself should be so much more powerful. He was so used to the feeling of invulnerability that the revelation that he could not only feel real pain, but be injured, or killed, had come as a profound shock.

"I'd forgotten," he said, more to himself than to Joni and Mee. "Forgotten what it was like to be hurt, or to know that anything that did hurt would keep on hurting. When Cochta was fighting me, I thought I was going to die, but it wasn't really me. It was like a lucid dream when Joni found me and woke me. But this, this was real. I could have died, I could have lost you both."

"But you didn't," said Mee. "And we're here. Let's go home."

With one last look at the spot where Fypp had stood, they turned and headed back to the path through the trees.

"Kaani must have been augmented by the Gyeuk in some way. I don't think she could have held her own against Fypp otherwise."

"What happens to Billy Joe now - and the massive guy with the enormous dick?"

"His name is Bok, Mee. Typical - that's the only thing you remember, right?"

"Well, you were the one who mentioned it."

"Fine. The truth is, I don't even know how I'd get a message to them. I guess Bok could follow Fypp here. I don't know."

Joni frowned.

"I don't think that route is open anymore."

She told them about the trap Kaani and the Gyeuk had laid for Fypp, the closed loop that no longer connected Earth and the other World Walkers.

"Then there's nothing you can do," said Mee. "It's over."

The next voice came from in front of them, and they all stopped dead when they heard it.

"It's far from over."

Fypp stepped out from behind a tree. She was chewing gum. She laughed at their expressions.

"Oh, come on. You seriously thought that pathetic attempt at a T'hn'uuth could hurt me? I've taken more difficult shits."

Mee raised an eyebrow on hearing a turn of phrase she would have been proud to deliver.

Seb smiled broadly.

"Well, it's good to see you, Fypp. And Kaani, she's...?"

"Oh, yeah. Blown apart into little tiny pieces. After which each little tiny piece was sliced up into even tinier pieces before being set fire to then stamped on. She's toast."

Seb put his arm around Mee.

"What's next for you? I mean, if the Gyeuk has sided with the Rozzers."

"I guess we're heading into an unpredictable, dangerous time. The Gyeuk will need to be confronted about its actions here. And it will need to be shown that such actions will have consequences. They've been very naughty."

Seb looked into Fypp's bottomless eyes. He wouldn't want her as an enemy.

"And the whole mystical tradition? What did you say about it? You weren't interested in the labels, you were interested in what's inside the bottles. Still interested?"

"You know it," said Fypp. "And the Gyeuk's involvement suggests it might be interested too. Perhaps it threatens the Gyeuk in some way. I don't know."

She grinned at them.

"I'll admit it. I love it when I don't know something. It happens so rarely these days. It happened three and a half thousand years ago, but it wasn't anything like as interesting as this is. Why would an artificially intelligent swarm mind be worried about the continued exploration of mystical exploration by short-lived carbon-based species? I mean to find out. Once we sort out the Gyeuk, we can come back and explore the whole subject some more."

Seb smiled back at Fypp. "Please tell Billy J—, I mean, Baiyaan, that I—"

Mee interrupted, her eyes fixed on Fypp. "What do you mean, *we?*"

Fypp gave her a look as if to suggest that she'd rarely heard a less intelligent question, then turned back to Seb.

"You're coming back with me. If there's a problem with the Gyeuk, we're going to need everyone. Particularly since we've lost Kaani."

"No." Mee. Seb and Joni spoke simultaneously.

Fypp shrugged.

"I'm sorry. I can't give you a choice in this. It's not as if there's another T'hn'uuth I can try instead. Try to remember we're the rarest creatures in the known universe."

She looked quizzically at Joni.

"Although she's quite a find. A shame her body wouldn't be able to withstand the stresses of Walking. No, it's just you, Seb."

Seb had heard Mee's long intake of breath as Fypp had spoken. He knew what was coming, but before Mee could launch into a rant of epic proportions, he put a finger on her mouth. Her eyes widened, and she struggled to stop herself, but with an obviously immense act of willpower, she managed to clamp her lips together, allowing only a solitary, and barely audible, "fucknugget" to escape.

"Give me sixty minutes," he said to Fypp. "I'll meet you all back at the Keep."

He planted a kiss on Mee's comically enraged and confused face, then took a step away and Walked, leaving the three of them wondering what they were going to talk about for an hour.

FORTY MINUTES Later

THE MOONLIGHT WAS STILL LENDING the quiet wood an almost fairytale quality when the man appeared in front of the old oak. In this clearing, only a few weeks previously, Joni had nearly been killed by Adam, saved by the reappearance of her father after a seventeen-year absence. Over seven years before that, the oak had been the cause of Joni's first *reset* after a nearly fatal fall from high in its branches.

There were no Thin Places on Innisfarne, an island which held no Manna at all. But some sites held an ancient sense of power which felt markedly different to the stores of nanotechnology seeded across the planet. Joni wasn't the only one who had found herself drawn to this clearing in the woods, the small area dominated by the oak. Visitors to the island, walking alone, had often stopped here, unable to put into words the sense of significance, of *rightness* about the place that made them pause, reluctant to move on.

There was something in humans that responded to a natural site like this. Mind, spirit, soul, chi, chakras...words and labels became hollow and meaningless here. It was not somewhere to come and think. Concepts considered in the shadow of these old branches seemed shallow, schedules unraveled, plans dissolved. It was a place of letting go. Of accepting and being accepted.

It was the place this man was inexorably drawn back to. Unsure of his very identity, the sense of belonging here reached through the branches, the dirt, the roots, the leaves, the air, the light.

He stood in the clearing, facing the giant oak, its silent presence a living witness to his decision.

He raised his arms.

The snow began to swirl, rising in a widening spiral, a miniature tornado turning darker as mud, rotted leaves, mulch and soil rose from the ground; spinning, dancing in the moonlight, a sufi whirl of creation singing its song of shit and rock, twig, bone and dark, soft mud.

It took no more than a few minutes for the figure to emerge, a sculpture suggesting human proportions and form, edges soft at first, fast gaining definition and detail. The hinged right-angle of an elbow, a snaking surge of spine, the shadows where eyes began to form, glistening. A gaping hole that became a mouth, the cold hard teeth, a rough tongue smoothing over moist lips. A scar on the fine-haired stomach, a face like so many other billions yet unique and perfectly imperfect. Virgin breath clouding the sub-zero air.

A moment of possibility. A pause, not born of hesitation, but rather an acknowledgment of the sacred, the unnamed, the *now* and the *always*. A silence, a stillness and a place where words were born, but could never describe.

The man held out his hands to his creation.

"Remember," he said.

The new hands rose and grasped those of its twin.

This scene had played out a generation ago, but one of the figures then had been a visitor who had crossed unimaginable distances, before waiting more than two-thirds of a century to save one human life.

This time was different, but no one was there to see it.

The fresh body trembled and shook, a series of shock-waves passing through it, waves of energy rippling across its form.

Increments of time passed, differently perceived by each of the two figures, the barn owl which swerved away from the clearing, the reprieved field mice, the woodlice in the leaves, the oak, the moon.

Finally, the first man spoke.

"You're sure, then?"

"I'm sure."

FYPP HAD SPARED Mee and Joni an hour of awkwardness by falling asleep in front of the fire in the Keep's large, flagstoned kitchen. All three knew that World Walkers didn't need sleep, but the pretense suited them equally, so no one pointed it out.

Joni and Mee did what British people have done in

times of great stress for centuries: they drank tea and played charades.

"It's a film," said Joni, as Mee pantomimed the operation of a movie camera.

"One word, although you're not supposed to hold up that finger, Mum."

Mee raised both eyebrows in mock-innocence.

"Alien?" said Joni.

"Bollocks. How did you get that?"

"I know you too well, Mum. Plus your last two were Starship Troopers and Close Encounters of the Third Kind. My go."

Fypp opened her eyes and stood up, facing the door. Mee joined Joni and took her hand as the door opened.

It was Seb.

Mee creased her forehead as she looked at him. Definitely Seb. Only…

Joni's expression so precisely mirrored her mother's it would have been comical under other circumstances.

Fypp said what they were all thinking.

"Who are you, then?"

Seb didn't answer the question directly, instead turning his back on them and walking out toward the outbuildings, leaving the door open. He called back over his shoulder.

"Someone I want you to meet."

They followed him out, Fypp uncharacteristically meek.

Standing outside John's workshop was another Seb.

"Oh, not this bollocks again," said Mee.

McGee, the island's resident goat, drawn out of his stall by the unusual activity, took one look at the two Sebs, bleated loudly in shocked disapproval, then retreated at speed.

The second Seb spoke.

"It's me."

"If you're you, who's he?"

Fypp had spent the time since she had initially detected Seb's return gathering Manna information and trying to build a comprehensive picture of what she was perceiving.

"Some kind of construct?" she managed.

"Well," the first Seb said, "usually, I'd be slightly insulted, but as we're gonna be spending lots of time together, I guess I'll let it pass. You can call me Sym."

He stuck his hand out. Fypp walked toward him, then straight past as if he didn't exist, heading straight for the other Seb.

"Charmed," said Seb/Sym, sticking his hand in his pocket.

Fypp slowed as she reached Seb, then looked him over carefully.

"You know what you've done?"

He didn't respond. Her Manna would have answered her own question before she'd spoken.

"There's no going back from this. Do you understand that?"

"I do."

She looked at him for another second, then beckoned, as if she wanted to whisper something.

Seb bent down, and Fypp whipped back her head before head butting him, breaking his nose with a loud crack which echoed around the stone buildings.

"Ow! What the fuck? Shit, that hurts."

"Yep," said Fypp, looking at him with a puzzled expression. "It's called physical pain. You won't have experienced it for a while. It'll heal eventually, but your nose will be a slightly different shape. And it'll ache while it heals. From now on. if you get sick, you'll stay sick. You can't even use Manna! What were you thinking? And when you die, you die. Which will be soon, Seb, since humans barely even begin to live before they drop dead. Why? Why did you do it?"

Sym/Seb walked over and shook his head at the state of Seb's nose, which was bleeding profusely.

"Here," he said, "let me just—"

"No." Seb waved him away. His voice was muffled and strained. "Fypp's right. I'm gonna feel pain again. Might as well get used to it. And a crooked nose will be a nice reminder."

Mee and Joni had joined them, Mee offering Seb a wadded ball of tissues. He held them up to his face, stemming the blood slightly.

Sym looked at him, and the blood stopped flowing.

"Hey, it's the least I can do. How you gonna explain what you did if no one can understand a word you're saying?"

Seb took the tissues away. His upper lip was slightly swollen, and dried blood covered his chin.

"Sexy new look," said Mee. "So, what's going on."

Seb pointed at his double.

"I made Sym an offer. He gets to be me. The World Walker me, I mean. He always was me, really, at the most basic level. He just developed differently - a mix of me, Walt, and a life lived as much online as in the real world. Kinda weird."

"Standing right here, buddy," said Sym.

Joni looked from one version of her father to another. She cautiously touched the arm of the one with the broken nose. It felt reassuringly normal.

"So…what are you? If he's you?"

Mee answered.

"You're a homunculus, aren't you?" she remembered the version of Seb which had gone willingly to his death to save her from Mason, back in New York two decades previously.

"A very sophisticated one, but yeah."

"Don't they fall apart after a few hours?"

Seb smiled, then winced as his nose spasmed in pain.

"Not this one. Guaranteed for a lifetime. A human lifetime, that is."

Fypp continued to stare. "I am unsure whether to admire you or pity you. Either way, I cannot understand. You were immortal, Seb Varden, a T'hn'uuth. A universe of infinite challenges, delights, and mysteries was open to you. And you gave it up for a flicker of existence filled with suffering. Why?"

Seb put one arm around Mee, the other around Joni.

"It wasn't a hard decision. Don't expect an explanation because there isn't one. There's no logic in this, just love. And I don't even know what love is."

Fypp stared blankly at the three of them for a long time. Seb wondered if she was genuinely speechless, or if billions of years of life had taught her to recognize the occasions when it was best not to speak. Either way, he was glad of her silence.

Sym stepped forward.

"Right, let's go unchain Baiyaan, wake Bok up, and kick some Gyeuk ass."

Very slowly, Fypp turned to Sym, then back to Seb.

"Well, he's probably going to be more fun than you, anyhow."

She stepped back.

"Shall we?" she said to Sym. "I'll have to recalibrate. It'll be a long trip by your standards. Not that you'll know it."

"Wait!" Joni ran forward and looked up at Sym. "Will we ever see you again?"

Sym pinched her cheek like an indulgent uncle.

"Sure you will. Once I'm off-planet, there won't be anything for my backup to ping against. So he'll come online. He'll be me - but he'll be missing the last couple of hours. You can tell him what happened when he shows up. And wish him all the best from me. See ya, folks, be good. Maybe I'll come and visit your great-grandchildren."

It was such a defining moment in all of their lives, that the lack of drama was almost a shame. No flash of light, no rumbling sub-bass ambiance, no special effects. Just a caucasian man and an alien child taking a single step, leaving a solar system and beginning an unimaginably vast journey to places humanity might never reach.

Mee wiped the blood gently away from Seb's face, before appraising the new shape of his nose.

"Well," she said finally, after checking from a couple of different angles, "I'd still give you one."

"Mum!"

Chapter 46

Many decades later

Five seconds after the old man replaced the receiver, the phone rang again. He stared at it thoughtfully. The antiquated landline was the only point of contact between Innisfarne and the world beyond. Only one person knew the number, and he had just finished talking to her.

He picked up.

"Did you forget something?"

The long pause told him the answer to his real question, the one he hadn't asked.

"Dad, I just wanted…" Another long pause. "I just wanted to tell you…"

He could hear her crying.

"There's nothing you can tell me you haven't already said a thousand times." His voice was gentle. "And we love you too."

"I know, Dad. And this day was always going to come. But it doesn't make it any easier."

"I understand. Of course I do."

After a long silence, he spoke again.

"Did you ever figure it out? As I have a theory."

"Figure what out?"

"Why there's only one World Walking Seb Varden, but he's in every universe you *reset*?"

"No, I never did figure it out, Dad. Okay, I'll bite. What's your theory?"

"I think your unique ability creates a new universe each time you do it. I don't think you're causing the universe you leave to collapse as if it were never there. I think your consciousness hops back to your *reset point* and both universes continue. Only, the universe you return from when you *reset* continues with me in it. The World Walker me. Well, until the day that version hangs up his cape, of course."

She laughed. "Are you trying to distract me?"

"Not at all. Just speculating that, since your birth, you have created a great number of universes where Seb Varden is a World Walker. Whether this is a good or a bad thing, is up for debate. We could prove this theory by asking Sym, but he's been as good as his word. If he's been back, I haven't seen him. You?"

"Me? No, no. He let us have a quiet life."

"Ha! Let me remind you that I've read all your books, young lady. I know you've seen plenty of Earth's Sym. Do the two of him not speak to each other?"

"If they do, he doesn't tell me about it. Of course, he's been so busy these past few years controlling the president."

"I'm not even gonna ask if that's a joke. Naturally, you realize all this means you're a time traveler too?"

"*What?*"

"Well, if each *reset* means you're starting again from a certain point, you've traveled to the past to start again. In effect, you are moving backward through time as the multiverse continues. Your first *reset* was when you were nine, you've been doing it all your life—again, let me remind you that I've read your books—so I calculate that the universe that continued after your first ever *reset* is now at least a couple of hundred years ahead of this one."

"And how long has it taken you to come up with this theory?"

"Oh, at least two and a half hours. I had gotten through a good few glasses of Lagavulin by then, of course. A few nights later, I finished the bottle and decided all of this is some kind of simulation, but a simulation of a type our brains cannot grasp."

"So which is it, Dad?"

"You choose, Jones. I think I'm happier not knowing."

They spoke for another few minutes, crying a little, laughing too. Finally, he reminded her of the promise she had made to him, decades ago.

"So tell me. When will it happen?"

She told him. They said goodbye.

⊏⊐

ONLY THE MOST generous cartographer would have described Innisfarne's highest point as a mountain, but that didn't stop it being marked as such on the maps handed out to visitors over the years.

Crab Hill was, in fact, not even a hill, being more of a gentle rise near the island's midpoint, reaching only eighty-seven feet above sea level. It was a popular location for visitors and, during the decade since Kate's death, Seb and

Mee had often slowly climbed the gentle incline to watch the sun set over the ever-changing sea.

It was late summer now, and the evenings were losing their warmth. The old couple wore heavy knitted sweaters as they made the climb to the top. Once there, they sat on the wooden bench their son-in-law had assembled many years previously.

———

IT HAD BEEN NEARLY thirty years since Joni moved to America. Long since retired from the foundation that bore her name, she lived anonymously with her husband, Odd, on a sprawling ranch near the west coast of California. A handful of rescued animals shared the space - two dogs, three cats and a slightly deranged horse called Django. Joni's cousin, Aaron, was the only regular visitor other than their children and, more recently, grandchildren.

Seb and Mee welcomed the entire clan to Innisfarne every Christmas and for six weeks most summers.

This summer, it had just been Joni.

Mee had finally been diagnosed in the Spring, after months of hints, prodding and—finally—commands from Seb.

"I know I'm dying; I don't need some snot-nosed sodding doctor to tell me how and when I'm going to pop my clogs."

She insisted her resistance to the latest advances in palliative care had nothing to do with stubbornness, fear or preserving her dignity, it was just that she didn't want "twats in white coats prodding me around."

In his darkest moments, during the long nights when Mee's tired body inexorably turned on itself, provoking gasps of pain, Seb felt predictable stabs of guilt at the

326

thought of how easily he might once have removed any discomfort. How simple it would have been to touch her and stop the pain. Even then, even as her cancer called her toward death, Mee knew what was going through his mind.

"Don't even think it, you clot-headed tit."

Terminal illness had diminished Mee's vocabulary in no way whatsoever.

———

THE LATE SUMMER sunsets could be remarkably beautiful on the island. Just like the clichéd snowflakes, no two sunsets were the same and, despite having watched many thousands of them, Seb and Mee still fell into awed silence as the sun turned the sea bronze and threw streaks of red, pink, and ochre across a darkening sky.

They sat on their bench and watched the day slip away.

Even more than the wonder they felt at Nature's daily display, Seb and Mee felt the power and beauty that came from spending their brief, fragile human existence deliberately bound to one another. Theirs was no romanticized airbrushed love from the plot of an cheap novel. If either of them had harbored unrealistic ideals of a maturing, deepening passion that would see them growing together in harmony, their differences blurring, faults forgotten or forgiven, a long life together had cured them of any such delusions. Life was far more interesting than that.

In his mid-fifties, Seb had nursed a nasty case of jealousy for nearly a year when Mee casually opened up to having around a dozen relationships during the couple of years they were apart after their first breakup.

"You should be flattered," she had insisted—typically,

maddeningly—while refusing to feel a jot of shame. "If you hadn't been the only man I've ever loved, some of those relationships might have lasted longer than a weekend."

Aged eighty-three, Mee had moved out to one of the guest rooms for a week because Seb had suggested Bob Dylan was overrated. Seb had been forced to learn *Tangled Up In Blue* by heart, so he could serenade her by moonlight outside her room. The nesting owls were singularly unimpressed, but Mee marched out, toothbrush in hand and followed him back to their bedroom, stifling giggles of triumph.

Their relationship had turned out to be as messy in the middle as it had been at the start, their love as ephemeral at the end as it was in the middle. Love was not to be pinned down, tamed, subdued or understood. It was wild, unpredictable, upsetting, boring, routine, uplifting, beautiful, and terrifying. It flowed through Seb and Mee, sometimes as distant as the rumble of faraway thunder, sometimes bursting from the core of their being like an exploding star. Love would not be understood, only experienced, and—even then—only in ways that defied categorization.

In their tenderest interactions—of which there were too many to count—they knew their love was an act of defiance, at the same time as being an act of surrender. In rare, unexpected moments, they felt the truth of finding eternity in impermanence.

In short, they had a long, happy marriage, with all the complexity such a bland phrase conceals.

Mee knew tonight would be the last sunset she would ever see. As did Seb.

There could be no words that could express anything adequate, so Seb said nothing.

After a few minutes, Mee leaned against Seb, her head on his shoulder.

When she stopped breathing, he didn't move for a while, just looked across the island to the horizon, as the colors bled out of the sky and the world became monochrome. The birdsong that had accompanied the sunset faded along with the light, as the nocturnal singers readied themselves to take over. The temperature fell quickly, and the speckled stars appeared, fading into view one by one. They were always there, waiting for the darkness to allow them to show themselves.

Briefly, Seb thought about the World Walkers. Out there somewhere, exploring, evolving, traversing unimaginable distances, taking care of the universe. Maybe. He smiled. It wasn't that he didn't care. It just didn't seem important anymore. He had chosen well.

He turned to his wife and placed a soft kiss on her cooling cheek. Then he closed his eyes and set in motion a subroutine he had placed in this body when he created it. He kept his last promise - the promise he had never spoken of to Mee.

No one was there to document the final moments of Meera Patel and Seb Varden. No one saw the old man's body crack and begin to crumble, no one saw the old woman's skin begin to change, beginning with the hand whose dead fingers still clasped her husband's. No one witnessed the silhouettes on the bench lose definition, become mere suggestions of human forms, then shift into abstract shapes before losing coherence completely.

The wind picked up as the temperature dropped, lifting the cloud of tiny dust particles, spreading them across Innisfarne, into the sea and out toward the horizon.

By the time the moon was high enough to dispel the shadows, the bench was empty.

⸺

FIVE NIGHTS PREVIOUSLY, in the gray-blue hour before dawn, between restless periods of semi-sleep, Mee had suddenly reached out to Seb and grabbed his hand, squeezing harder than she had managed in months. Seb reached for the light switch, but she stopped him with a single, softly whispered, "Don't."

"Can I get you anything?" he had asked, but her only answer for a few, long minutes had been a gentle squeezing of his fingers. When she did finally speak, after he had helped drink a few sips of water, her voice was a dry, cracked parody of the rich tone she had spoken with for most of her life. Seb could still hear the music there, but he knew no one else would be able to.

"So, did you do the right thing?" she asked. He didn't need to ask her to clarify the question.

Fifty-three years previously, he had stood in front of the oldest known being in the universe, while his daughter watched, and he had rejected immortality. Fypp offered an endless life of exploration, discovery, challenge and the responsibility of preserving entire galaxies of sentient species. Earth offered a short life, suffering, and death. But it also contained Mee and the daughter he had never known.

In the darkness, he reached across with his other hand and softly stroked the dry, liver-spotted skin of his wife.

"Absolutely," he said. He didn't need a light to know she was smiling.

THE END

Author's Note

Join my (very occasional) mailing list, and I'll send you the unpublished prologue for The World Walker: http://eepurl.com/bQ_zJ9

Email me ianwsainsbury@gmail.com

It's a bit hard not to feel bereft after writing The End this time around. Seb, Meera, Joni, Sym, (and now, in particular, Fypp) seem so real to me that it's hard to leave them. However, the observant among you—and the emails I receive suggest my readers are *very* observant (intelligent and good-looking too, naturally)—will have noticed that there is some scope for further books. There's a long, long gap between Fypp leaving with Sym and the end of Seb and Mee's lives. And, of course, there's the entire period of Earth's Manna-rich history up to the point the Unmaking Engine dropped. Joni and Odd will have to *earn* the quiet life we find them enjoying at the end of The Unnamed Way. Plus, there are Sym's missing years. Options, lots of options...I have a feeling I may return to this world one day.

Okay, a quick word about death. If Seb was going to *choose* love and, therefore, mortality, I knew I had to follow that through to its inevitable conclusion. At a ripe old age, but there was no getting around it. I wrote the final chapter weeks before finishing the novel. One morning, bright and early, it all seemed so clear, so *right* that I knew I had to write that scene straight away, or risk missing the moment. It was very like songwriting. Sometimes an idea comes along, and if you don't snatch it out of the ether as it floats by your face, you may lose it forever. Other songs will get written, but that particular song? Never. It's of the moment, and all the more precious for it.

Having said that, this particular book was the hardest to write. In a spirit of casual, carefree and misguided optimism, I had assumed it would flow out in an unstoppable torrent since I had already planned most of it before writing The Seventeenth Year. I was wrong. Really, really wrong. Could hardly have been wronger. It wasn't that The Unnamed Way was hard to write. It was no harder, or easier than the other books in The World Walker series. It was just that I hadn't allowed for the gestation period.

(I'm not sure anyone other than a mother should be allowed to talk about a "gestation period." At the end of a couple of months' thinking, I wrote a book. After nine months of weight gain, swollen ankles, and hormone swings, women poo a basketball. Still, it's a handy, familiar metaphor and I can't think of a better one. Sorry.)

This book—working title The Gyeuk Egg, think yourself lucky I finally saw reason on *that*—just wouldn't let me start until certain tectonic mental shifts had taken place. Huge, slowly turning gears were grinding their cogs inside my head, and there was no way to get going until everything major had fallen into place. I filled a notebook and a half with scribblings, made voice notes on my phone and drove my family to drink, which is bad for the under-tens, apparently. I was wandering about the house lost in an imaginary universe of my own making. That may sound cool, but try being married to it. I briefly considered buying a smoking jacket and drinking absinthe before lunch, but Mrs. S drew the line.

When I finally got started, progress tended to proceed along the lines of fast, fast, slow; fast, fast, stop. Back up a bit, what the hell was that? Slow, slow, very slow, fast, faster, aargh!

You can thank me later for this in-depth and thorough examination of the craft of writing science fiction. It's all part of the service. Education *and* entertainment, folks.

The simulated world inside the Gyeuk Egg became intricately detailed. Too much so. I had to dial it all back a bit, make sure there were a few missing pieces, a few seeming shortcuts (the measurement of time, for instance. Why would an alien planet use months, weeks, days and hours?). Sopharndi's world was never intended to be fully developed in every detail. Ultimately, it had been constructed by the Gyeuk as an elaborate, beautiful, but deadly, trap for Seb and, by implication, Baiyaan. But Sopharndi and the People seemed very real to me, despite the fact there was much about them that never left the pages of my notebooks. They were a simulation within an illusion within a particular branch of the multiverse within a work of fiction. A work of fiction that would, for the most part, be read as a digital file, therefore never having a physical presence in the so-called *real* world.

Mrs. S, bring forth the absinthe immediately!!

I hope this book goes some way to answering a question that was often the subject of my own idle speculation years ago, particularly as I watched movies, or read comics and graphic novels featuring superheroes. Why was Batman more fascinating than Superman, particularly as I got older? Notice, I said "got older" rather than "matured." I'm still reading the graphic novels and watching the movies, after all.

The answer, as a couple of reviewers of my own books pointed out, is that making someone too "super" was a problem. Where's the jeopardy? The danger? If your hero can sneeze and accidentally kill an elephant, how can s/he be hurt?

There was an answer in the first two books: to hurt this superhero, just hurt his friends. Mee and Bob were endangered by Mason, Seb couldn't prevent Mee's torture or Bob's death. But this was just a partial answer. Before I'd finished the first book, I knew where the whole shebang had to end. Seb would, ultimately, choose to be human, to lose his power.

This, for me, is why Superman II is the best Superman movie (I'm geeking out now, I know.) Mostly because of Zod, Ursa and Non and that scene with the redneck in the diner. But also because, at its heart, it's a tragedy. A proper tragedy. (Skip the rest of this paragraph if you've never seen Superman 2. Although, if you haven't seen Superman II, why are you even still reading? Go and watch Superman II!) Superman gives up his powers to be with Lois, but the tragedy comes at the end when he regains his powers in order to save the world. And loses Lois again. Forever. Great ending for the world. Great ending for me when I first saw it, as a kid. Even a great ending for Lois, as she remembers nothing after a memory-wiping superkiss (a *what?!*). But for Superman? Tragedy. Proper gut-churning, heart-rending tragedy.

If only Superman had been able to keep his powers *and*

be with Lois, right? But this was back in the day, there were rules, and those rules said that was never going to happen. But, hey, this is my book. My rules. Okay, Seb doesn't get to keep his powers *and* be with Mee, but he finds a way he can be with her and not leave the universe unprotected.

I knew this was the way it would all end before I started writing The Unmaking Engine. I knew Seb wasn't, actually, *too* super. He could meet more powerful beings (hello, Kaani and, possibly, the Gyeuk) and be injured, or killed. But, ultimately, he could, and would, choose absolute vulnerability to be with Mee and Joni. Now, that's the choice of a hero. Just don't tell my Superman II-loving twelve-year-old self.

Finally, there was the question of religion, spirituality, and mysticism - running themes throughout all four books. Did Seb live up to Baiyaan's hopes sufficiently? What does his eventual choice mean for his spiritual progress, when it seems that Baiyaan exhibits the traits of an advanced mystic?

(I'm not answering any of those questions, by the way.)

One last thing, for those of you who have followed me since The World Walker, as I slowly realized that, as unlikely as it seemed, readers were, overwhelmingly, responding positively to my first novel - so much so that I was able to write a second, then a third, and now a fourth. I hope you'll permit me this slightly self-indulgent anecdote. We leased a car recently, and the salesman sat down with me to fill out the forms.

"Occupation?"

I only hesitated for a second and a half, tops. I swear.

"Author," I said.

More books to come, I promise. Thank you, *thank you*, for reading.

Ian W. Sainsbury
Norwich
June 12th, 2017

My blog is ianwsainsbury.com and I'm on Facebook too -
https://www.facebook.com/IanWSainsbury/

I'm on Twitter as @IanWSainsbury

Also by Ian W. Sainsbury

Made in the USA
Coppell, TX
16 August 2020

33204546R00204